CW01647624

running into *forever*

JENNIFER
RODEWALD

A Love on Sanctuary Shores Novel

Rooted Publishing

Running into Forever

Print ISBN: 979-8-9874510-6-9

First printing edition 2024.

Rooted Publishing

McCook, NE 69001

Email: jen@authorjenrodewald.com

https://authorjenrodewald.com

CONTENTS

The name of the LORD is a fortified tower; the righteous run to it and are safe.

Proverbs 18:10

For those who wrestle with disappointment. You're not alone.

One

"Taylor, a moment of your time please?"

Though Gretta's voice was all politeness and calm, her dark eyes held snap and fire. Taylor sighed, twisting his mouth to the side. This afternoon kept poking him with irritants, and if it didn't stop, he'd need to drink calamine lotion.

Ick. Drink calamine lotion? Who would think of such a thing?

A truly frustrated man, that was who.

Keeping his shoulders taut and square, allowing the lines of his dark livery—his driving uniform, as worn by the three generations of Everests before him—to fall in their striking crispness, Taylor followed Gretta past the high, polished wooden front desk of Shore View Palace and toward her office.

Curtis raised his carrot-colored brows and cleared his throat. "Now you've done it," the man muttered.

Great. This wasn't the first time Taylor had been called into Gretta's opulent office, located at the back of the historic island hotel—the most famous of lodgings on Sanctuary Island. It wasn't even the tenth. But it was the first time Curtis hadn't chuckled about it. And Curtis chuckled about everything—he had since they'd been grade school students. Everything from the alphabet to road apples was funny to Taylor's red-haired counterpart, who loved to play up his Irish heritage.

Except not this, apparently.

Taylor's breath puffed through his lips as he exhaled before he passed through the door separating the concierge desk and the management realm.

"Shut the door, please." Gretta sounded as grave as she ever did. Then again, that was expected. Gretta Fellenbaum was a consummate hostess of impeccable quality. Courteous. Steady. And always serious. If she was older, Taylor would have claimed it was her advanced years that made her so, but Gretta was no more than ten years older than him, if that. She was simply a woman born out of time and would have fit more suitably a hundred years before.

"Please." She gestured with one sweeping hand, as though her invitation was not an instruction. But make no mistake—whatever Gretta combined with *please* was, indeed, a command. Dressed in her pressed gray pantsuit, complete with a peach rosebud pinned on the narrow lapel of her jacket, Gretta was all business, all the time. And no one was to defy her authority. "Sit down."

Like being called into the headmaster's office at school.

Taylor tugged on his dark suit lapels, rolled his shoulders back, and shook his head. "I'd rather stand." Wasn't he brave? "There's work to do at the stables, and I—"

Gretta planted her long fingers on her trim waist. "This is not a courtesy visit, Mr. Everest. Nor is it likely to be quick. You will hear me out, and then—"

Taylor cleared his throat. "Just get to whatever you're stewing about, Gret. The horses don't unhitch themselves."

"Gretta. Or better still, Mrs. Fellenbaum, as I am your boss."

"I contract with the Palace, *Gret*." Just so she didn't think she intimidated him. For the record, no one did. At least, no one that he'd let on about. "I don't *work* for you."

She crossed her arms while her chin lifted in stern arrogance. "That contract is currently in severe jeopardy."

Taylor scowled. Gretta wasn't joking—the woman wasn't capable of such a thing. Humor was as foreign to her as laziness was to Taylor. But she couldn't be serious either. Not about his contract as the carriage driver for the Palace being in jeopardy. Who else was she going to have haul her spoiled, uppity clientele during the tourist season? Though the Palace was outside of town limits and vehicles were technically allowed, few tourists brought them. Not to the historic resort where half the charm was a step back in time.

Were all those visitors simply going to ride the resort's bikes? Doubtful. For one thing, over half were on the silver end of the age spectrum. And second, of those who were younger, most had never broken a sweat in their lives—unless it was done so in front of a full-length mirror, in skintight clothes, and paid for with some sort of expensive membership. They weren't going to start pedaling places during their high-priced vacation to a tiny resort island in the Great Lakes.

Taylor matched Gretta's stance—arms tucked tight across his chest. "Enlighten me, dear Mrs. Fellenbaum. How do you expect to transport—"

"I'm asking the questions in this interview." With a sharp pivot, she spun to her massive desk, retrieved her cell phone from its straight and tidy position in front of the high-back leather chair, and marched her way directly in front of Taylor. "I require an explanation."

Taylor held her fierce stare for several heartbeats. Then he dropped his attention to the phone she'd shoved into his chest. He nearly ripped it from her grip and then tapped the Play button.

There was his carriage, clean and polished, shining in the late-July sun. And there he was, pristinely clad in this suit. And there were his great matched Friesians—Albert and Victoria. When it was just him and the animals—which was how Taylor preferred it—the two gentle giants were Al and Vicky. But everyone around the Palace knew them by their royal names.

And there, in that stupid video, was that blasted tyke who'd tried to get himself stomped on not one hour before.

In the video, Taylor swooped down, snagged the five-year-old by the back of the shirt, and pulled him out from beneath the horses' bellies. The child screamed and kicked. Taylor kept a firm grip and dragged the boy to his well-dressed and entirely too-made-up mother. He leaned forward, pressing the tyke to the woman's legs, and said something.

"Well?" Gretta huffed.

"Well what?"

"What do you have to say for yourself?"

"Nothing. The kid was lucky."

"I beg your pardon?"

"He should have gotten a good paddling on his backside." Taylor passed the phone back to Gretta. "And he was lucky my horses are steady."

"What did you say to that woman?"

His arms folded against his chest again, Taylor rocked back on his heels. "I told her she'd better keep her son in check, or he was going to get himself hurt."

Gretta's eyes bulged. "You *threatened* a guest?"

Brows pinching, Taylor shook his head. "Threatened? No, Gret. I *warned* her. It's dangerous to be running under the horses. And really stupid."

"Your animals are dangerous?"

Tipping his face up toward the coffered ceiling, Taylor growled. "No. My horses are not dangerous, and you well know it." Leaning toward the woman, Taylor let his scowl rest on her for a few beats. "But they are animals. Say the boy tickled Albert's belly and he kicked, thinking it was a fly? Or heaven forbid, both horses are spooked because some little tyke isn't supposed to be running around beneath them? Then what, your greatness?"

Gretta thrust her chin forward. "Don't talk to me with such impertinence."

"Don't accuse my horses of being dangerous."

"Don't threaten my guests."

"Don't have guests who do dumb things."

Gretta stared at him. Then huffed. It was the most undignified thing he'd ever witnessed the woman do. With rolled fists she spun, rounded her fat desk, and sat in her chair. "Sit." She pointed toward the upholstered Queen Anne chair on his side of the desk.

"No *please*?"

Her brows lifted as she glared at him. "Sit down, Taylor. You need to see this." Reaching for a file positioned to her right on her desk, she swiped it up and passed it over the great distance of oak that separated them.

Taylor leaned forward to grasp it. "What is it?"

"Your contract."

His heart stalled, and his mouth went dry. She wasn't actually going to—

"You'll find that on at least two counts you are in breach of it."

"What?"

"First, line three. You will treat every guest with the utmost courtesy. By the complaints I have in this file"—she tapped another folder that had rested beneath the one Taylor now held—"you cannot possibly deny that you are in breach of that."

Taylor held out his hand, a silent ask. Gretta complied, passing him the folder full of notes, each one dated, each one with some sort of quoted grievance.

Carriage driver failed to smile when offering his services. Smiling was not in his contract. Was he to go everywhere with some ridiculous grin plastered on his face, like a masked actor in some stupid comedy? Nope. No thanks. Not for him.

Man driving horses cursed under his breath when lifting luggage. He did *not* curse. Taylor didn't use foul language. The one time he'd done so when he'd been barely a teen, his mother had told him it was a sign of a stupid person, and he'd never done so since.

The ogre in charge of carriage rides did not respond to questions. He could imagine exactly what sort of person had submitted that one. The flirty, obnoxious sort who had asked him things like *What time does your shift end?* And *What does it take for a girl to find your smile?* They weren't real questions, and therefore he was not required to answer them.

Taylor tossed the file onto the desk. "These are ridiculous. You can't possibly take them seriously."

The contents slid helter-skelter across the tidy space. Gretta frowned and quickly set about straightening the notes and replacing them in their folder.

"I take everything seriously."

"No argument there." He mocked her with the tilt of his head.

"As if you don't, Taylor Everest."

Her pointed response set him back. She was right. Taylor wasn't the funny guy Curtis was. Even so, some things didn't require serious attention.

"Now I have to deal with this video situation. Do you know what will happen if this guest posts it on her social media, as she's threatened?"

"Everyone with half a brain will think she's a bad mother for allowing her five-year-old to run under horses like that?"

"No, because she won't post that part, genius. She'll clip it down so that people will only see you manhandling her son and whispering your threats." Palms braced on her desk, Gretta leaned forward. "Even you can't fail to see how that will ruin the Palace. And if we go down . . ."

He went down. Taylor couldn't deny that. He didn't have a business without the Palace.

Leaning back hard, he huffed. "What do you want me to do?"

"We'll get to that in a minute. Right now there is the matter of your second violation of contract."

"What?"

"At the end."

Taylor flipped the three pages until he came to the page he'd signed. Looked the same it always did—a whole bunch of unnecessary words declaring that this agreement was binding for the season and blah, blah, blah . . .

"Section eight, Mr. Everest."

Ah. Back to highfalutin formality. Taylor scanned the page until he came to section eight.

The Palace desires all employees and contractors to behave with absolute dignity, to live in such a way that is above reproach. As such, an unmarried individual cannot continue employment or contract beyond the age of thirty.

What on earth? This was inconceivable. Implausible. Utterly . . . absurd.

It couldn't be legal.

Taylor lifted his stare to meet Gretta's.

"I recall you had a birthday in May."

All he could do was glare at her. Harder.

"Remind me, Mr. Everest. How old did you turn?"

This just couldn't be legitimate. It was . . . insane. Who would put that in a contract?

Who would sign a contract with that in it?

A man who didn't read the contract.

"How old, Taylor?"

He ground his jaw. "You know how old I am."

"I do, in fact." She folded her hands primly. "As of May 17, you are thirty-one. Which means that, though you can argue the validity of those complaints, you can't say you are not in violation of our agreement."

Taylor looked back to the papers he clutched in his hand. The blood in his veins pulsed hot and fast. Anger ballooned bigger with every breath. Not to mention disbelief.

"Why would you do this?" Dropping the hand that held this insidious contract, he pinned Gretta with the heat of his rising anger.

She looked away—and was that a flinch? Her mouth moved with discomfort. Then she swallowed and returned eye contact. Suddenly her uppity coolness moved toward something else. Something much worse.

Pity.

Shaking her head, Gretta leaned toward him. "You've been unhappy for far too long, Taylor. It's making you grumpy. It's time for a change. For your sake as much as for everyone else's."

"You think losing my contract with the Palace is going to fix my being grumpy?"

"No." One brow quirked in challenge. "I think you finding a wife will."

"That is irrational and opaque." Shaking his head, Taylor jumped to his feet. "This won't stand."

"I assure you, it will. I've already checked with our lawyers." Gretta stood, her motion significantly calmer than Taylor's. Then she strode round the desk and stopped beside him. She dared to lay a hand on his arm. “It’s time to let old wounds heal. And to find a hopeful future.”

Taylor scowled at her. What the heck did she know about old wounds? Then with a flick of his wrist, he tossed the idiotic contract toward her desk. Without another word, he spun toward the door and stormed out.

Married? Who was he going to find to marry? Some flippant female tourist who thought life with him on the island would be terribly romantic, only to bail when she found out how harsh and isolated winter could be?

He’d tried that once before.

No thank you.

Two

"We're engaged!"

Sonora gritted her teeth and plastered on a smile as she absorbed the giddy young woman's announcement. A wave of dizzying disbelief made her head light and her balance iffy.

Engaged? After two weeks?

She slid her gaze from Arabelle, the beauty-queen heiress of the Pine Creek Resort, and locked it onto Donovan. His light-brown eyes met Sonora's, and for a brief moment, she saw a flash of . . . pity? Regret? Apology? She wasn't sure. His wide grin—the one Sonora knew he practiced for the cameras—faded for a breath. And then there it was again. Full blast. A mix of sly charm and puzzling humor.

Donovan had always looked like he had a secret, one that made him smile. In that moment, Sonora knew exactly what that secret was. Donovan Arlington *always* got what he wanted. By way of charm or position, he found a way to mold the world to his liking.

Not so long ago, that realization might have made Sonora swoon. Because not so long ago, Donovan had wanted her.

"That was fast, Arlington. Afraid that this one will get away too?"

Like it had appeared to have happened with Sonora?

Donovan had set that one up with precision, though it hadn't been exactly clear to Sonora why he had led everyone to believe that *she'd* done the breaking up, until he'd been spotted out with Arabelle a mere two weeks after *he'd* broken up with Sonora.

"I have nothing to offer you, Sonora. And a woman like you deserves a man who could give her the world."

His theatrically humble words burned in Sonora's mind as she glimpsed the big shiny rock on Arabelle's left hand. Donovan was a gold digger. He didn't mean that he'd had nothing to offer Sonora. What he had actually meant was that what she had—a strong work ethic, a deep love and thorough knowledge of horses, and a commitment to Jesus—wasn't enough for him.

Now it had all become clear. All it had taken was her broken heart.

Arabelle had returned from college less than a month before. Within a week, Donovan detached himself from the resort's head wrangler—that being herself—ending a two-year relationship between them. And the good-looking, sweet-talking, and recently *heartbroken* director of guest experience and marketing found his way into the boss's daughter's sights.

And now there they were. Two pretty people who would, when they spoke their vows, make excellent photo models for the new images Donovan had been seeking for the Pine Creek Resort's wedding package pamphlet. How convenient was that?

When exactly was that going to happen?

Sonora keyed her mind back to the celebration and to the conversations between the betrothed and their delighted audience.

"We just knew from the first glimpse this was right." Arabelle's manicured hands snaked around Donovan's arm. "Sometimes the stars just align." Her pink-glossed mouth smiled with sweetness up at Donovan. "And ours lined up perfectly."

Donovan lowered his head to kiss all that sugar.

Sonora looked away. A mix of anger, humiliation, and heartache rolled through her chest, its progress slow, heavy, and stifling. The room was too hot, the people too close. This moment too . . . much. She needed out of there.

"When's the wedding? I assume it'll be in the lodge."

"Of course it'll be in the lodge!" Much more of Arabelle's high-pitched happiness and Sonora might go into sugar shock. "And we're not waiting. I've been planning my wedding since I was twelve years old. We've set the date—August 13." She eyed Donovan with a playful, secretive look. "And don't say the thirteenth isn't a lucky number. I don't believe in that silly business."

Hadn't this bubbly young woman fresh out of college just claimed that her and Donovan's stars had aligned? She was ridiculous.

But beautiful. And likely of more interest to Donovan, rich.

Who got themselves engaged to a man they had only met a pair of weeks before? And who married that near stranger only a second pair of weeks after? Shouldn't Arabelle's dad be a little suspicious? How was everyone apparently okay with this?

Two weeks. Ugh.

Sonora turned away from the circle of the gathering, mostly coworkers. She wove her way through bodies—a handful of cowboys who worked under her as wranglers, guest support staff, and kitchen staff. Breaking free from the small crowd, she came to the edge of the dining hall.

A hand landed on her arm as Sonora reached to push open the door. With a startled glance, she found Nina watching her with concern.

"You okay?" Nina asked.

"Of course." Sonora's mouth hurt from the continued fake smile. "I'm happy for them. I wish them all the best. Hope they'll be deliriously happy."

"So . . . you're not angry at all." Nina's voice was all sarcasm.

Sonora let that painful smile fall. As her shoulders sagged, she shook her head, met Nina's gaze, and then moved to exit the hall. The intense late-afternoon Wyoming sun hit her eyes with a brightness that made the tears burn. She lifted her cowboy hat, covering her dark-blond braid and using the wide brim to shade her eyes.

No. She wasn't okay. She'd given her heart to a man who had found her lacking.

And now? He was getting married. In two short weeks. To a woman who was as beautiful as she was rich and, in all ways, made Sonora feel deeply her own insufficiency. How was she supposed to be okay with that?

Wind pounded on the log walls—a common sound on this western Wyoming ranch. Sonora stretched out on her bunk, praying that the long day in the saddle, along with the extra hour of unloading the hay truck, would render her body and mind exhausted. She couldn't stand thinking about *the engagement* anymore. Which was inconvenient because not only had everyone talked about *the whirlwind ranch romance* incessantly for the past three days, but in the moments of quiet, nearly every one of her own rebellious thoughts wandered back to the stupid topic as well.

Donovan is getting married.

Married! To the boss's daughter. To a woman he'd known for like five minutes.

Who cared?

She cared. To an annoyingly, painfully extreme.

Swallowing against the sudden surge of emotion, Sonora squeezed her eyes shut. *God, I loved him* . . . At least she'd believed she had. Worse, she believed that *he'd* loved her. How could she have had such a tremendous misjudgment?

Suddenly she thought of her mother, and a fresh, unwanted understanding of Mom's pain sank in deep. Involuntarily, Sonora's sharp inhale shuddered.

A hand covered her ankle and shook her leg. "It's okay, girl. No one here but you and me." Nina's soft voice accompanied her touch. "You can let it out."

"I don't want to." Sonora covered her face with both hands. "Crying over such a man is . . . stupid." Yeah. It was stupid to fall in love with such a man too. Apparently that hadn't stopped her—though she should have certainly known better. And there the lingering resentment toward her father rose up to join the emotional riot.

Sonora sniffed and clenched her jaw. Then she sat up, careful not to hit her head on the bunk above her and leaned on her elbow. "Donovan doesn't deserve my tears."

"No. He doesn't." Nina sat on the end of the bed, swiveling to lean her back against the foot of the frame. "But that doesn't mean that you don't need to cry them."

Crying hadn't fixed anything six years ago when her world had spun off course, so there was no reason to believe it would now. Sonora shook her head, gripping the stubborn streak that came from being born on the harsh Wyoming prairie. Least, that was what her mother claimed. *This un-*

repentant land of extremes makes for some fierce and stubborn souls.

Fine. Sonora would be fierce. And stubborn. "I ain't."

"You *ain't?*"

"No. I *ain't* doing it. Not for him."

Nina chuckled at Sonora's resolve. "Okay, girl. Have your own way. You usually do." She reached across the narrow bit of floor in the bunkhouse and grabbed an equestrian magazine from her bed. "I'll just sit over here and read while you sit over there and *ain't.*"

Despite her muddled emotions, and the tears on the verge of finding freedom no matter what she'd declared, Sonora chuckled. Nina was like that. Gentle and genuine. Ready to laugh or cry with her friend. And willing to hang out, even if there was no conversation involved.

Sonora rolled back and let her head fall onto the pillow again. Her shoulders and back ached from carrying square bales and tossing them into stacks behind the big barn. They had tractors for such things—a fact that Harley had reminded her of when he'd caught her doing manual labor. But she'd opted for the sweat, for the sore muscles. For the exhaustion. That way she'd be too tired to think about—

Dang it! There he was again. Sonora wanted to growl in her frustration. And might would have, but for Nina's soft giggle.

"This is nuts," her friend murmured.

Sonora peeked down to the foot of the bed at her friend. "What's nuts?"

Dark-brown eyes lifted over the edge of the magazine and met Sonora's look, mocking laughter dancing in them. She leaned forward, holding out the magazine for Sonora to take. "Check out the help-wanted ad." She tapped the page—a full spread with an image of a beautiful resort in the background, similar to the nice hotel in the old movie *Somewhere in Time*. In front of the beautiful, three-story white building, a matched set of Friesians, hitched to a handsome dark carriage, claimed center stage.

Come work at one of the most exclusive resorts in North America.

That was the bold print at the bottom of the page.

Sonora read it out loud and then pinned a raised-brow look onto Nina. "That's funny?"

"Read the small print."

Sonora complied. *This position requires a female horsewoman, skilled at driving. Must be willing to live on a remote island in a small apartment above the carriage house . . . and marry her boss. Both are nonnegotiable.*

Marry the boss? Holy smokes! Sonora blew out a snort.

Nina's soft giggle blew up to a full belly laugh. "Can you imagine someone answering that?"

"What on earth?" Sonora shook her head. That was some kind of desperation right there. Or a joke.

It had to be a joke.

"What sort of man would run that?" Nina flopped onto her belly, leaning on her elbows.

"Maybe he has some sort of facial scar or something. You know, like the *Phantom of the Opera*?"

Nina jumped up, pressing her hand forward. "No, wait! He's a reformed criminal! He's desperate for a new shot at domestic life, but no one on the island will have him because of his past."

Sonora crossed her legs. "Maybe he's sick and this is his one last stab at marriage."

"Ohh . . . he's sick *and* rich!" Nina plopped onto her bunk on the opposite side of the small room. "He is *so* rich, and he needs someone to pass on his inheritance to. All the local girls don't like him, because he's the wealthy snob who was never nice to them. But he's discovered, too late, that what he really wants in all of the world—before he dies—is a woman to love him."

Nina laughed at her own fiction. "Or maybe he's just a grump and no one can stand him. So if he's gonna find a wife, he's got to hire one."

Sonora recovered from her fit of giggles and nodded. "That's the most likely." She passed the magazine back to Nina.

With a gentle smile, Nina took it and shook Sonora's arm. "See, it could be worse." She winked. "At least you don't have to run an ad to find love."

"Who says the guy is looking for love? Love is . . . a fiction." Sonora lay back again, the momentary reprieve from her misery gone.

"Aw, come on now. You don't really believe that."

Sonora sighed. In that moment, she didn't know what she believed about love. All she knew was that she felt heartbroken and humiliated, and she never wanted to land there again.

Ever.

Clenching her jaw and embracing the stubbornness over the urge to cry, Sonora stared up at the underside of the bed above her. "Anyway, maybe he's got it right and the rest of us are fools."

"Why would you say that?"

Sonora pinned her lips together and shut her eyes. *Fool. Exactly. She'd been such a fool.*

"Sonora?" Nina poked her side.

"At least he's honest, you know?" Not like *dishonest* Donovan, who had whispered promises beneath stunning starry night skies. Meaningless nothings like, *the Milky Way is nothing compared to what shines in my heart for you.*

Lesson learned there. Never trust a man given to cheesy hyperbole. Pretty words were merely a disguise for a cold and vacant heart.

"The ad guy?" Nina propped up on one elbow.

"Yeah. He printed exactly what he wanted. A wife."

Nina drew in a long breath and sighed. “Oh, Sonora.” She shook Sonora’s arm. “I think you need a good cry and a long sleep.”

Probably true. Maybe just this once, she’d set the stubbornness aside for the tears. Just a few. After both—the cry and the sleep—she’d forget about it.

About dishonest Donovan.

And about that ad.

Three

COULD A MAN EVER trust again the One who had so keenly disappointed him before? Or was the damage too severe, too permanent?

In Taylor's case, the second seemed the more likely. Specifically, because *disappointed* was a tame and innocuous description of what had actually happened. One could miss the ferry and be disappointed. That wasn't life altering. Heart damaging.

Dreary thoughts for the pleasant early morning. He instead could be savoring the gentle oranges and pinks that were streaking across the eastern sky, their hues becoming more vibrant as the sun stretched upward toward their existence. After all, it was his morning off—a few hours every week offered as a reprieve from the otherwise work-maddened life of a seasonal tourist community.

Inhaling the crisp breath of lake-seasoned air, he pushed his attention toward the hilly stretch of grass in front of him, banishing the wandering, melancholic thoughts that often darkened his mood.

Taylor stood to the side of the fairway, hands tucked behind his back, while Curtis took a crisp swing with his driving wedge. Firm contact made, the little white ball soared at a low arc and landed near the first green.

"Nice drive." Taylor nodded.

With his trademark grin, Curtis plucked off his cap and bowed, then held his driver out toward Taylor. "You're up."

Taylor lifted one hand. "No thanks."

Golf had never held his interest. The only reason he ever came to the course was because Curtis was his longtime best friend, and Curtis loved taking advantage of the early Sunday morning front nine made available to the Palace staff. Given their limited time before they were both required to be at their respective jobs, Curtis never got through the first nine holes on his own. He rarely played through three. Adding Taylor's pathetic attempts to play golf would be frustrating. For both of them.

Curtis lifted his brows. "You sure?"

"As always."

His friend chuckled, sliding his club into his golf bag. "Same answer. Every time. You are like a Swiss watch, Everest. Unrelenting in your reliability."

"Hmm." Taylor took the bag of clubs and slipped the wide strap over his shoulder.

"You don't have to caddy for me," Curtis said.

"I believe you say that every time."

"I mean it every time."

"Then we are the same. And for point of clarification, I doubt I could qualify as a caddy. I don't know anything about this maddening game other than I'm bad at it."

Curtis cast him a wry grin. "You could *try* having fun."

Meeting that teasing glance, Taylor shrugged. "I'm bad at that too."

Chuckling, Curtis elbowed his arm, then shook his head.

Taylor took no offense to the jab. Everyone knew that Taylor was the serious one. The responsible one. His friendship with Curtis was one of opposites. When Taylor had been home studying as a schoolboy, Curtis was out packing snowballs and stashing them in great ammunition piles. While Taylor preferred a quiet evening with a long book, Curtis wanted to meet all the pretty girls in the town square.

Somehow they got along though, and their friendship was nothing but sincere.

Both men strode the one-hundred-plus feet toward the waiting golf ball. A sweet morning breeze stirred the deep leathery leaves of oak and maple lining the fairway, scented faintly of lake and seasoned with a touch of rose. The morning sun winked through the hillside of scattered trees and shrubbery, reminding the men that their recreation time was limited.

After a typically busy weekend—this past one themed Summer Garden Tour, which would come to its conclusion at four that afternoon—another week of tourists lay ahead of them. Check-ins began at seven tomorrow morning. That meant Taylor needed to have the carriage at the docks by eight, and Curtis was required to be at his post to expedite the early checkouts.

"Well?" Curtis asked.

"You'll be lucky to tuck in two holes this round."

"One of these days I'll get all nine."

"That's an extraordinarily unlikely event. You'd need to start by four."

"I can do that."

"I will not be joining you."

Curtis chuckled. "Know what else is an extraordinarily unlikely event?"

Taylor bent a mild scowl toward his friend. He knew exactly what irritant his friend was going to itch. "Leave it alone."

"Fellenbaum will not be appeased with an *attempt.*"

Unease rammed through Taylor's back. "She'll have to be. My lawyers say it should do. And anyway, it was *your* idea."

An absurd one at that. Taylor could hardly believe he'd taken the advice of his redheaded mischief-maker friend. Whoever heard of taking out an ad for a wife?

No one in this century.

"What if someone answers the ad?" One dark-red brow rose, adding to Curtis's perpetually amused expression.

"Unlikely." *Please, God in heaven, let it be no one.* Issues with a contract was one thing. Slogging through an unstable woman who showed up ready to marry her boss? Not on his wish list.

And make no mistake: any woman who answered that advertisement would certainly be unstable. Taylor wasn't in the market for crazy. Actually, he wasn't in the market at all.

"Extraordinarily unlikely?"

"Yes. We live in the modern world. What woman in her right mind—or otherwise—would agree to such employment terms?"

"I still think it's a risk." Amusement lit up Curtis's copper eyes. "Or perhaps a possibility." He bounced his eyebrows.

Five feet from the ball, Taylor pulled to a stop and lowered the bag of clubs. Then he scowled and shook his head at Curtis's last statement. "A *risk*. And so is trying to play golf before work. Yet here we are."

"My version of risk taking isn't nearly as risky as yours." At that, Curtis laughed. "Who would have imagined that? Of the two of us—the class clown and the clockwork coachman—you would be the desperado?"

Taylor selected an iron and passed it to his friend. "Running an employment ad hardly qualifies me as a desperado."

Mentally, he scrolled through the various definitions of the term.

A bold outlaw, especially one from southern portions of the Wild West. Nope.

A person who is desperate for love or romance. Absolutely not.

A criminal. Heaven forbid.

A reckless person who enjoys doing dangerous things. Reckless . . . perhaps the ad was that. But Taylor certainly didn't enjoy doing dangerous things. He didn't even enjoy placid, innocuous things. Like golf.

Curtis smirked. And laughed. "I'm looking forward to the *possibilities.*" Then he took his stance, eyed his target, and swung the club.

Ball on the green. With a solid putt, he'd land a birdie. Taylor wasn't surprised. Curtis rarely missed.

"Sonora, right?"

A gentle, feminine tone snagged Sonora's attention from the saddle she was securing. With one hand on the paint pony, she turned from the cinch to see who spoke.

Ugh. Turning back to the animal, Sonora put her attention on her work so she wouldn't have to give Arabelle her attention. "Yes, that's me."

"Donovan said you were the wrangler."

"I'm sure you could have asked anyone for that information."

"You've been here two years?"

"This is my third season with the ranch." Cinch secured, Sonora tested the saddle. Not too much wiggle. She moved on to the next animal at the hitching post.

"Could you give me a moment of your time?"

There was too much sugar in that. Way too much. Sonora didn't have a moment for sugar—especially if it was the imitation kind. Sonora hefted the next saddle from the post and settled it onto the next trail pony, a little bay who should probably retire after this season. "I have a trail ride scheduled in forty minutes and three more horses to saddle." She brushed her hands, and dropping them to her hips, she turned to face the princess of Pine Creek Guest Ranch. "I doubt your daddy would appreciate it if I dillydally."

Arabelle's perfectly plucked eyebrows arched. For a moment her violet eyes clamped onto Sonora's with a warning chill. Just as swiftly, the younger woman smiled. "I only need a minute, Miss Hillary. And rest assured, my daddy is aware of our little meeting today. I doubt a few minutes tardy will be a bother."

Sonora's stomach sank as suspicion entered her mind. She could think of one reason this little miss would come seek her out.

One. Reason.

She refused to duck her head. Instead, Sonora kept firm, unflinching eye contact with the beautiful heiress.

By the widening of her eyes, Arabelle was caught off guard by Sonora's lack of . . . simpering. Yet again, that was a fleeting thing. She cleared her throat and lifted her chin. "I'll get right to it. Given your previous . . . association with my fiancé, Dad and I have agreed that it would be best for you to seek other opportunities."

"Other opportunities?" Sonora didn't need it clarified. She just wanted to hear this woman say it plainly.

"You cannot work here anymore."

"You mean I'm fired."

"That is . . ." Arabelle looked down at her designer jeans and brand-new boots. "That isn't entirely accurate."

"Because you have no cause to fire me. Other than the fact that Donovan dated me for two years."

Cold anger darkened Arabelle's gaze, causing her brows to pinch into an ugly scowl. "I don't need a cause."

"Think that will hold up?" Sonora had no idea of such legalities, nor did she have any intention of chasing them down. But to walk away, face to the ground, back broken? Not in her nature. Maybe it was that fierce, stubborn Wyoming girl in her.

Or maybe it was *the woman scorned* part . . .

Arabelle drew back, and the color in her pink cheeks drained. She looked over her shoulder, back at the main lodge. Likely where Donovan was tucked safely in his office, away from the trouble he'd made.

Spineless man.

Jaw stiff, and with a far less haughty air, Arabelle returned her attention to Sonora. "There will be a severance package." She swallowed, fiddled with her fingers. "Dad will make sure it's more than fair."

For three breaths Sonora stared at the woman who fidgeted and refused to meet her gaze again. Though her stomach twisted with sickening knots, she snorted and shook her head. "Don't bother, princess."

"What?"

"Don't bother with a severance package."

"But . . ." She bit her lip. "Does that mean that you're not—"

"I'll go. Without a fuss. Without a word to anyone."

Those perfectly made-up eyes lifted again. "You will?"

"After this ride, I'll pack up and head out."

Arabelle's breath left in an audible rush. "Thank you." Again, she swallowed. "I hope you know there's no hard feelings."

Sonora laughed. What a patronizing, if not ignorant, thing to say. "Of course not." She shook her head and turned back to the animal she'd been saddling.

Arabelle stepped away.

"I hope he's better to you," Sonora said.

"What's that?" Arabelle turned back to face her.

Sonora lifted her eyes and studied the younger woman for a moment. So pretty. So full of life. Spoiled. But innocent. Arabelle hadn't plotted this. Donovan had.

A sudden wave of pity washed through Sonora, wiping away the spitefulness. She blinked and lowered her challenging stare. "I hope he makes you happy, Arabelle."

Four

She might be a woman rejected, but she could choose to be a woman of her word. Even if Donovan deserved for her to spill the story to everyone before she left.

Sonora stuffed her last pair of jeans into her large canvass laundry bag and slung the thick cords over her shoulder. That was it. Her clean clothes had been packed. The three books she'd brought to Pine Creek—her Bible, a well-worn copy of *The Complete Guide to Horse Care Manual*, and one of her mother's many copies of *Anne of Green Gables*—had been tucked inside her large suitcase. Her personal items had been cleared from the bathhouse. All had been tossed into her pickup.

Just her dirty clothes and her church boots, both of which she held in hand.

Sonora stopped at the door and took once last look at the room she'd shared with three other young women. Two were new this season. They got along well enough. Nina she'd known since her first year at the ranch. Her friend worked in the big house—guest relations—under Donovan.

Must feel awkward for her. Sonora felt a pinch of guilt for having not thought of that before now. She'd send her a text, apologizing for being so self-focused, and then she'd tell her best friend that she just couldn't stay.

It was the smoothed-over truth.

A bulge grew in her throat. Sonora swallowed against it and pivoted toward the door again, when a glossy page caught her eye.

The magazine, pages folded back and the advertisement facing up, rested on Nina's bunk.

Would it hurt to make a call? Likely whoever had listed it hadn't been serious. Not about the marriage part.

But the job?

Rather than stepping out the door, Sonora reached for the magazine.

She knew horses. She could ride, and she could drive. And she knew the tourist industry. Maybe with the reference Mr. Stone had most willingly—if not guiltily—provided, she could land the job part.

Not the wife part.

Maybe her new chapter would be far, far away from the fierce and stubborn wilds of Wyoming. From all the memories there.

From the heartache and humiliation.

Yeah. A remote island sounded like just the ticket.

She ripped out the page and replaced the periodical on Nina's bed, then swept out the bunkhouse door.

The truck engine turned over, and her radio, set to a country station, blared "There's Your Trouble" by the Chicks. Sonora looked over her shoulder toward the main lodge just in time to see Donovan and Arabelle sweeping through the double front door, arm in arm.

There was her trouble indeed. She was done with it. She wasn't running. Just moving on.

Turning up the volume, Sonora let the sass override the sadness as she pulled out of the drive. One chapter closed. Time to find a new life. Somewhere where she'd never have to think about Donovan again.

Taylor stared at the contents of the large manila envelope.

Not. Possible.

I am excellent with horses, proficient at driving, experienced in the tourism industry, and I do well with people. In short, perfectly qualified for the job. As for the other . . . my heart is as cold as stone and unavailable. If you want a proficient driver, I'm your girl. If you're truly looking for a wife in this absurd way, I am afraid I'll disappoint you. Love is not in my story.

This Miss Sonora Hillary certainly had some spunk.

And he did need a driver, someone who did "well with people." By her words, and the letter of recommendation that came with her response, Miss Hillary was that girl.

On the other side of his table sat the troublesome contract he was currently in breach of. How could Gretta possibly be serious about this?

She couldn't.

And even if she was, he could say that he'd tried. That should count.

Fellenbaum will not be appeased with an attempt.

Curtis's words, tainted with both amusement and warning, bounced around in Taylor's mind with the annoying persistence of crickets chirping in the dead of a sleepless night. With a growl, Taylor reached for the contract. If he'd read it once, he'd read it a hundred times, but even so, he studied the words that spelled out his doom yet again.

Married by thirty. What a demand.

He wouldn't acquiesce.

As he often did, he pulled up the meaning of his unique choice of words. *Acquiesce: accept something reluctantly but without protest.*

Perhaps he would not *acquiesce*. But likely he'd be forced to accept the terms of the blasted contract, no matter how much he protested. Gretta Fellenbaum was equally stubborn as she was formal. Both of which Taylor usually admired about the woman.

Until now.

Taylor shifted his attention back to the cover letter bearing the name Miss Sonora Hillary. *Love is not in my story.*

Nor was it in his.

That seemed promising . . .

Though possibly insane, a touch of hope stirred. If Miss Sonora Hillary had reached out wanting this job, she likely had a compelling reason—after all, the terms were bizarre. And if that compelling reason was as serious as his compelling reason, perhaps they could come to an agreement.

One mutually beneficial. And mutually benign.

Benign: kindly, gentle.

No, not that meaning of the word. Well, perhaps that too—he was not an ill-tempered man, no matter what was said of him by some of the island residents—but not predominantly.

Benign: (of a disease) not harmful in effect.

Yes, that definition. Perhaps he could enter into a benign understanding of mutual benefit with Miss Sonora Hillary.

They should meet. And then . . .

Then he would see.

Five

Taylor scanned the peppering of people at the ferry dock at Havensport. The trip across the lake had been uneventful, but even so, his stomach churned with what could have been named as sea illness.

That would be a lie. Though he'd never enjoyed being on the water—a quirk Curtis enjoyed poking at because every other islander seemed to love boats, water, and surf—Taylor didn't get sick. Particularly not on the ferry.

Still, he felt his stomach twist with painful nausea. Might have something to do with his reason for traveling to the mainland.

Lifting his cell phone, he tapped the photo app. The first image bloomed on the screen—the one he'd stared at during most of the crossing from the island.

Why was this woman lovely? She wasn't supposed to be.

Unease rocked his resolve. This was a bad plan.

Feet firm on the dock, Taylor looked over his shoulder, back at the dark, cold waters of Lake Huron. A foreboding northern wind pushed the waves, rolling whitecaps onto the shore. A picture of his internal affairs, if there ever was one.

"Mr. Everest." A crisp voice snapped his attention away from his emotional metaphor.

A sharp pain jabbed the front of his brain as he stiffened his already perfectly straight posture, and he barely withheld the growl that vibrated in his throat. Turning, he found Gretta Fellenbaum's curious scowl fastened on him.

"Gretta."

"What are you doing away from your post?" she demanded.

"It's Sunday evening. My night off."

Her pinched brows remained crumpled. "You rode the ferry over with our guests?"

Crossing his arms, Taylor leaned in. "I did. Don't worry—there was not an incident."

"I didn't imagine so."

"Didn't you? Your demeaning expression would say otherwise."

She shook her head. "I am merely shocked you are off the island. You never leave, except to see Al and Vicky safely across for the off-season."

Another gale of discomfort thrashed in his gut. "Yes, well." Swallowing, he stepped back. "I have business here today."

"On a Sunday evening?"

"Yes."

"What is it?"

"You do realize that you are not in charge of every aspect of my life, don't you?"

Gretta lowered her pointed gaze, a dusting of pink coloring her cheeks. The rare glimpse of humility was short lived, as within two breaths, she had her chin pointed back up at him. “This is the last ferry for the evening.” She pointed to the boat she was more than likely about to board.

“Then may I suggest you get on it?” Taylor swept his hand toward the gangplank in a grand, overplayed gesture.

“What about the morning?”

Taylor’s hands fell to his sides. “I’m sure you’ll reach Sanctuary’s shores well before the sun makes a full trip around the other side of the globe.”

Her sharp eyes pinched. “That is not what I mean. What about *your* job in the morning? Mondays are always busy.”

“As I’ve been driving coaches since I was a teen, I am well aware of that, Gretta.”

She raised her eyebrows. “Well?”

“The morning is covered. Your guests will have transportation.”

“When will you return?”

“That is my business.”

Gretta huffed. “As your—”

“Enough.” Taylor shook his head and took a step away. His lifted vision crashed into a white cowboy hat with an attractive woman beneath its wide brim. The involuntary lurch in his chest only served to irritate him further.

A cowgirl. She’d said nothing about being a cowgirl. Though he’d never really met anyone who claimed to be a cowgirl, Taylor felt certain one would be trouble. Wild, flirty, brazen . . . He didn't run a rodeo and had no interest in some sort of buckle bunny—though he wasn't exactly sure what that was.

"Taylor?"

Wearing a full scowl, Taylor glanced back at the woman who had become the curse of his post-thirty life. "What?"

Gretta blinked, drawing back, as if he'd threatened her. Her jaw worked as she swallowed, and then she leaned into her all-business, in-control-of-everything persona. "I expect to see you returned tomorrow."

If this introduction went the way his gut told him—a total disaster and a waste of the blasted ferry crossing—he'd likely be back on the *Haven* before it left dock in twenty minutes. But Gretta didn't need the satisfaction of determining his plans.

"Expect what you want. I'm not promising you anything of the sort though." He turned away, his long stride stamping against the stone walkway toward the Havensport Inn. He might have been stomping. His heart was sure pounding.

Not with the eagerness to meet the lovely Miss Sonora Hillary. Certainly not that.

The man moved like a beast. His strides long and powerful, his tall form stiff. The dark suit jacket only made his appearance more severe, which was not aided by the hard scowl engraved on his face.

And he came directly toward her, stormy eyes set on her like a cruise missile locked in on its target. She was the target.

Lifting her chin, she refused to let her growing alarm about this meeting bleed into her expression. After all, she was like the Wyoming prairie—fierce and stubborn.

She hoped the echo of her mother's proclamation would act as an anchor in this uncertain moment. Fierce and stubborn.

Or crazy and foolish. Dear Lord in heaven, what was she doing?

Sonora batted away that accusation. It wasn't helpful. And as to the prayer . . . she'd come back to that later, though it was certain she should have consulted God on this decision a whole lot sooner.

"Miss Hillary." His deep, quiet voice held the quality of one who did not joke. Perhaps he didn't even smile.

So naturally, she smiled up at him, meeting his dark solemnity with light cheer, even though she didn't feel it. "That's me."

He stared at her, freezing her with the arctic quality of his icy-blue eyes. Something about being held in that unwavering gaze spurred her heart into a gallop. Even so, she refused to drop eye contact. "You are Taylor Everest."

A slight nod. Nothing more—not a waver in his look, a twitch on his firm mouth.

Was this man stone?

"I'm afraid this was a mistake."

She inhaled sharply at his low proclamation. "I beg your pardon?"

"I have no use for a cowgirl." At last his eyes shifted, but only to her hat.

Blinking, Sonora tried to make sense of his words. A joke. He had to be making a joke. She snorted. And then chuckled as she removed her white straw hat. "I believe you wanted a horsewoman." The cool breeze coming off the choppy lake chilled the sweat beneath her dark-honey-blond braid.

"That doesn't necessarily mean a cowgirl."

"Are you afraid of cowgirls?"

His firm mouth pinched severely. He was serious? Sonora's smile faded. She tucked her hat under her arm. "I've traveled a long way, Mr. Everest. Maybe you could save your judgment for after our interview."

His brows quirked upward. A good sign? By the darkening of his already foreboding eyes, no.

Likely she should walk away. Who would want to work for this jagged chunk of glacier? No wonder he had to take an ad out for a wife. A woman would have to be stone to work for this man and desperate to marry him!

Was she desperate? For marriage, no—and she'd already been clear with him about that in her response. She wasn't in the market for a relationship, period.

For this job? Yes. Though she couldn't define why. She was an able-bodied, intelligent woman. She could find another job. Didn't even have to be with horses.

But . . .

But what? Sonora couldn't say for sure, other than she was anxious for an escape. One to a remote island where Donovan and Arabelle would be as far away as the moon, for all intents and purposes, seemed ideal. Even if the man she was toe to toe with was far less than ideal.

Actually, perhaps that was even better that she didn't like him. There was no risk then, was there? Not to her heart, at least.

Ah, stone. She could be that.

Sonora tipped her head to the side and matched Mr. Everest's stoic look. "I am qualified, and by your response, likely your only applicant. Do you think there will be many more women who meet your spelled-out specifications? After all, you have to admit, your parameters are on the far side of—"

"You don't meet my parameters."

Sonora rolled her eyes. "You didn't specify 'no cowgirls.'"

"No, but I did specify marriage. You've indicated that was out of the question."

Was there a touch of color in his sun-kissed cheeks? Interesting . . . was the flush because of the mention of marriage or because she'd challenged him? As to marriage, if there was no danger to her heart . . .

"I said love was not in my story. That didn't automatically rule out marriage." What was she saying?

She didn't need this job *that* badly. This well could be the wrong side of stubborn at work here. Act now, pray later was a really bad life policy. Maybe she needed to pause and—

"You would agree to a marriage of convenience?" Mr. Everest lifted one brow, as if intrigued. Which was, by itself, intriguing.

"That would depend on the terms." *Lord, get me out of this if it's a bad idea.* What an insane request—of course this was a really bad idea! God wasn't supposed to be insurance against intentional stupidity.

Taylor's expression flickered toward consideration. One hand came up to rub his shadowed jawline, displaying long fingers and drawing her attention to the angular lines of his face.

A handsome face. Or at least the potential to be handsome. Certainly on the cold side of good looking. Like an arctic scene. Nice to look at in a picture. Maybe even breathtaking. But chilling enough to be certain one would not like to try it in real life.

Breathtaking?

Sonora swallowed against the sudden fluttering in her chest. Such a silly reaction to a purely aesthetic observation. Handsome men were as common as a tumbleweed on the prairie. Cold handsome men were a safer option than the slippery charm of the other variety. If Taylor Everest must be good looking, at least he was also frigid.

Anyway, it hardly mattered what the man looked like.

Stone.

Apparently satisfied with whatever he'd pondered in that pause, Mr. Everest nodded toward the building behind her. Then without a word, he strode around her and toward the long front porch of the Havensport Inn.

Was she supposed to follow him? To discuss terms?

Very well then. Let the negotiations begin. First bullet point on her requirements, the iceberg must learn to use his words, for heaven's sake. She wasn't a mind reader and wasn't about to attempt an acquisition of the skill.

Without a backward glance, Mr. Everest led her to the double front doors and opened the one on the right. To her surprise, he held it wide and gestured for her to pass through before him.

Huh. The iceman had some manners. At least one.

Sonora stepped inside, then followed the tall man through the lobby and toward another set of double glass doors.

The warm aroma of grilled meat—predominately steak, with an undertone of fish—made her mouth water. When her stomach rumbled above the quiet din of the lobby, Sonora hugged her belly and fought back a blush. Now at her side, she felt Mr. Everest's gaze on her. She caught his smirk—and the passing amusement in it.

Ah, so the man could smile. Sort of.

"Let's see if we can find something to sedate your stomach."

"Thank you very much." Sarcasm rolled off her tongue as easily as dryness did his.

Once again in silence, he led her to the back tavern, which was all red brick and dark-stained wood, balanced by a solid bank of windows that let in a stunning, unobstructed view of the lake. Sonora paused midway through the restaurant and gawked at the vastness of water and sky.

Mr. Everest was at the table and bending to sit before he observed her pause. After a silent look, one that felt like disapproval, he stood straight again, then moved toward a table next to one of the paned windows.

Hmm. Another subtly kind gesture. Perhaps this man wasn't frozen solid.

Not that it mattered either way.

Sonora made her way to the chair opposite where he'd planted himself and sat, setting her despised cowboy hat top down onto the seat of a chair not in use. Her braid slid over her shoulder, and she mindlessly fingered the thick twists of hair as she stared at the vast water below the rocky shoreline.

For the second time in five minutes, the image before her eyes stole her breath.

"You've never seen the Great Lakes, have you?"

Startled by his less sharp tone, Sonora peeled her attention from the rolling white waves and looked at the man across from her. "No. Nor the ocean. I've lived landlocked my whole life."

"Never took a vacation to the beach?"

"No. Our vacations consisted of a camper and the Platte River. My dad is an avid fly fisherman and a bad traveler." She gestured toward the lake. "That is stunning."

Taylor grunted, and his frown deepened. His extended silence seemed like a tense warning. "The lake can be brutal."

Was this his way of scaring her off, since his aversion to cowgirls hadn't done the job? Sonora chuckled. "So can the prairie."

His icy-blue eyes pinned on her with warning. "Winters are long, cold, brutal, and lonely."

"So you love it?" Sonora held his look, raising her brows in challenge. "You fit there perfectly."

"What?"

She snorted softly. "You work in the tourist industry?" No wonder he was looking for a new driver. He was about as welcoming as a late-winter blizzard.

"I—" He shook his head. "You know what I do—drive a horse-drawn carriage for a resort hotel. Why are you changing the subject?"

"I thought that *was* the subject. At least the one we were supposed to be discussing. Terms of the job, remember?"

He scowled. "We were discussing the lake—and that its beauty is deceptive."

"You sure know how to send a person packing for a guy in the tourism industry."

"I want you to be aware of the reality at the other end of that ferry."

Sonora leaned back. "I know how to use Google." She let an amused grin poke at one corner of her mouth as a server stopped beside the table.

Mr. Everest's solemn scowl did not ease.

"Welcome to the Tavern." The young man standing beside the table said. "Will you be putting this on your tab with the hotel?"

"No." Taylor hesitated before he shifted his attention from Sonora to the man with pen and pad at the ready. "We're not guests."

"No problem." The young man nodded easily. "Can I interest you in the pan-fried perch? The batter is a local specialty. You won't get anything like it anywhere else."

Mr. Everest eased his gaze back to Sonora. Suddenly his eyes weren't darts of ice, and his features relaxed.

He *was* handsome. With that one intrusive thought, all others faded, and the heart she'd instructed to be stone became flesh.

"Miss Hillary?"

"Hmm?" Had he asked her something? Heat drifted into her cheeks. Why did this man hide those mesmerizing blue eyes behind a cold front? Did he not know how captivating he could be if—

"The perch," he said flatly. "Do you want to eat the perch?"

Like a brief warm spell in February, the momentary gentleness in his gaze vanished. Once again he was frowning, spearing her with his sharp glare. Worse, there was a hint of his thinking she was stupid in that hard look.

She wasn't stupid, even if that moment of fogginess was silly. Fine. Rather than giving him the satisfaction of her embarrassment, Sonora grinned and turned to look up at the cute young man waiting for her order. "I'm new around here. How about you choose for me?" And then she winked.

The boy's grin widened. "Perch it is, for the pretty lady. I'll have them double batter it for you." It was an extra moment before he turned his attention back to Mr. Everest. "And you, sir?"

Mr. Everest turned an unfiltered glare and locked it onto the poor server. "I will have the sirloin. It had better be juicy, and not overdone. A side of dressed greens—use the balsamic vinaigrette—and a baked sweet potato topped with cinnamon and brown sugar."

The young man wrote on his paper pad, his grin wilting. With a repentant expression, he made brief eye contact with Mr. Everest, nodded, and then mumbled that he'd get that in immediately. He didn't look back at Sonora as he scurried away like a rebuked lad.

"That was impressive." She didn't temper one ounce of her sarcasm.

Mr. Everest didn't flinch. "I was thinking the opposite."

"He did a perfectly fine job."

"I wasn't referring to his performance."

Sonora drew back. "I beg your pardon."

"I think this has been a waste of both of our time. You clearly are not suited for the job."

"How on earth have you determined that?"

"Flirting with the waitstaff?" He shook his head. "I need a reliable driver. Not drama."

Shoot. She hadn't considered that he'd think she was a flirt in general—because she wasn't. She'd just wanted to . . .

To what?

Make him wish that her smile was for him. To make him jealous?

How childish. And ridiculous.

Sonora straightened in her chair, knowing well the fire in her face probably made her glow. Folding her hands, she leaned against the table. "Forgive me, Mr. Everest. I am not generally a flirt. That was badly done. I . . . I was aiming to make *you* smile."

He blinked, and the spot near his right eyebrow twitched. As if dumbfounded, he looked to the side, out the large paned window and toward the rolling waves of the lake. "Why would you do that?"

"To see if you own one."

One long finger tapped against the table, then he slowly brought his face back to her. "Your aim is significantly off."

"I see that."

Silence settled at the table. Mr. Everest looked down toward his hand resting near the fork at his place.

"Do you?"

"Do I what?"

"Own a smile?"

He looked back toward the lake.

There was something unsettled with him—which seemed odd for a man so forceful and sharp. What was this armor he wore? Why would he feel the need for it with her—a stranger? And how did he expect to maintain it in a marriage?

Marriage.

Oh yes. That was the term of this arrangement they were there to discuss, wasn't it? She'd been clear in her response to the advertisement about that. Well, at least about her heart.

Sonora sighed, following his gaze back to the lake. Perhaps he was right—this was clearly not going to work. Why would she even want it to?

SIX

WHAT WAS IT GRETTA had said? He was a grump—and was getting worse.

Taylor's gut clenched, and he balled his fist against the table. Why was he doing this? It had been bad enough that he'd been suckered into Curtis's absurd ad scheme. But to agree to meet the questionable woman who had answered the thing? Not wise. Especially when he'd seen her picture and had an immediate shot of adrenaline rush through his veins.

That should have ended the whole thing right then and there. But rather than issuing a *thanks but no thanks*, he'd offered an interview. Because he'd thought her lovely.

His vision caught the movement of her hand as she reached to finger that thick braid resting against her shoulder. Irresistibly drawn, Taylor's eyes followed the trail of her hair up to her neck and then on to the outline of her profile. Her skin was creamy, kissed with a warm touch of caramel by the sun.

He tightened his fingers against the impulse to know for himself if her flesh was as soft and warm as it looked as she sat in the soft golden light of the fading day. He should look away. Not skim the curve of her jawline and seek the shape of her mouth with his starving eyes.

Her mouth did not smile as she continued to stare out the window. A pity.

That grin . . . the one she'd planted on the kid taking their order. What would it be like to have it for himself? His heart flipped as he imagined it.

It would be . . . trouble. Nothing but trouble. No, it could be worse than trouble. He'd already known the ripping of his heart at the hands of a young, flighty, and flirtatious woman.

Never again.

"Well?" She brought her attention back to him.

Was she asking what he was staring at? *You. Because I can't stop myself.* Heaven help him. He clenched his jaw. "Well what?"

A sad tilt of her mouth proceeded her headshake. "That is a no, then."

A no? Some kind of measure of grief fell through his core, and suddenly he wanted to take away whatever made this woman sad by any means necessary.

What was it that made her sad?

His smile. She'd asked if he'd owned a smile . . . and then took his taciturn silence as a no. Taylor blinked, caught in a juxtaposition of desire and logic. He wanted to experience the sunshine of her grin again. But he didn't want to expose himself to her charm—that would be far too dangerous.

Foolish. So with an effort that seemed extreme, he stuffed away the longing to make her glad and added chill to his eye contact with her.

"Don't waste your time fishing in waters that are barren."

"That's sad."

He hardened himself against the gentle compassion in her tone. "That brings us to the terms of this arrangement."

Clearing her throat, she straightened her shoulders. "Very well."

"The job is twelve hours a day."

"Seven days a week?"

"That is life in the seasonal tourist industry—though Sunday mornings and evenings are usually our own."

"And I would be driving tourists around the island?"

"Only to a few predetermined places within a small radius of town. Vehicles are not allowed in that part of the island. Predominantly, you'll be going to and from the docks, making a few stops along the way on occasion. Vehicles are allowed on Harbor Way, so you'll have to deal with that—and some make their way to the Palace, but for the most part, the tourists come on foot."

She nodded, her demeanor now all business. "I take it you will not be driving?"

"Why would you think that?"

"Did you have another driver before you took out that ad?"

She was a smart one, this pretty lady. "No."

"And you're needing one now because . . ."

Taylor leaned back hard against his chair. By the content of their conversation earlier, she'd figured it out. "I am not good with the tourists."

A small, knowing grin poked at one side of her mouth. "Ah, now we are being honest."

"Fine." He pressed his arms against the table and leaned against them. "Here is the truth: I am under contract with the Shore View Palace—the resort. The contract is older than I am, and I have never thoroughly read the details of it before I sign it every year. This year my negligence has come back to bite me."

"Because you're not good with tourists."

"Correct."

"I find that odd, Mr. Everest. Have you suddenly lost your ability to deal kindly with people?"

"What?"

"Is this sour front a recent development?"

"What are you talking about?"

"I am wondering why, now, after all these years of driving tourists, the fact that you are a grump has become an issue?"

Gretta's proclamation stabbed his memory again. *I think you finding a wife would make you happier.*

What if Gret's infuriating meddling was dead on? An absurd moment of surreal possibly clamped on Taylor as suddenly he imagined Sonora Hillary as his wife. Without reason, and without rebuke, the desire for it took unrelenting hold of his heart. The emotion was as powerful as it was stupid. As unshakable as it was foolish.

He silently fought to dispel the surge of longing while he maintained his stern business front.

"There is a different issue with the contract," he said, lowering his tone so that what was shared would only fall on her ears.

Interest piqued in her gaze, and she leaned in to hear. "Ah, we come to the real mystery. Your layers are intriguing, Mr. Everest."

Her move nearer to him sent a waft of feminine scent—something with sweet lemons and floral qualities—straight into his already muddled senses. Combined with the playful glint in her mesmerizing eyes, a powerful wave of dizzying delight nearly took him under.

"I need a wife." He swallowed, heat rising at the intimacy of his whisper. Good heavens, that sounded like . . . like a proposal. Like a real one.

She blinked. Then her delightfully curious expression hardened into something closed as she looked toward her lap. "That is . . . odd."

"Yes." Taylor cleared his throat. "But it is in the contract."

"Thus your strange ad."

"Exactly." Ah. The firm ground of business only again. Much better. No more staring. No more speaking in hushed, intimate tones. No more . . . flirting.

Their interview paused as their waiter returned with a tray full of food. He passed plates to both and refilled their waters, before asking if there was anything else needed. There was none, and so he left. Thankfully, without summoning Sonora's captivating smile.

"Mr. Everest, perhaps you were right. This has been a waste of our time."

Taylor gripped the fork near his left hand hard while his gut clenched, as if experiencing the force of a blow. "What?"

"I was clear in my response. Love is not . . ." She motioned between them. "It's not possible between us."

He let that sink in. Stinging. Burning. Smashing that near-euphoric sensation of her nearness and scent and the imaginings of her as his wife had summoned.

A rejection before he'd even had the chance . . . His heart twisted.

That was ridiculous. He didn't want the chance. What was going on in his frenzied mind? Putting iron back into his demeanor, he merely nodded at her toxic words. "I don't require love." Love was all untethered emotion and impossible expectations anyway. Could such a thing truly last under any circumstances? No. "Frankly, it's not possible from my end either."

Sonora met his momentary pause with eyebrows lifted, a silent *Well then?*

"I do, however, require marriage, as it is in my contract, and I haven't been able to find a way out of that clause."

Her expression didn't fold. Instead, the corners of her mouth seemed to twitch upward. "What sort of marriage would that be?"

"One that is legally filed."

"And?"

"And the rest stays between you and me."

"What exactly are those expectations between you and me?"

Fire flared up his neck at her pointed question. He knew exactly what she wanted to know—would they share a bed? Not if they intended to dissolve the legal union in the spring, as he planned.

But what if he let her squirm on that for a bit?

Taylor shook his head. Such a thought! Why would he wish her discomfort—or worse, risk her rejection just when she seemed to be willing to play this charade?

"My contract renews every spring—I will sign a new one in April. One that I will read thoroughly and negotiate accordingly."

"That's lovely. Not what I asked though."

"My expectations are that you and I remain married—for legal purposes only—until that time. After the first of April, we can file for an annulment. Or whatever."

"That's all?"

He tilted his head. Was she in?

"How about I put down my terms." Her voice was as removed from a question as she was currently from her Wyoming home.

Taylor liked her boldness, though he wasn't willing to express that. "Your terms? I think you've turned this interview around."

"Indeed. But you can't expect me to go into this sort of arrangement without having certain things stated plainly." She folded her hands and placed them on the table. "I won't sleep with you."

Didn't get plainer than that. Though a blush—again—climbed to the tips of his ears, Taylor refused to allow his expression to change. Rather than giving her any hint that she could fluster him, he simply nodded. "Let me be clear with you about that. I won't be seeking intimacy with you."

Did she flinch? He hadn't meant to be insulting, but perhaps his dry tone came across as such? As usual, Taylor was gauche.

Gauche: tacky, graceless, tactless, rude, boorish, or awkward and foolish . . . He ran through the definitions and matched the one that most closely related to his typical behavior. Awkward. No, maybe tactless.

He sighed quietly. "Forgive me, Miss Hillary. That did not come out the way I intended—which was as a reassurance, not an insult."

Hands having slid to her lap, and her face cast down toward them, Sonora peeked up at him, and to his shock, she chuckled. “You are very formal, Mr. Everest.”

“Stiff and serious and as boring as plain toast, Miss Hillary. And shockingly honest.”

Her cheeky—flirty—grin set on him, and his heart did a flip as her copper eyes danced. “We might do okay.”

Interesting that she would find that list of his character flaws reassuring. Sitting backward, Taylor crossed his arms. “What’s in this for you?”

A thoughtful pause weighed the space between them—one in which he suspected she considered how much of the truth she would tell him.

All of it, he hoped. Though he didn’t know why.

She cut into the fried perch and took a taste. “Better than I expected.”

“You’re not a fan of fish?”

“No. Not really.”

“Then why did you order the perch?”

“I am here to find a new life. I’ve had sirloin before.” She nodded toward Taylor’s untouched plate. “But never perch.”

Had she answered both of his questions with that?

Taylor wasn’t up for trying to dissect subtleties. “Why would you need a new life?”

She shrugged, and a shadow passed through her expression. “The old one didn’t work out the way I’d hoped.”

Taylor picked up his fork and steak knife and sliced off a grilled hunk of meat. The inside was still pink, but not bloody. Mentally, he congratulated the nervous waiter for getting his order right. "You're not a criminal, are you?"

"Do I strike you as someone who would commit crimes?"

"No." He chewed the bite he'd shoved into his mouth—a touch salty, but good nonetheless—and then swallowed. "But they say psychopaths can appear normal."

"I have never heard that."

She couldn't be a psychopath. *God, please don't let her be a psychopath.* Any sort of marriage—convenient, fake, or otherwise—would be a disaster with a psychopath.

"Don't worry. I feel bad when I hit a rodent on the lonely roads back home." Full sweetness, and a touch of fun, filled her voice. "I won't kill you while you sleep."

"Good to know." A smile teased his mouth. He schooled it with a reminder of the seriousness of this interview while he cut another bite of his steak. "You're not in danger?"

"No." She speared a side of asparagus that had come with her fish. "Though I would prefer some people didn't know where I am."

"Which people?"

She sipped her water, leaving him in dangling curiosity—one that, absurdly, felt a whole lot like concern.

"A man I dated."

Something feral and deeply protective overtook his sensibilities. He could think of one reason a woman wouldn't want a man she'd been involved with to find her. Taylor held the next bite of meat away from his mouth and pinned a stern look on her face. "Did he treat you badly?" Why was every muscle in him taut? Where was this anger boiling up from?

Soft appreciation made her natural loveliness even more compelling. "No," she said calmly. "Not the way you're implying." She sighed, looked at the lake as the sun began to sink into the land far across the horizon, and then squared back to him. "He broke my heart, was all."

Taylor stared at her. Such a pretty young woman. Eyes that could make a man feel rich, a smile that could make him dizzy. And obviously smart—witty enough to spar with him.

It didn't make sense that a man who had claimed her heart would be foolish enough to break it.

No, what didn't make sense was that he cared. Her heart wasn't available—she'd been perfectly clear about that. Now he knew why—some stupid man had claimed it and then broken it.

The world seemed plagued with idiots.

A general truth, but Taylor brushed away the rising irritation. He wasn't interested in her heart anyway. And if she had the sense to leave an idiot rather than chase after him, all the better for her. And him.

Perhaps he should finish his steak and find a bed. This tossed-about thinking could be nothing except a touch of boat sickness. After all, he'd never enjoyed the crossing.

They both finished their meals while the late-summer sun spilled a vibrant orange streak across the graying sky, leaving a reflection of color against the dark vastness of the lake.

"Well?"

Taylor looked away from the sunset, startled by the voice across from him. "Well what?"

"I'm game if you are. Do I get the job or not?"

"You agree to *all* the terms?"

"Is that your way of asking if I'll marry you?"

Once again heat infused his cheeks. How often had this cowgirl provoked a blush in the brief hour since they'd met? Too often. That couldn't be a good sign.

But those copper eyes clamped on him, a hint of a smile in them. Warmth pooled in his chest, and without conscious thought, his fingers slid across the table toward hers.

He stopped just short of touching her. Thank goodness. Clearing his throat, he drew back and pinned his shoulders straight. "If you want the job, we'll go to the courthouse in the morning and catch the noon ferry."

Her smile bloomed full, and she held out the hand he'd nearly touched. "Deal."

Seven

THAT MUST HAVE BEEN the world's worst proposal ever. And who shook on a marriage agreement?

Sonora lay on her back against the too soft mattress in her dark room. A mixture of amusement and anxiety had her staring up at the ceiling, certain not to sleep at all that night. Amusement, because of the deep blush Mr. Everest had been unable to control when the woman at the front desk of the inn had asked if they would like the honeymoon suite.

"It's all we have for double occupancy for the night."

He'd shaken his head too emphatically. "Certainly not. We will need two rooms tonight. Two *separate* rooms."

The clerk's surprised look, combined with Mr. Everest's fluster, had nearly provoked Sonora to laugh out loud. How was he going to make it through a marriage ceremony at the courthouse in the morning?

Scratch that. How was *she* going to get through it?

As the query settled in her mind, she squeezed her eyes shut. This was . . . madness. Who ran off to marry a stranger for a job because her former boyfriend was getting married?

Panic raced through her veins, and Sonora tossed the stiff blanket from her legs. Sitting up, her feet hit the chilly floor, and without stopping to talk herself down, she gripped the doorknob, flung the door open, and scurried across the carpeted hallway to tap on Taylor's door.

In less than three breaths, he stood before her. Dark hair disheveled, blue eyes dark and pinched, he stared down at her with an intensity that caught her breath.

"Something wrong?" His low voice came deep. Almost intimate.

A shiver rippled along her arms. Sonora forked her fingers into her loose hair. Taylor's attention followed her hand, and then his eyes drifted over her form. A mixture of pleasure and hunger passed through his expression.

Sucking in a breath, Sonora shrank back and crossed her arms. She hadn't considered a simple tank top and thin sleep shorts to be revealing, but under the warming watch of Taylor's gaze, she suddenly felt . . . exposed. And oh so foolish.

Taylor stood straighter, pulling his shoulder off the doorframe. Coolness reentered his gaze. "Is there a problem, Miss Hillary?"

Yes. Many problems. At the moment, the foremost was that she wanted to experience the way he'd just looked at her again, which was insane because it sort of frightened her. In a thrilling way.

Clearing her throat, Sonora crossed her arms. "I think this is a bad idea."

"It's after three in the morning. You're just now deciding our agreement might need reconsidering?"

"Yes. Well, you know, they say to sleep on it, and . . ." Where was she going with that? She hadn't slept.

His long fingers buried into that mess of dark hair. Oh man. Taylor Everest was a good-looking guy, even if he didn't own a smile.

"For the record, I've not slept a moment." His sharp blue gaze pinned on her face. "And I would bet that you haven't either."

Sonora bit her bottom lip.

"It's understandable to be nervous before you get married. Or so I'm told."

"This is a little more than that."

"Is it? I thought our agreement was *less* than a real marriage."

"I don't know you. You could be a con artist. Or a serial killer. How do I know you're not going to haul me off to Siberia or stuff me in a trunk or something?"

"I assumed an intelligent woman like yourself had done her homework before agreeing to meet me."

Ahem. She had. Called the Palace and asked about the man in charge of the carriage. Taylor Everest, they'd said. A lifelong resident of Sanctuary Island. About thirty years old, no criminal record. Tall, dark hair, serious. Harmless, unless you thought brusque words and a sharp tone could cause injury. But he didn't mean harm. And he adored his horses.

That was the clincher right there. A man who was kind to his horses was a man Sonora believed she could trust.

"Tell me about Albert and Victoria."

One dark brow lifted. And was that a trace of a smile? An effort at least. "My Friesians? So you did do some investigations."

"The man I spoke to said if you judged a man's heart by the way he treated his animals, yours was pure."

Taylor frowned. "Who did you speak with?"

"Curtis something."

The scowl turned to an eye roll. "Of course Curtis would say something that maudlin."

Maudlin? Who used that sort of word? Sonora wasn't even sure she knew what it meant, exactly.

But that was not the focus of this long-after-midnight meeting in the hall. "It isn't true?"

"What? That my heart is pure?" Taylor shrugged. "I don't know that I can say. I'm a man, full of flaws just like any other."

"But not a serial killer?"

"No."

"A con artist?"

"I told you . . . I am brutally honest."

"Right." Sonora nodded. Then she considered a way to test that claim . . . She would do it, though it might be humiliating. "Then tell me, Taylor Everest. What exactly were you thinking when you found me standing here, knocking on your door?"

He swallowed visibly, his stare heating while the color of his neck grew crimson. "My exact thoughts?"

"Yes. No editing."

Clearing his throat, he leaned nearer. "You're beautiful. That's what I thought." He rubbed his neck, and his stare drifted toward the floor. "And it would be a fortunate situation to have your lovely face be the first one I see every day."

His compliment came like a shy little boy telling his crush that he liked her, all timid and endearing. Sonora wrapped a section of hair around her finger and dared to catch his eyes again. At his blush, she grinned. "That's sweet, Mr. Everest."

"It was raw. Not an invitation to flirt."

Man, that tone was harsh. Curtis hadn't been lying. She sighed. "I did ask for honesty."

His lips pinched, and his brow furrowed. Was he irritated with her or with himself?

"Do you think we'll work well together?" she asked.

"As . . . as husband and wife?" Was there a touch of hope in his quiet voice?

"As employer and employee."

Relief seemed to sag through his tense posture. "Yes. I think you'll do well. So long as you can handle the animals." At that, he frowned. "Your letter said you have handled horses and have driven before, right?"

It was amusing to see this uptight and self-possessed man off balance. Sonora chuckled. “Yes. I grew up in the saddle, and I’ve started at least a half dozen young horses on my own. And my dad taught me how to handle the reins from a wagon. I’ve been driving a wagon for a dude ranch for the last three years.”

“Albert and Victoria are not just any old rodeo horses.”

Sonora shook her head. “Clearly you don’t know anyone who rodeos.” She raised her brow in challenge. “I’ve never met a cowboy or cowgirl who didn’t love their animals heart and soul.”

Taylor had the decency to look put in his place. “You’re right—I’ve not. Forgive me.”

“How long have you had Albert and Victoria?”

“Since I took over the contract with the Palace from my father. They were a gift to me before he and my mom moved to the winter grounds in southern Michigan.”

“The winter grounds?”

“Where I send Al and Vicky after the tourist season—before the ferry services close.”

“You don’t keep them all year?”

“No. Winters are brutal on the island, and keeping them there would be hard for them and difficult for me. My small acreage doesn’t put up enough hay for them.”

“So it’s just you through the winter?”

“No. I have Molly and Pete. And Mr. and Mrs. Kline.”

“Who are they?”

"Molly and Pete are my Haflingers—smaller, hardier animals that don't require as much feed. And the Klines are my nearest neighbors. Mrs. Kline is my housekeeper. Mr. Kline leases the ground from me during the tourist season, in exchange for putting up hay that will see me through the winter."

His formal, stiff demeanor had faded, and Sonora felt more comfortable with him as they stood there. "I look forward to meeting Al and Vicky—and Molly and Pete."

Those firm lips relaxed, and did he *almost* grin?

So close.

This could be a fun new pastime, trying to summon the impossible from this formidable man. Though she would have to figure out a way of doing so without him perceiving her as a flirt, as clearly he found any trace of flirting irritating.

"Feel better now?"

She blinked at his question. "What?"

He stepped forward, meeting her just outside his door in the hall and crowding into her space. She nearly jumped at his touch when his fingers brushed her bare arm. When her gaze flew toward his face, his fingers fell away, and his expression reverted to cool sternness.

"Forgive me." He stepped back again. "I think we've stood here long enough. It is the middle of the night, after all."

"Right." She swallowed. Had he just been . . . tender toward her?

Suddenly new goals popped up like spring seedlings. *Find Taylor's grin. Summon his tender touch.*

Stupid. Neither of those items had anything to do with seasonal employment. Worse, both of them had the potential to create problems.

"I think we'll do well together, Sonora."

Have him say my name with that low gentleness.

Mentally she drew a line through that. And the two previous goals as well.

Sonora nodded, turning back to make her way to her own room again. As long as she kept her heart and mind in check, they'd do just fine.

Taylor sat on the edge of his bed, the side lamp still on. He stared at his bare toes, replaying the interaction that had happened twenty minutes before. Particularly the part when he'd allowed yearning to overcome logic and let his fingers slide over the warm silk of her arm.

His middle clenched.

They weren't even married yet, and he'd already been unable to resist touching her.

Growling, he flipped his feet onto the bed and sagged against the stacked pair of pillows. Through the inch gap in the curtains at his window, he could see the pale light of breaking day. Another hour and the sun would be fully up, and he could stop imagining that he might catch some sleep. At this point, it wasn't even worth trying.

He snatched his phone off the nightstand and tapped the screen to view the text conversation he'd had the night before with Curtis.

Well? Curtis had sent that question long before the dinner interview had been completed. What had he been expecting? That Taylor would propose the moment he met the woman in person?

Not quite. Though, insanely, not that far off.

She's beautiful in real life, isn't she? he'd texted, not long after that first intrusion.

You're a goner. Just admit it. What was his friend doing? Hadn't been helpful.

And no, Taylor wasn't a goner. He'd decided well before he'd crossed the lake that he was not going to be a goner. Ever.

Come on, man! That had come through sometime during Taylor's shower, after they'd checked into their *separate* rooms.

Taylor had finally answered at that point. Short and to the point. *Getting married in the morning.*

Curtis replied with a set of firework emojis and a stupid question about a honeymoon.

None required. Be back on the noon ferry.

Taylor replayed the way Sonora had looked, standing there in her jammies, hair spilling around her shoulders, and vulnerability in her beautiful eyes. And that momentary touch. Tipping his head back, he let his eyes slip shut as he sighed.

"God, it's been a few years . . ." Ache twanged in his chest. The questions he'd pondered on the golf course several days ago whispered back to mind.

Could a man ever trust again the One who had disappointed him?

No, he'd not been aiming that curiosity at a woman, though her flippant inconsistency had been the catalyst. But ultimately, God had let it happen. If He could, as Scripture proclaimed, establish times and seasons, set up kings and depose them, then He was sovereign over Taylor's life. He'd allowed Taylor's heart to be broken. And not only once.

For no reason, as far as Taylor could determine. He'd not been stiff necked and rebellious. So he was like Naomi, returning to her old life and asking to be called Mara. For it was God who had dealt harshly with her.

With that, Taylor had decided years ago he couldn't trust the One who had disappointed him. And he wouldn't miss Him.

He'd been lying to himself all this time. An ironic truth, since Taylor prided himself on being honest.

Well then. It was time to be honest with himself.

He missed God. Mornings spent in prayer. Evenings reading the Psalms. A sense of being known, though most people thought him closed off and unknowable. And he missed having someone to be honest with. One to whom he could pour out his rather stiff and awkward heart.

And what would Taylor say now, if he was being honest?

Taylor opened his eyes and watched while the light of day brightened through the crack in the curtains.

"I'm scared."

Terrified, actually. Significantly more than he should be for a business deal.

He was knee-quaking scared. Of the beautiful young woman who would soon be his wife. And of the cracking of his cemented heart. Seemed a collision course had been provoked, and Taylor felt helpless to stop it.

Eight

The skinny three-story building before her held a small-town charm. Or so Sonora told herself as she took in the three tall columns on either side of the nine-foot heavy wooden doors that centered the pristine white-sided building. In a moment she would pass by those six columns and beneath the portico, through those century-plus-old doors, and find herself standing before a judge to promise forever to a man she barely knew and had no intention of staying with.

She'd lie. That fact wiped all the charm away from the otherwise endearing setting.

As her stomach roiled, Sonora swallowed.

"You all right?"

Taylor's quiet question held more concern than she'd expected. Pulling her attention from the covering upheld by those columns, she met his eyes.

Pinched. Wary. Scared? Layers of silent emotion stared back at her. Her pulse throbbed, and she couldn't summon a smile to cover her fear. Instead, she clamped her jaw to quell the surge of emotion.

A girl only had one wedding. Well. That was what her mom had told her. "Make a good choice, Sonora. It's a one-shot deal." Her mom's exact words.

Sound in theory. But in practice? Statistics told a whole other tale—her parents being among them.

And what about this? Had her mom ever considered a business-arrangement/fake-marriage situation?

Um, no. For obvious reasons. And Sonora was about to become a statistic. *But, God, we're being honest and up front about it with each other—and You. Does that count for anything?*

Long, cold fingers touched Sonora's elbow, causing her to suck in a sharp breath.

"Sorry." Taylor's hand immediately dropped to his side. He looked back toward the park across the road, his expression every bit as tight as her stomach.

"It's okay. I'm just jumpy, I guess."

"Nervous?" His attention came back to her.

"Yes," she breathed. "You?"

He swallowed visibly. "Very." His eyes drifted toward his clenched fist and then slowly found hers again. "It's not forever though."

"Right. Even though that's what we'll tell the judge."

Taylor flinched.

"You don't like that any more than I do, do you?"

"That I'm about to go tell a bald-faced lie?" He shook his head. "No. I don't like it at all."

"But you and I know the truth." Sonora exhaled slowly. That was a measure of comfort, wasn't it? After all, they were the ones who would be most affected by this charade. They were being honest with themselves. That *did* count for something.

Didn't it? Heaven seemed silent on the matter.

Taylor's response was slow in coming, but he finally nodded. "You and me and God." He turned square to her, and once again his hand found her elbow. "Can we just say it out loud? This marriage isn't a marriage. It's business, and before God, I promise that I'll honor that agreement."

Ah, something honorable in the charade.

Gentle warmth eased the twisting discomfort in her gut, and Sonora found she could smile at that vow. She slid a half step nearer, holding his intense gaze. "It's business, and before God, I'll honor that agreement."

The corner of his mouth twitched. Was that . . . almost a smile?

Good enough for now.

Taylor maintained his hold on her elbow and guided her under that portico, through those double doors, and into the charming small-town courthouse. And everything went as a business deal should go—uneventful.

Until the justice asked if they would be exchanging a symbol of their commitment.

With a slight nod, Taylor pulled a ring from his pants pocket and slipped it onto Sonora's left finger. "With this ring, I thee wed."

Emotion welled up against Sonora's throat as the justice recited, "Let this ring serve as a reminder of your affection, sincerity, and loyalty to each other. May you remember this moment of love and promise all through the coming years. May your burdens be lighter as you carry them together. May your days be sweeter as you enjoy each other's companionship. And may this new, shared life be filled with joy."

Sonora trapped a shuddering cry in her chest as the power of this stranger's blessing sank in. The cold metal of the simple, narrow band felt foreign and weighty on her finger, and suddenly the vows to love and care for the man who had just slipped it on her finger became a mass upon her soul.

"By the authority given to me by the state of Michigan, I proclaim you partners in marriage." The woman, who had been rather stern faced and all business, allowed a grin to break free. She winked at Sonora. "You can kiss your husband, young lady."

Nothing about this ceremony had been as Sonora had dreamed for her wedding. And yet it felt more powerful than she'd imagined—or hoped for, particularly for a business agreement. Feeling caught, and certain her blush made her cheeks blaze crimson, Sonora looked up from the ring and into Taylor's stoic face. Did he feel this weightiness too?

Taylor watched her, the intensity of his gaze adding to this already suffocating moment. To see if she'd do as the justice advised?

What else could she do?

Curling her fingers over his, Sonora took a deep breath, stepped near enough to brace her free hand on his chest, and lifted to her toes.

To her shock, those blue eyes widened and then softened. Taylor bent to meet her mouth with the barest touch. His breath—minty from the gum he'd tossed in the garbage right before the justice began this farce—curled over her lips. He did not immediately pull away. Instead, he held still. And then his hand curled around the small of her back, tucking her closer still.

And in a warm exhale, his lips met hers for a second time.

A lovely, dizzying sensation filled Sonora's head as his kiss lingered. It was not at all an impassive, stony connection. Not as she would have expected—like a handshake, only with lips. No. This was . . .

Sweet. Tender. Emotional?

The headiness lingered even after Taylor lifted his face from hers and stepped back. Cool air filled the space between them, and Sonora blinked as she tried to convince herself that nothing remarkable had just happened.

She'd just gotten married. To a stranger whose unexpected kiss had made her head swim. Nothing remarkable at all.

"Well done."

The woman's voice shot reality back into the heady moment, and bride and groom separated farther. Taylor released her hand, suddenly making her aware that he'd held on to it even when he'd broken their kiss.

"You'll need to both sign, and then the paperwork will be filed."

Taylor's stare didn't waver as the justice spoke. This time wonder joined the layers of emotion in those blue eyes.

Sonora's heart jumped, sputtered. Galloped. And then a shiver quaked through her middle.

A kiss was not the way to seal a business deal. Not if one wanted to walk away with their heart intact.

What had she just done?

You're a goner.

He couldn't get that line out of his head. Curious, though Curtis had been the one to say it—or rather text it—the voice speaking the words over and over in his mind was his own.

Taylor faced the oncoming wind as the *Haven* bounced against the rolling waves, allowing the brusqueness of the lake-chilled air to claw against his face. Hands on the polished railing of the ferry, he shut his eyes in an effort to vanquish the three troublesome words haunting his mind.

You're a goner.

Closing his eyes was a mistake. For in that space of darkness, tinged with orange as the power of the sun seeped through his lids, he found a commanding reenactment of the ceremony he'd participated in an hour previously. Particularly, the end of it.

That kiss.

Had he truly kissed a woman he'd known less than twenty-four hours? Yes. Yes, indeed he had. He'd *really* kissed Sonora Hillary-Everest. The hyphen their agreed compromise, as he'd asserted that no one who knew him on the island would believe their marriage real if she didn't take his name, but Sonora asserted, rightfully, that dropping her name would make matters infinitely more complicated when they executed their planned separation.

So Sonora Hillary-Everest she'd become. And he'd kissed her as though there was emotion between them. Kissed her as though his name attached to hers would be an everlasting thing.

And here was the real kicker: He wanted, unreasonably, but powerfully, to do so again.

Taylor crammed his hand into his wind-mussed hair.

You're a goner.

He couldn't be a goner. This was supposed to be a neat and tidy solution. A satisfactory resolution to Gretta's infuriating interference in his personal life. One that would *not* be personal at all. Wouldn't involve any more emotion than a business transaction. Like making a deposit at the bank.

Sign the paper. Submit the exchange. Walk away. No heart palpitations involved.

Palpitations? *Irregular heartbeat due to agitation, exertion, or illness . . .*

Was that the right word?

Taylor turned, looking over his shoulder at the woman he was, in about twenty minutes, going to introduce to everyone who'd known him his whole life as his wife. Down the railing about fifteen feet, and face tipped up as if to gather the warmth from the sun to combat the cool gusts swirling off the lake, Sonora stood. Her profile slammed against his vision, causing his heart to gallop. Not palpitate. Gallop.

His wife was a beautiful woman.

His wife.

His beautiful . . . *wife.*

The kiss haunted his lips, the effects of it rippling through his veins yet again. Warmth rushed over his limbs and infused his cheeks, working against the chilly lake wind.

And his heart? Pounding. Definitely *irregular* and *agitated.*

How had he ever believed this was a good—and innocuous—idea?

Nine

Would he always *watch* her?

Sonora stepped off the bobbing vessel and onto the equally unstable gangway. The movement of the ferry in rhythm with the waves didn't bother her, but even so, she wrapped a light grip on the metal handle attached to the gangway. As she took in her first glimpse of Sanctuary Island, she intentionally let her survey dawdle. There was the dock line, thick and matte gray against the thick billows of white clouds set off by a deep-blue sky. She followed the cable to the docks, finding thick planks kept in pristine condition leading the way to solid land.

And there . . .

Her breath caught.

The scene before her was like one of those puzzles her mom pulled out during the dreary winter days back home. The ones featuring paintings by Charles Wysocki. Yesteryear ambiance, small-town charm.

The frantic flutter of her heart eased, melting away a bit of the anxiety that had accompanied her on the ferry ride. *That* was the setting she was about to step into? Gorgeous. Rolling green hills interrupted by clusters of deciduous trees and seamed by curving roads paved with brick. Sanctuary spread before her on a canvas that seemed to rise with layers of detail, each one pressing a sense of peace and beauty where she'd only felt panic moments before.

First layer contained the rocky shoreline of the island, sprinkled with a few small buildings, most of which flew an American flag on a raised post near the front door. Down the pebbled beach, off a ways into the distance, a lighthouse rose toward the blue sky, a beacon of safety that, for some undefined reason, touched her heart.

The Lord is a strong tower. The righteous run to it and are safe.

The verse from Proverbs whispered in her heart, and questions trailed in its wake. Sonora tucked away the thoughts carefully, keeping them safe to examine later.

Next came a layer of countryside, all green and warm, dressed in full late-summer glory. Blooming shrubs lined sections of the road, and Victorian lamps spaced at even intervals lent to that yesteryear feel. Mopheads of pink-white blooms bounced cheerily in the shoreline breeze, making Sonora think that the land was waving a kind welcome to her.

How lovely was that?

Then there was the heart of Sanctuary Island—the town that was all of a handful of blocks. The epitome of a sweet small town if ever there was one. From where she stood on the dock, Sonora looked right toward the lighthouse and found a glimpse of the sweeping red roofline of the largest building on the island. The Shore View Palace, she would guess. That long covered front porch, which she knew ran beneath that red roof from the web page she'd studied, would offer stunning views of the peaceful and lovely island countryside and then the far-reaching greatness of the lake. Not to mention pristine gardens renowned for their epic beauty and a nearby golf course ranked high on the list of best in the nation.

"You look like a tourist." Taylor's quiet voice seemed neither critical nor pleased. A simple observation, was all.

Sonora peeled her attention from the glorious scene that had greeted her and looked up at her *husband.* "It is breathtaking."

The corner of his mouth twitched. "Glad you appreciate it."

She couldn't help the playful spirit that had her leaning her shoulder into his arm. "Come on now, Taylor. Take it in for a minute. Don't let your familiarity steal the wonder of it."

The man at her side held an inscrutable gaze on her. Then he swallowed visibly and turned his face to do as she'd asked. He took in the wide view of his home. After a moment, he nodded. "The island is a sight this time of year. Although my favorite is fall, when the trees turn to fire and gold."

Then he shifted the bag he carried—her luggage, which he'd insisted he'd attend to, and wasn't that gentlemanly of him?—and nudged her forward with a firm hand on the small of her back. "The carriage only waits for ten minutes. We'd best get to it."

Questions about his island comment sprouted in the back of her mind, but she focused on the waiting carriage. "I thought you were the only carriage driver?"

"I am. Was. Now we are two." He glanced down, his tight lips attempting a grin. It looked . . . painful. "Curtis knows how to handle Al and Vicky, in a pinch. He took my duties last night and this morning."

"Curtis? The man I spoke with about you?"

"Yes."

"He's a friend of yours?"

"Yes."

"Hmm." She'd inquired about this stranger and had unknowingly gotten a recommendation from a friend of his. Not the best plan. Then again, Sanctuary Island was small. Odds were, everyone who resided there knew each other. "How many are you?"

"Come again?" His scowl indicated offense.

Sonora chuckled. Her question had sounded off. Like she suspected him of multiple personalities, or something worse. She looped her hand through his arm, hoping he'd lighten up and try answering her questions with more than the necessary basics.

"On the island, how many people are here year round?"

"Oh. About seven hundred." Taylor led her to the side of the carriage and held a formal hand out to offer assistance so she could step up to the backseat.

She looked at his hand, then shifted her gaze to meet his eyes. "Are words hard in general, Taylor, or does being married have you tongue tied?"

Deep crimson crept up from beneath his stiff white collar and flared onto his cheeks.

Sonora didn't even try to bottle her quiet giggle. "I think making you blush might be a good pastime for me."

"I'd prefer not."

She arched an eyebrow, then moved her attention toward the red-haired man at the front of the carriage. Dancing green eyes were already watching her, mirth toying with his expression. The man winked, then pinned his attention on Taylor. "Your wife, I presume?"

Taylor shifted, rubbing his neck, and then cleared his throat with the energy that came with annoyance. "Move over, Curtis, and hand me the reins."

"Not a chance, my friend." Still grinning with mischief in every line of his expression, Curtis shifted back around to face the waiting horses. "You'll ride next to your bride, obviously. Albert and Victoria are in good hands."

Taylor climbed into the carriage behind Sonora. "That is questionable."

"That is false." Curtis flicked the reins and called a soft "walk on" to the animals hitched to this gorgeous carriage.

"You wouldn't let me near them if you didn't think I'd do a good job."

Sonora had no doubt that assertion was 100 percent accurate—and she couldn't blame Taylor for that. The charge of horses was not to be taken lightly, and particularly when there was to be a mixing of animals and people.

And a beautiful set of animals they were! Black Friesians, perfectly matched and, by all appearances, well cared for. Gleaming coats. Long, flowing black manes without a trace of tangle or burr. Braided and tucked tails, showing no trace of a falsie. Both Albert and Victoria held their necks in a lovely arc, and at Curtis's command, they pulled the weight of the carriage with strength and ease, creating a smooth ride.

Oh! Sonora nearly clapped with anticipation. She'd get to work with these lovely creatures! Marriage to a stoic stranger might just be worth the privilege.

She peeked at the man holding himself rigid near her right shoulder. Tight jaw. Eyes trained forward. Pale skin.

Was that about her or about his horses being handled by another?

Tapping her own mischievous tendencies, Sonora slipped her hand over his. Taylor sucked in a breath and nearly jumped from the soft red velvet of their shared seat. Then he swallowed hard, fixing his startled eyes on her.

"Nervous?" she asked, hearing the ironic echo of his query aimed at her earlier that morning.

He cleared his throat.

Sonora leaned in close, loving that her proximity clearly made this man's nerves vault toward the heavens. Why was it so entertaining to see a grown man squirm?

"We didn't discuss how to play this off in front of all the people who know you."

"We did." He leaned against the backrest of the seat, an amusing attempt to put space between them. "The details of our marriage are ours alone. That was clearly specified before." His whisper cracked.

"So we should be stiff and indifferent?" A playful grin teased her mouth. "Will that be believable, do you think?"

Another visible swallow. "I'm not . . . not the . . ." A fresh streak of red climbed the length of his neck. ". . . the tender sort."

Sonora leaned in closer. "Our wedding kiss would seem to offer contrary evidence."

A snort sounded from the high seat in front.

Taylor scowled at Sonora, then straightened from the seat back again. "No comments from you, Curtis. I'm in this mess because of you."

Ah. So Curtis *was* in on it.

"You never do anything you don't want to do, Everest." A grinning Curtis glanced back, his look falling directly on Sonora. "And I would hardly call your wife a *mess*." He winked at her again. "Actually, I'd say you've landed neatly on your feet, my friend."

An ally? Or was this redheaded mischief maker going to be trouble?

A question that would require some investigation. But his first comment—the one about Taylor never doing anything he didn't want to do—that one seemed to hit the target dead center, even if she had only known her husband for less than a day.

She turned her chin to seek Taylor's attention again. When his eyes met hers, it seemed almost involuntarily on his part. A spark fired in her veins, and she extinguished it before it could send off a second, more potent flash. It was one thing to tease this man because watching him blush was amusing. It was another to allow her emotions to chase after something more than that.

"Can we manage dignified appreciation for each other, do you think?" she asked.

The wary reserve dissolved from his expression, and he nodded. "That would be wise, I think."

"That would be boring, I think," Curtis inserted.

Taylor eyed his friend's back with stern irritation. "Don't let him influence you. I only put up with him because we grew up together."

A pure smile settled on Sonora's mouth. "I am not easily influenced."

He held a doubtful look on her. "Perhaps not. But I think you are a tease." That last part was spoken with a bite.

Sonora flinched. While she was, perhaps, a tease in the sense that she loved to laugh, she wasn't interested in causing harm. And she wasn't interested in triggering this harshness from Taylor Everest, even if she did wonder why he responded so.

What she wanted was his smile. *And maybe another go at that kiss . . .*

Banish the thought! No kissing.

Sonora sat back, releasing Taylor's arm. She felt the man suck in a breath. Relief? She looked up to gauge his expression, but his face was turned away.

Well then. She'd settle for the sweeping view of the Palace as they drew near. That wide red roof sheltered a long white building. Massive full-length windows slated the front of the resort, with a covered front porch acting as their protector. The wooden floor planks gleamed with polish, and the many white rockers that dotted that sheltered area would offer any visitor a stunning view of the lake.

The carriage rolled into the wide circle drive, the horses' shod feet producing a rhythmic clip-clop against the bricks. At Curtis's gentle "whoa now," Albert and Victoria eased to a smooth stop.

"Stand." Taylor spoke the command. To her?

She lifted a raised-brow look toward him, and his cheeks pinked.

No, of course the command hadn't been intended for her.

"Hard to let someone else take the reins?" she asked.

Curtis hopped down from the front, a cheeky grin on his teasing face. “He’ll have to get used to it now.” Another wink dropped over one green eye.

Ignoring Curtis’s offered hand, Taylor jumped from the carriage and then turned to offer his hand to Sonora. She looked from Curtis, who still stood with a hand stretched out, and then to Taylor. For a moment, she hesitated, lifting a teasing brow.

Taylor scowled. Then dropped his hand.

Sonora’s grin fell. Was he angry at her? For teasing him? Boy, this could be a long marriage. She glanced at Curtis, who shook his head, as if to tell her to not let it bother her.

How could being married to a grump not bother her?

With a puffed sigh, she jumped to the bricked ground, sans assistance from either man, and strode to the back of the carriage to retrieve her luggage.

“I’ll get it, Sonora.” Taylor’s low voice was all demand.

“I’m capable.” Forget gentlemanly. He was just being . . . overbearing.

“I’m sure you are.” He stepped in front of her, as if boxing her out in a basketball game. “But I’ll get it just the same.”

Still imposing, though all done in a near whisper. Was this an ego thing? Or perhaps this tall, unsmiling man had never met a Wyoming-grown cowgirl who could wrangle her own stuff? Sonora shot Taylor a scowl, which he most certainly saw and answered with a turned shoulder and silence. Next thing she knew, the man was walking toward that wide covered deck at the front of the opulent Palace, not another word to her, and carrying her stuff.

How was that for a *welcome home*? So much for charming.

"He's just scared to death."

Sonora turned, startled. Curtis lifted a half grin, his expression still mostly amused.

She smirked and crossed her arms. "Is that what that is? I thought he was simply a taciturn man."

Curtis laughed. "Taciturn? He'll love that."

"What?"

"Taylor likes big words that no one ever uses. He used to read the dictionary in his spare time."

"I find that hard to believe. I've had mostly monosyllable answers, if not simply a movement of his head." Not entirely true. They'd had a few exchanges that slipped toward the deeper end of conversation. Which, frankly, made Taylor's brusque actions just now even more irritating.

She'd seen he was a decent human—him asking if she was nervous before they married and reassuring her that this was *only* a business deal and he'd keep it that way.

And then there was that kiss . . .

Banish the kiss!

"Well, my dear Mrs. Everest, I just told you. Taylor is scared to death."

Sonora snorted. "That would imply that he felt something in that closed-off heart."

"It would." Curtis's grin mellowed to something sincere rather than outright entertained. "You can trust my word, Mrs. Everest. Your husband feels deeply. He rarely let's anyone see that, but I promise he does."

"Sonora." Rolling her shoulders straight, Sonora corrected the man's use of her fake married name even as the term *husband* ricocheted around her mind like a Ping-Pong ball. "Just Sonora."

Curtis held out his right hand. "Glad to meet you. I'm Curtis O'Connell, but you've already got that."

Sonora shook his hand as the sound of heavy footfalls banged down the front steps and onto the cobblestone walk, coming toward them.

"Might have warned me Gretta was hyperventilating today." Taylor's frown was aimed at Curtis, but his glance at Sonora indicated she was included in his rapidly disintegrating mood.

"Figured that would be stating the obvious."

Taylor shoved a hand through his dark hair. "She know?"

"That you got hitched?" Curtis laughed and clapped Taylor's shoulder. "Nope. Left that happy news for you to share. But please make sure I'm present when you do." He walked away chuckling, heading toward the Palace.

Sonora fixed her attention on her grumpy *husband*. "Is this you normally?"

"What?"

"Are you always this . . . *pleasant*?"

He looked away, but not before his mouth tugged into a deeper frown.

"I see. So you were on your best behavior on the mainland, hmm?"

Silence.

"No wonder you had to put an ad out to find a wife."

His scowl whipped straight back to her, and now fire snapped in his eyes. "I didn't actually want to get married, in case you somehow missed that in our exchange. This wasn't my idea."

"Your friend seems to think that if you didn't want to do it, you wouldn't have."

"I don't want to lose my contract."

"That seems flimsy."

"Look around, Sonora. This island, though beautiful, is small. Everyone who lives here has their place, and they stay in it. Me? I drive the carriage for the Palace. Just like my dad did, and my grandfather before him, and his father before that. It's our legacy and our position here. I have the team, the equipment, and the experience. But without the contract, I don't have the clients. I don't have a job. Maybe you can drop everything and leave a job because things got uncomfortable, but I don't have that luxury."

That last sentence was like a shot fired. Did he know how much it stung? And *uncomfortable*? That was understating it. Watching Donovan fall all over himself for a pretty heiress two seconds after he'd dumped her had been devastating. And having that heiress dismiss her? Humiliating.

But what would this egotistical man of stone know about it?

Her heart pounded with furious heat, words of reprimand ready to launch from her tongue as she matched his glare. Their gazes locked, and Sonora determined not to be the first to flinch as she dared step into the small gap between them. "Do you always feel sorry for yourself?"

He flinched. And she felt bad in spite of his brutish behavior.

"Mr. Everest." A curt feminine voice broke into their heated deadlock. "A word please."

Sonora looked away from the mesmerizing, infuriating blue of his eyes and toward the sound of that demand.

A short woman in a charcoal pantsuit strode toward them, head held stiff, fists curled, mouth stern. Her attention was narrowly focused on Taylor, and for a moment Sonora wondered if this woman had been entangled with *Mr. Everest* on a more personal level. Why else would she come out fuming so?

"You did not request permission to vacate your duties."

Taylor spun toward the carriage where his Friesians, good animals that they were, stood patiently. "Curtis handled my duties just fine."

"That is not the point. And he has a job of his own to attend to."

"Gretta, it's been a day. Lay off."

"It's barely noon."

He swiveled his jaw around and pinned a warning on this feisty bit of a pest. So this was Gretta. The woman who wielded the sort of might that forced Taylor to find a wife. Sonora took her in from head to toe. All five foot nothing of her.

Gretta met Sonora's inspection. "Please excuse us." She feigned a congenial smile. "My carriage man and I will take this discussion inside. Unless you have need of his services?"

Sonora stared for a beat, and then a laugh burst from her chest. "She is formidable, Taylor. I'll give you that."

Taylor's shoulders dropped, and he groaned.

"I'm . . . sorry?" Gretta looked from Sonora to Taylor, who still stood with his back to them, and back to Sonora. "Have I missed something?"

Sonora employed her widest smile. "Yes, actually, you have, Gretta." Stepping forward, she held out her hand. "I'm Sonora. Sonora Hillary-Everest."

"Ev—" Gretta didn't finish the name as Taylor turned around.

Sonora watched his face. Disappointingly, he remained impassive. But Gretta's reaction . . . well, her stunned, open-lipped silence was fun. Perhaps Taylor was enjoying it behind his cold, unaffected veneer?

For some opaque reason, Sonora hoped so. "Everest," Sonora finished for the mute woman. "As in Taylor Everest."

"You . . . you're . . ."

"Married," Taylor said.

Silence rolled out like wedding bells. Loud, clanging, and jarring.

If Sonora had scripted this moment, she would have had Taylor lift a sweet smile, step to her side, and slip a hand around her waist. She would have had him say "Meet my wife," and maybe even he would have called her beautiful. For authenticity.

Her heart fluttered at the imaginary moment.

Taylor did none of that. He simply stood, rooted to the ground in his distant severity. Sonora tried to ignore the drop of disappointment in her chest.

"Well." Gretta lifted her chin. And was that an attempt at a pleasant smile? "Well indeed." She folded her hands in front of her. "I suppose getting married is a reasonable excuse for missing work." That odd grin brightened. It was like she was trying to be pleasant while chewing pure salt. "We'll have to celebrate, won't we?"

Taylor remained stoic, though color crept up his neck.

A fact that did not seem to escape Gretta's notice. "Yes. A celebration will be just the thing." Gretta turned to Sonora. "Mrs. Everest, dear, welcome to the Shore View Palace."

"Sonora."

"Very well. Sonora." Gretta patted Sonora's shoulder and nodded. "Don't worry about a thing—I will see to every detail."

"Of . . . what?"

"The celebration."

Oh yeah, that. Was she serious? Sonora glanced at Taylor. He shut his eyes, as if this nightmare just kept getting worse.

Sonora brushed her bright smile back up and looked back at Gretta. "That would be lovely." Knowing that Taylor would not love her for it, she moved to his side and slipped her hand around his arm. "Wouldn't it be lovely, Tay?"

"Taylor," he whispered.

She pushed up on her toes and planted a kiss on his cheek. "Say thank you," she whispered.

He scowled down at her. She held his stern look with a stubborn grin, gripping his bicep hard.

Finally, with a smothered sigh, Taylor shifted his unhappy gaze from Sonora to Gretta. "Thank you, Gret."

"It would be my pleasure." The woman smiled, as if she'd just swallowed a raw fish and was trying to be pleased about it.

There was most certainly something more substantial than a working relationship between those two. Sonora wasn't sure if she was more curious or jealous.

Scratch that. Jealous would be stupid. So curious it must be.

Ten

Taylor strode into the cool darkness of the carriage house and made his way into the back stall. Pete and Molly looked up from their hay bunks, staring at him, as if to ask what was wrong.

Everything. That was what.

He leaned against the thick post that held the stall door, tipping his head back and staring up at the ceiling. Up there, in the living quarters above, Sonora was unpacking her things into *his* room.

Man, he landed himself in a stupid ordeal. A mess.

Absolute chaos.

Was that an exaggeration? *Chaos: complete disorder and confusion.*

Everything in his head was that exactly. And his heart?

Despite his resolve not to allow it, the recent memory of his mouth taking a tender tour of Sonora's lips whipped his pulse into a gallop all over again.

So not an exaggeration. He'd landed in chaos. Added to all that foolish mess, there was Gretta. Offering to plan a party? No.

He wasn't going that far.

Pushing his weight off the stall post, Taylor set his jaw and turned his determined stride toward the hotel. Sonora would be down soon—her bag wasn't large and wouldn't take long to unpack—which, come to think of it, was odd. The woman was coming to live there for the foreseeable future. Didn't she need a little more?

Her business, not his. Right now he had his own to attend to. He'd put an end to this celebration nonsense now. He despised attention in general—he certainly didn't want it focused on him while he was in the midst of a disaster of his own making.

An image of Sonora surfaced in his mind's eye: strong, happy disposition, pretty. Could he truly label her a *disaster?* That would be unkind.

Maybe he'd stop at the kitchen and have lunch sent up for Sonora before he marched into Gretta's office.

Taylor did so, ordering a sandwich and lemonade to be delivered to the living quarters above the carriage house. At Rachel's—the kitchen manager—questioning look, Taylor said nothing.

"Delivered now?" Rachel clarified, brow raised, tone piqued, as if he'd lost a step.

"Yes."

"But you're standing right here."

"It's for my wife." He let that bomb drop and then turned and walked away as Rachel's mouth swung open.

Between Curtis, Gretta, and now Rachel—which would include, by natural extension, Rachel's sister Candi, the town blabbermouth who conveniently owned Hook, Line and Scissors, the salon in town, every permanent island resident should know his new relationship status by sundown. Who needed Facebook?

Taylor sighed. Or growled. He wasn't keen on being the subject of town gossip. But it was just as well. That eliminated the need for a party, didn't it? Deed done, he could move on to the next task.

He passed through the frosted glass door labeled *Gretta Fellenbaum, Resort Manager* without knocking. As he expected, Gretta sat behind her mammoth desk, typing something into her laptop.

"No party." He didn't stop until his legs pressed against her desk.

Startled, Gretta jerked her gaze up. "I beg your pardon."

Taylor bent to press his hands against the polished oak. "No. Party."

Gretta leaned back, a momentary flash of fear passing through her eyes.

He felt bad about that. Sort of.

Standing he stepped back and turned to leave.

"Taylor."

"What?"

"Sit."

"I'm busy." He gave her his back and took another step toward the door. "My *wife* is currently unpacking, and then I need to make sure she knows how to handle Al and Vicky."

"Your wife." That tone held as much suspicion as the lake held water.

Taylor turned, finding that Gretta had stood, arms crossed, scowl folding her brow.

"Yes. My wife."

"I'm to believe that you actually got married?"

"You can check with the county courthouse if you'd like."

Her scowl morphed into concern. "Taylor. What have you done?" she whispered.

He pressed his lips firmly and shifted his attention to the window that overlooked the back gardens. And beyond that, the carriage house. *My wife* . . . A lump swelled in his throat as the weight of this reality pressed hard. "I got married. Just as you demanded." He looked back at her.

Gretta sucked in a breath. "I didn't—"

"You most certainly did."

"Do you even know this woman?"

"That's my concern, not yours."

"But—"

"It's done, Gretta. Your contract is appeased, and you'll be glad to know that she'll be handling the carriage. If she can, in fact, handle Al and Vicky. And if not, she'll accompany me, do the interacting with the tourists. As you saw, she has a pretty face and a pleasant way."

"Does she have any experience with the horses?"

Taylor nodded. "She was a wrangler at an upscale dude ranch in Wyoming."

"So you at least vetted her?"

Taylor rolled his fists. "I told you, Gretta. That's my business. Not yours."

Gretta's shoulders rounded as she slumped into her chair. For a moment, she simply stared at her computer screen. Guilt scrawled over her expression.

Which helped nobody. In fact, it only made Taylor angrier. Enough so that he didn't trust himself in the same space anymore. He was an unlocked vault of emotions that afternoon, and he hated the sense that his self-control was rapidly slipping.

He finished the pivot toward the door and marched to it.

"Taylor."

He growled, tipping his head back until the ceiling came into view. "What, Gretta?"

"I didn't mean for this."

"What do you mean, you *didn't* mean for this?" As he looked back at her, his grip on those roiling emotions slipped further. "You said I had to get married to keep my job. What did you expect me to do?"

"I thought you'd try . . . dating." She stood again and rounded her desk toward him. "I thought you'd try letting go of Iris, and maybe you'd find someone who was more worthy of your heart. And that would have been—"

"Good enough?" His voice came out low and deadly chilled. At the mention of Iris's name, Taylor felt his gut clench. How dare Gretta drag that memory into this moment? "That is not what you said. What you *demanded*."

Gretta looked toward her shiny black stilettoes. When she raised her face to him again, a sheen glazed over her eyes. "I'm sorry, Taylor. I never imagined you'd *marry* a stranger. That is entirely beyond your normal, steady personality."

Nor had he imagined it. Not for real.

But it wasn't real. He and Sonora had agreed on that.

He could ease Gretta's consciousness if he let her in on that part. But he didn't. And oddly, he felt little comfort in repeating that fact to himself.

Taylor opened the office door, his back once again to Gretta.

"It's done." He moved to exit, glancing back at the small, imposing woman as he went. "No party."

He took her wide-eyed silence for an agreement.

Sonora finished half of the shredded turkey salad on a croissant, telling herself that eating at least half of the meal was required.

It'd been thoughtful of Taylor to send it up. And shocking. Was this man bipolar? How could he one moment be all brisk winds and sharp quills and the next thoughtful and kind?

Should she be worried about his rapid shifts in mood and action?

Wiping the crumbs onto the supplied napkin, she took a slow turn around the tiny table where she stood. It had been placed near a south-facing window, the view offering glimpses of a cobblestone walking path that led into a gathering of pines and maples. Beyond that, she couldn't tell where that trail led, but she hoped to discover it soon. Removing her attention from the outdoor vista, she took in the small living space of the upper part of the carriage house. Tiny kitchenette supplied with an electric teakettle, a small refrigerator, and a microwave. Opposite that, an equally small front room with space enough for a small couch and wooden coffee table. The couch faced a fireplace.

Then there was the stairway that led below to where the animals and carriage resided. If she had forgotten that she was to live above the animals, the occasional stomp of a hoof or rump-bump against a wall would remind her. But that part made her smile.

There was something delightfully intimate about sharing a roof with those magnificent horses.

Speaking of intimate . . .

Past the stairway, a wall portioned off the back third of the area. Taylor's bedroom. Sweat beaded at her hairline, and heat bloomed in her chest as she thought the words. *Taylor's bedroom.* Where she'd hurriedly unpacked her things—a couple pairs of jeans, three nice button-down plaids, a handful of T-shirts, and enough underwear and socks to last a week before washing would be required. Not much, but enough, though she wasn't sure what she'd wear to drive that beautiful black carriage. Curtis had been wearing a dark suit. She didn't own such a thing.

But that was the second of her concerns, and a distant second at that.

Taylor's bedroom.

The itemized list of her meager belongings, and concerns over the things she didn't have, did not distract her from those two stamping words.

She swallowed. Hard.

As her focus narrowed on the open doorway to that back room, she swallowed again. One queen bed.

She eyed the couch. Narrow and less comfortable than a bed. But—

The sound of footfalls hard against the stairs jarred her from her worrisome thoughts. Taylor's unsmiling face met her as he strode into the room. He stopped three feet short of where she stood.

"I see lunch came."

Sonora wondered if he could see her racing pulse as it throbbed through her neck. "Yes," she squeaked. Then she cleared her throat. "Thank you for ordering it."

He dipped a silent nod.

"There is some left, if you want it."

"You didn't like it?"

"I liked it. I just had enough." She placed a hand on her churning stomach, willing herself to calm down.

Taylor stared at her, his expression stern but unreadable.

A tremble shook her core. Would he always be so formidable and intimidating? Where was the kindness that had prompted him to order her some lunch?

She summoned a wobbly smile. And then forced it to stop wobbling. He didn't need to know that he intimidated her—nor that she was a little terrified of how this situation was to work out. Putting brightness into her voice, she said, "Rachel seems nice."

"Rachel delivered your lunch?"

Could this man please stop glaring?

"Yes. Didn't you ask her to?"

"I did. Only she doesn't normally deliver food. There are others who do that."

"Oh."

"I told her the lunch was for my wife."

"Oh." A fresh burst of heat flared toward her face. Guess he wasn't going to beat around the bush about them. Were they a *them?* Their marriage. Whatever. "Well then, obviously that prompted some curiosity."

"Yes."

A strange pause lingered between them. This man liked big words? Curtis might not be trustworthy. Taylor barely used small words.

"Decided to get the news out right away, did you?" Sonora tried to tease away the discomfort stuffing the room.

"News?"

"You told Rachel I was your wife."

Taylor offered a small shrug. "Seemed the best plan. The sooner everyone knows, the sooner the gossip will die down."

"Gossip bothers you?"

He held a wordless stare on her. So that was a yes?

"Are you embarrassed of me, Taylor?"

"Of you? Why would I be? You're a beautiful woman with a cheerful attitude. Perfect for the job."

The carriage-driver job or the wife job? "Hmm." Whichever the case, his words were nice. His ongoing frown was not.

"I told Gretta no party."

Sonora lifted her brow. "How did she take that?"

A streak of red crawled up his neck.

Suspicion slithered through her mind, accompanied by a sense of . . . jealousy? She'd already settled that question—couldn't be that. Even so, she was bothered. "As your wife, even if a temporary one, I think I should know if there's something going on between you two."

"What?"

Finally a real emotion. Though Sonora wasn't sure if that reaction was anger or insulted shock. Maybe both?

Taylor snorted and shook his head. It almost sounded like a laugh. "Something between Gretta Fellenbaum and *me*?" This time he did laugh.

Was that a laugh of astonishment? Or a cover-up laugh? Sonora gave him a look of expectation.

"Only if you count ongoing irritation. The pestilential woman has been a pain in my neck since the moment I took over for my dad."

"Pestilential?" Huh. Out of nowhere, the big word cometh. Sonora barely kept a giggle buckled in.

The edges of his mouth nearly poked upward. "Yes. Pestilential: 'giving rise to vexation or annoyance.'"

He really just pulled that definition from his memory? This could become quite the fun game. But Sonora refocused on the Gretta question—which did still bother. Crossing her arms, she tilted her chin at a sassy angle. "Enemies to lovers, perhaps?"

Lover? Could this man ever bear that title, with his stiff manner and curt ways? Seemed unlikely. Then again, his kiss had been . . . memorable. Or perhaps unforgettable would be more accurate.

"If that hasn't happened yet—and it hasn't—it's not going to. You and I are more likely to fall in love than the chance of Gretta and me being anything but animus coresidents of the island."

Animus. Sonora snorted.

"And besides," Taylor continued, ignoring her amused smirk and unladylike nasal sounds, "I'm married, and so is she." He arched one eyebrow, as if to put the punctuation on his statement.

Was that a teasing light in his too-serious blue eyes?

Sonora rolled her eyes, enjoying this unexpected banter. "That rarely stops anyone."

Taylor's look immediately darkened, and the silent glare he held on her was fierce. She immediately missed the near smile from only moments before.

That was definitely a wrong turn. And wow. She'd really insulted him. She wasn't sure if that should please her—that he was a man of honor and didn't appreciate a woman *impugning* that honor. (Should she ask him that exact thing and see if he was impressed with her vocabulary?) Or if she should be irritated with him and worried that the man was so touchy?

Hmm . . . what would be a better word for that? *Maligned*? No, that wasn't quite right, though she didn't have the ability to pull up a word-perfect definition. How about *affronted*?

Yes, that.

"I apologize, Mr. Everest. I didn't realize you would be so easily affronted." Sonora couldn't help the lift of the right corner of her mouth.

Taylor studied her, his heated stare cooling and those pinched lips softening. A heartbeat passed. Then another. Still, his blue gaze held hers.

And she was captivated.

"I am not an easygoing man. Some may say I'm a grump." He lifted his hand and laid it flat on the table, near the half-eaten sandwich. "But I am a man who keeps his word."

He was so close—enough that she could see the stubble of his afternoon shadow coming in along his jawbone. Sonora swallowed and wondered why warmth flooded her veins. Because she'd thought for a moment that he was lifting his hand to touch her? Or was it simply the nearness? Neither should make her system ooze with pleasure.

"Faithful?" She squeaked out the word, hoping to divert herself from her stupid visceral reaction.

His expression softened, and yearning weighed his stare. "Yes. That's what I aim for."

The bulk of Sonora's anxiety died right there under the sincerity of those blue eyes. She could deal with grumpy. With intensity. With big words interrupted by long stretches of silence. With an awkward man who wasn't great with people.

With an unconventional relationship.

All of that would be nothing if he was what he said.

Faithful.

That was a rare find.

Eleven

Taylor emerged from the bedroom dressed in a long dark suit that made for a striking contrast against his white button-down shirt. His face had been washed and his hair combed, neatly, and in his hand he held a bowler cap.

Sonora couldn't help but grin. "Don't you look like you just stepped off the set of *Downton Abbey*."

His stony expression didn't change. "This is what we wear for work."

The costume begged for some teasing. "Oh, you mean I get to play dress-up too?" Her smile grew wide, and she wished that even a hint of his would surface on that implacable expression.

Taylor frowned. More.

Man, what would it take to get his smile?

"We'll see how you do with the horses first." He slipped the hat over his hair. "Worry about clothing once I know for sure you can do the job."

Sonora tamed her grin and tossed him a sassy look. "What will you do if I'm terrible? After all, we're already married. Will you find yourself a new wife?"

Taylor looked away, pinching the bridge of his nose, as if pain had shot through his head.

Not what she was going for. She edged near him enough to place her fingers on his arm. "I promise you—I know what I'm doing with the animals."

His sigh left his chest with a frustrated rush. "I hope so. I can use one less disaster today." He looked down at her, those serious blue eyes cutting her mirth into worry, then walked away from her touch.

Had he just called her a disaster? He'd known her all of a day. He didn't have enough information to judge that one way or another. And anyway, this had been his idea. He'd been the one to place that advertisement.

What business did he have deciding *she* was at fault?

Just as her ire had risen high enough to find her voice, Taylor's stride continued to the stairs and then down and out. She supposed she should follow him.

"Mr. Everest." Her curt call made it from her lips as she reached the bottom of the steps.

Taylor jerked to a halt just before he stepped into the sunny afternoon. He turned slowly. "Probably should call me Taylor," he mumbled. "We are married."

"Should I call you something more endearing? Honey lips perhaps?"

No grin. Not even an eye roll. Just an unflinching—and unamused—stare.

Ugh.

Sonora marched forward, only stopping when she was directly in front of him. "This wasn't my idea, you know."

He merely raised one eyebrow.

"I'm not a mistake." That wasn't the right word. "A . . . disaster." Yes, that was what he'd called her.

That stoic blue gaze grabbed her eyes and held. What was in the mix of that storm she saw there? Frustration. Exhaustion. Doubt?

No. Maybe . . . hope?

Maybe she needed to banish all romantic, and otherwise silly, ideas from her imagination. Would be easier if she didn't have that kiss lingering not so far in the back of her mind.

After who knew how many heartbeats, Taylor released her from his silent stare, nodded, and continued down the brick drive that led around to the front of the Palace. There waited the carriage, the horses still hitched and standing, as if the most well-trained animals in the world.

Taylor stopped and turned abruptly. He motioned with one hand. "That's Albert. This one is Victoria. They always drive this way, Albert on the left, Victoria on the right. Don't mix them up."

Shifting her attention from Taylor's infuriatingly impassive face to the beautiful creatures, Sonora shed her irritation in favor of delight, making her way to the horse's noses. "Albert." She reached for his big jawline and scratched beneath the bone.

The big boy lowered his head and looked at her, then nudged his nose at her shoulder.

"He doesn't know he's not a lap dog. Don't let him get too nosey."

"Personal space issues, hmm?" With the back of her knuckles, Sonora ran her fingers along his nose. Then she stepped back to where she'd left Taylor standing, stopping beside Victoria. "Hello, Vicky. Can I call you that?"

"Only when tourists aren't around." Taylor's low voice came from just over her shoulder. When had he stepped so near? And why would his quiet tone send a ripple of goose-flesh down her arm.

Taylor reached past Sonora to run a large hand down Vicky's sleek neck.

"I wouldn't have guessed you would have personal space issues too." Sonora turned her smirk at Taylor.

He froze. Swallowed. Let his arm fall to his side as he stepped back. "I don't. I mean, I usually—" He seamed his lips, cleared his throat, and fell another pace away. "Forgive me."

Sonora was one part amused and another part pity. This man was coiled up like a spring. Did he ever tease? Or laugh? Or just . . . breathe?

Before her thoughts ran a full course, Taylor had moved to the side of the carriage and held out a hand toward her. "Let's get started."

His words were a command, but his tone seemed . . . gentle? Was that possible for this all-edges-and-prickles guy? Sonora sighed inwardly. She was ridiculous, this determined search for calm sunshine when clearly the man she'd temporarily married was all clouds and wind.

Brushing away the thoughts that threatened to pull her into panic—because *good Lord, what had she done?!*—Sonora accepted his gentle offer, slipping her fingers against his palm, and climbed up the carriage step and onto the front seat.

She settled on the far side of the top seat, behind Albert, while Taylor set himself beside her. His movement into the carriage was smooth and easy, a tell he did this often. He reached for the reins, gathering them evenly, hands held forward, ready to drive. Albert and Victoria perked their ears, their lifted heads indicating they were ready to work.

But rather than flicking the reins or giving a verbal *get up* or *walk on*, Taylor froze, drew a breath, and then shifted his hands toward Sonora.

She looked first at his loose fists, now pressed in her space, and then up to his face. A pensive stare met her.

"Me?" she asked, interpreting his silence.

"Might as well see what you can do." He punctuated that hesitant response with a visible swallow.

Sonora held his worried look. "You don't trust me."

"I married you."

The corners of her mouth lifted. "Yes. You did do that. But passing me the reins?"

His brow knitted. "Seems I must."

"I think Curtis is right. This is hard for you."

Taylor held in a wordless trance. She could see the pounding of his heartbeat through the throbbing vein in his neck. This terrified him. Because of the horses he clearly loved? Or was there more to it?

Sonora glanced at the animals, both still holding in a ready and willing posture. Then she met Taylor's unmoving look. "I wasn't lying to you before. I do know what I'm doing, Taylor."

He blinked. Lowered his gaze to the reins he still held, and then passed them into her hands. "Please don't," he whispered.

Rather than flicking the leather straps, Sonora met his blue eyes again, her silence an understood question between them.

"Please don't let me down."

His plea settled in her heart. Much deeper than it likely should have.

"Tell me their cues."

Sonora's question jarred Taylor as he sat transfixed next to her. Had he really just begged her to not let him down? And did she sense that he wasn't talking about the job. Well, not only the job.

Muddled. Addled.

He drew in a breath and stretched his neck one way, then the other.

"Taylor, I need to know what they're trained to respond to if you want me to be successful."

"Walk on," he blurted.

Albert pressed his head forward, and Victoria followed suit immediately, and with that, the carriage was in motion.

"Nice."

Sonora sounded pleased . . . Taylor thought. Wait. Was that a sarcastic *nice*?

"Sorry," he muttered.

"For what?"

"You have the reins."

"Don't think I need them." She watched the horses pull with puppy love on her face. "They know exactly what to do, don't they?"

Taylor's heart settled back into the normal, apathetic spot where it belonged. Nearly. And then he sat back, relaxing his tight shoulders. Sonora was right—Al and Vicky knew exactly what they were doing.

This was going to be fine.

"They were Amish trained, and they've been working the tourist season for me for a decade."

"This should be easy-peasy, then." They passed by a hedge row of blooming hydrangeas, and Sonora studied them with admiration.

The island was loaded with flowers. Sanctuary Island was renowned for the stunning displays from May until frost. And apparently Sonora liked flowers.

Ignoring that observation—because why should he care?—Taylor nodded. "The driving part, yes."

"Ah, but we have to care for them too, right?" She nudged him with her shoulder. "Don't worry. I know how to shovel manure and work a brush."

"I wasn't worried about that, though it's good to know."

"No? That's not the real work?"

"The real work is with the tourists."

Sonora sat back with a small gasp. "Whoa." She pulled back on the reins—gently, with respect. "Wow. That is a stunning vista."

Vista. He liked her word choice. Taylor took in the canvass of water meeting rocky shore, the lighthouse a charming fixture to the left. In the foreground, near the road, another hedge of white-lime blooms bobbed in the breeze. In the far reaches of the background, wispy white clouds broke apart the long stretch of deep-blue sky.

It was a picturesque scene.

Taylor turned to say so, but his voice died in his throat as he took in her profile. Sonora had lifted her face to the afternoon sun, shut her eyes, and soaked in the warmth with a peaceful smile.

Stunning vista indeed.

He swallowed, annoyed that his chest had done a strange pleasure leap that caused his heart rate to trot. Clearing his throat, he turned his gaze back to the road.

“Sorry.” She didn’t sound repentant. Only happy. “Walk on,” she called to the horses.

Both resumed their progress, as if they’d not been interrupted in the first place.

“What were we talking about?” she asked.

Taylor’s mind launched into a frenzied search, shoving past the looming image of her lovely expression moments before. How irritating that it refused to fade into nothing as it should. “Tourists,” he blurted. He nearly sagged with relief.

“Ah. Yes, the real work. Exactly why I’m here—right?”

He nodded.

“That, and that pesky little stipulation on your contract.”

Rats. He’d almost put that out of his mind for a whole second. What was with this playful teasing she kept reaching for? Was that her way of dealing with the discomfort of this situation?

He felt, more than saw, her glance. And then once again, she was pressing her shoulder into him. “Are we not supposed to talk about that part?”

Did she have to be so touchy? And man, why did that little grin of hers have to be so . . . adorable?

No. Not adorable. He was not the sort of man who found things *adorable.*

Bewitching? Ugh. Please, heaven, not that. Never again with that.

With a chill worthy of an arctic front, Taylor turned to answer Sonora's playful question. "I'd rather the situation with my contract not get out."

"Just our little secret. Me. You. Curtis. Gretta." She gave him a raised-eyebrow look. "Will they keep our secret, do you think?"

His throat constricted, and he swallowed against the rising panic.

"Perhaps we need to work out a story."

"What sort of story?" Story meant lie. He wasn't keen on lying. Not as a habit. Which contradicted the whole disaster he'd jumped into here.

"For how we met."

"It's not anyone's business." No story, no lie. That would be easier—to maintain and to bear in his conscience.

"Wow. No wonder you have a hard time with the tourists."

"What does that mean?"

Sonora guided the animals around the final curve that would take them to the docks. "You clearly do not understand people."

"No." No secret there. Though it was not pleasant to have this playful creature simply lay that fact out in broad daylight.

Sonora did not take his hint to drop it, given with a pointed glare. "They're going to ask. It's natural for people to be curious."

"I think it's natural for people to mind their own business."

"No, my dear husband"—gripping the lines in one hand, she laid the other on his arm—"it is not."

Iron entered his spine at the term *husband*. Why must she use it? He was not husband material. Iris had made that clear. He did not possess a heart that was worthy of more than a summer fling. He was good looking, and that was all. No, it wasn't all. He was cold. Grumpy. Unlovable. Not worth staying for.

He'd accepted all this. Embraced it, actually. Particularly after his attempt at being different had proven a categorical failure.

With intention, he removed her touch from his arm—and no, he did not immediately miss the warmth of her fingers, thank you—and returned her hand to the reins. Then he pointed to the carriage loading area. "Stop at the top of the docks, where we found Curtis when we arrived."

Sonora nodded and executed the task as though it were nothing.

Granted, Albert and Victoria knew the drill. But even so, Sonora guided them to a stop with the sort of confidence and ease that came with experience.

She would do fine. More than fine.

"Well?" She looked at him.

Taylor met those eyes and found expectation. The longing for approval. And the iceberg named his heart softened. "Perfect," he whispered.

She rewarded him with a look that could summon spring from a January blizzard.

Or he was ridiculous. Who thought such sappy things? Not Taylor Everest.

With a frown firmly fixed, he jumped from the top seat. Once on the ground, he pivoted to help her down, only to spin into her. Knocked off balance, she stumbled back. He reached to steady her, but rather than simply laying a hand on her shoulder, his maverick hand slipped around her to land on the small of her back. At the same time, her palms braced against his shirtfront.

One solid heartbeat. Then two.

Her eyes were such a beautiful metallic copper. Joy danced in them and offered an invitation to join in. A man could find contentment staring—

Staring!

Taylor dropped his arm and stepped back. "I beg your pardon."

An amused smirk twisted her mouth, but she looked away. "You are pardoned." She began to move away, but before she'd gone three steps, she glanced over her shoulder with a sassy grin. "Husband."

And then she winked.

There was that pleasure-squeeze thing again.

This must stop.

Oh, he hoped it wouldn't.

No, that wasn't true.

Rats. What was wrong with him? Shaking his head and clenching his fists, as if that might remind his hands to behave, Taylor leaned into the back of the carriage to tug down the step.

"Welcome to Sanctuary Island." Sonora's cheerful greeting drew his attention. At the end of the carriage, he found her with a couple. The man carried two bags. The woman held one hand against the back of her head, bracing her white floppy hat against the lake breeze.

"Heading to the Shore View Palace?"

The woman grinned. "How did you know?"

"Lucky guess." Sonora reached toward the bags. "Can I take your luggage, sir?"

"Oh, no, little miss. If you just show me where to store it, I'll see to it."

Sonora nodded, pleasantness fixed on her face. But before she could answer, Taylor came to the back. With a nod, he took the luggage and made sure the bags were securely stored. Then he moved back to the sidestep.

Sonora seemed unbothered. "Just the pair of you?"

The woman, still holding her hat in place, turned her happy expression up to the man. "Yes. We're on our honeymoon."

Taylor would have guessed. He'd seen it a million times. He'd also seen at least half that many times the adoring couple not so adoring at the end of their visits, having given them a ride back to the ferry dock in stilted silence. Seemed marriage was a bit like the island—all charming beauty for a season. But year round?

Winters were harsh. Not many could endure them.

But what did he really know about marriage?

"Congratulations!" Sonora gushed, as though she knew these people personally and was so delighted for their happiness. "What a lovely way to experience the island. The Palace will be a perfect place for you to celebrate your committed love."

Huh. She was good at this.

At Sonora's gesture, the gooey couple stepped toward Taylor. Like an extra in a movie scene, he was simply there. When the woman moved to step up, he held out an impassive hand. She took it only as long as it took to enter the carriage, and then her husband bounced in behind her. Taylor wordlessly folded the step back in and shut the carriage door. Then he moved toward the front and held a hand out to Sonora. She accepted his offered help as she climbed up top, and then he followed her into the front seat.

Business as usual. Except Sonora kept up a friendly chatter, whereas everything would have been done in silence had he been there alone.

With a gentle "Walk on," Sonora had the carriage in motion.

"Your horses are magnificent," the woman said.

"They're Mr. Everest's." Sonora nodded toward Taylor.

"Ah." There was puzzlement in that response. "What kind are they?"

Was he required to answer?

"Friesians," Sonora supplied readily.

So no, then. How nice.

"They're so big. I assume they are well trained."

"Very well. Mr. Everest takes every care with them. And Friesians are gentle giants by nature."

They climbed the hill to the first curve on the road, and Sonora handled the reins with expertise. Really, Taylor was superfluous.

He was not sure how he felt about that.

Sonora dipped her head near his to speak low between them. "Do you want the reins?"

He shook her off.

She did not return to her own space. "I can do the talking, if you'd prefer to drive. Wouldn't bother me."

"I hired you to drive."

Her eyes caught his, and he found amusement in them. Why was that funny? It was the truth. Some of it.

"Oh! What a sight!" The woman sat forward in her seat. "Could we stop?"

"Sure." Sonora eased back on the line with a soft "Whoa."

This was not normal. Taylor never stopped in the middle of a ride.

"Would you like me to take your picture?"

What was she doing? This wasn't part of their job. He was a taxi driver, only with a shiny carriage worthy of a Cinderella live-action retelling and a pair of beautiful black Friesians. He wasn't a tour guide. Or a personal photographer.

Which might have contributed to the complaints. And lack of decent tips.

Sonora hopped off her seat, her boots hitting the cobblestone with a firm clap. Then she reached up to take the woman's phone and walked around to the other side. There, she held up the phone, fiddled with the screen, and then said, "Smile!"

Several clicks later, she was handing the phone back and climbing into her seat.

Taylor scowled at her. She winked, then clucked at the horses. "Walk on."

And they were back to doing what they were supposed to.

The man and woman oohed and aahed on the half mile to the Palace. Every now and then, they'd ask a question, which Sonora fielded.

"Have you been here long?"

"No, ma'am. It's my first season. But Mr. Everest grew up on the island."

"What are the horses' names?"

"Albert and Victoria."

"Oh! Like the queen. How fun!"

"Will you stay after the tourist season?"

"I'm taking Albert and Victoria back to their winter grounds after frost."

Standard questions. Things Taylor had heard and answered a million times before. But it was a relief not to have to converse. And a delight to hear Sonora do so instead.

A delight? That must be an exaggeration. It wasn't as if she'd said anything brilliant. Or even meaningful.

He needed a nap. Or a good night's sleep. Which could be hard to come by now, as Sonora would be in his bed.

Not with him. He'd be on the small couch in the living room. Had he clarified that with her?

This sudden course of thought, and having Sonora in his space, and the sleeping arrangements that he hadn't explained had his heart strumming in high gear again. Also, he was pretty sure he was blushing.

"Whoa." Sonora stopped the carriage.

Startled, Taylor blinked and lifted his empty stare away from the pair of black rumps in front of him. She'd stopped them in the circle drive, in between the big circle fountain and the wide front porch of the Palace. Exactly where she should have, and she hadn't needed instructions to do so.

"Well?" she whispered.

"Perfect," he muttered. Man, he needed to quit using that word. *Adequate* would have worked fine. Better than *fine*, as it was a much more interesting word, even if it did fall short of the truth.

He scrambled to the ground, tugged his suit straight, and played the part of footman. Silent. Stiff. Efficient. Exactly him.

Sonora played the part of . . . of perfection. Easily conversing. Taking a few more pictures of the snuggly couple, who tipped her generously. Wishing them a happy honeymoon.

Yes. Of perfection.

Taylor wondered why it bothered him so much.

TWELVE

"CONGRATULATIONS!"

Sonora's heart stuttered, and a chill raced through her limbs as she stopped just inside the employee dining hall. The man at her side—her husband—drew in a sharp breath and became more concrete statue than a bridegroom.

Great. She'd married a concrete statue. After two days as his wife, this shouldn't exactly catch her by surprise. He'd been aloof from the first introduction.

But there had been moments when Taylor had given her a glimpse at a softer layer. Like when he'd ordered her lunch that first day. And told her she'd done well when they'd unhitched the horses and worked together to get Albert and Victoria brushed, fed, watered, and settled in for the night.

And when he'd insisted she take the bedroom and he'd be fine on that miniature couch. That had actually been a tender moment.

"I got us into this," he'd murmured. And had his hand raised a little? As though he wanted to touch her? Perhaps that was her imagination. "The least I can do is make sure you have somewhere comfortable to sleep."

And so that had launched their marriage. She, alone in the warm comfort of his bed, and he, duking it out with the sofa that was at least a foot too short. Together they'd readied the horses and carriage for a new day of service. Together they'd eaten a quiet breakfast in a tucked-away corner of the employee dining hall. And together they'd trekked through the charming little village and to the docks, giving rides to tourists.

And she'd assumed they'd gotten through the worst of this strange beginning that would have a planned and quick end. Until this moment.

Someone started clapping, and the gathering of Palace employees all quickly joined in. A few whistles cracked the air. And strangers crept nearer.

Sonora looked up at Taylor. His glance found her, revealing a deep scowl, and then shifted with purpose, searching. As Sonora followed his traveling gaze, she found the target of his inspection. Gretta Fellenbaum.

Meeting Taylor's glare, Gretta shook her head.

Sonora swallowed, guessing that the woman was telling Taylor this had not been her doing. A mix of responses swirled within Sonora—one part jealousy at whatever this relationship was between Taylor and Gretta, as clearly they *did* have one. And one part pity for Taylor.

The pity took the bulk of space in her churning emotions, and Sonora stepped closer to his side, slipping her hand around his arm. Immediately his attention fell back to her.

She offered silent reassurance and a gentle squeeze of his arm.

Huh. That bicep was pretty firm.

"We couldn't let this occasion go uncelebrated!" Rachel, from the kitchen, emerged from the applause, stepping forward from the little crowd. "And it's just like you, Taylor, to go get married in secret."

Sonora doubted any of this was *just like* Taylor.

Suddenly they were engulfed, being tugged deeper into the room. A glass of something pale and bubbly was pushed into her hand, and Taylor's as well.

"We all said we had to see it for ourselves," a man wearing a service uniform said. "I'd bet there were a few wagers lost just now."

A low round of snickers followed.

Pity grew. Sonora leaned into Taylor, tipping her head against his shoulder. He looked down, his eyes holding a touch of panic. And maybe hurt?

She did her best to portray a girl smitten as she fit a small grin. Then for good measure, she pressed up on her toes and kissed the corner of his mouth.

He sighed. Relief? Irritation? Who knew with this man. Either way, the stage was set, the curtains drawn, lights shining on them. She'd promised the details of their marriage would remain between them, and for her own dignity as much as Taylor's, she was gonna make sure that happened.

"I'd bet on you every time, Taylor." She winked.

He simply held her in his unreadable stare.

"Seems you've already placed that wager." This merry comment came from a voice she knew. Curtis pushed his way to the front of the semicircle around them. "And we're all thrilled." He raised his champagne flute. "To the newly-weds!"

"To the newlyweds!" everyone echoed, raising their glass-es.

Sonora turned, lifting her glass to cheer with Taylor. Relief spiraled into her stomach when he clinked his glass with hers, and warm pleasure chased it when his stern mouth softened.

That was very nearly a grin, right?

Such a simple thing seemed silly to feel victorious about. Sonora felt victorious nonetheless.

The room became noise and motion. Some sort of piano music became the backdrop for this surprise party. One that Taylor had said specifically he did not want. Even so, when Sonora let her hand fall from his arm, he sought it out with his and wove his thick fingers with her smaller ones.

Why would his holding her hand feel so . . . intimate?

"Tell us how you met!"

Of course they would want to know that. Hadn't Sonora told Taylor they'd need a story? He'd said he wasn't a liar, and that ended that.

But were they truly going to say she'd answered his ad for a driver/wife? No. That defied their agreement.

Taylor's hand clenched against hers, and she took his reaction as panic.

"We were both in a chat group about horses in the tourist industry, and Taylor made a comment about how the general public often behaved dangerously around the animals."

A few chuckles sounded, along with a comment from the back. "I'll bet he called them stupid."

"No, Taylor would use *foolish* over *stupid*."

"So you corrected him, I assume?"

"Corrected him?" Sonora looked at Gretta, who seemed to be attempting to help with this fabrication.

Sonora didn't feel that was particularly helpful.

"For being harsh to his clients."

Sonora laughed. As if she would have, if this scenario had actually happened. "Not at all." She looked at Taylor and held his gaze—and yes, that hand squeeze had been panic. "I agreed with him. People can be very foolish around horses. And difficult to work with."

His tense jaw eased.

"And from that, you fell in love?" A snort punctuated the doubt statement.

"From there we started talking. That led to a meeting. And the rest, as they say . . ."

". . . is history," Taylor finished, his tone so low it was almost inaudible. His blue gaze remained steady on her.

A round of clinking jarred Sonora from staring. She blinked as understanding flooded her whole body with heat.

A kiss. They wanted to see a kiss.

With as much flirty energy as she could summon, she rose on her toes to press her lips to his. She didn't mind—after all, this was the charade they'd put themselves in.

But would Taylor—

Before she had time to work through that question, Taylor's hand slipped around her waist and pressed the small of her back. Holding her against his side, he leaned down to meet her mouth with his.

His kiss was more than convincing. By far.

Cheers erupted around them.

Sonora's head swam in a current of pleasure as an intoxicating heat flooded her whole being. Which was accompanied with the most unfortunate confusion and the odd but compelling wish that all this wasn't a lie.

This wasn't supposed to be confusing. This was a business deal. They'd promised it was so. A job, and nothing more. But kissing wasn't in their agreement—though one could argue that she'd started it. But . . .

Was Taylor merely playing the part?

The tingle in her lips and the sweet throbbing in her chest indicated that she hoped there was more to it than that.

Sonora told herself that was stupid—after all, Taylor barely smiled, was aloof and chilly, and most importantly, nearly a stranger—not to mention her boss. All good reasons to keep business business and personal feelings locked up tight.

Even so, there was that insistent whisper in the back of her mind. Though it was so quiet the word was hard to make out, it seemed a whole lot like . . . *maybe.*

They had settled into a routine.

While tugging on his boots, Taylor smiled at that. At least, as much as Taylor was accustomed to smiling. There was a tightening at the corners of his eyes and his mouth, so that must mean at least a grin.

Resisting the urge to finger his face to see if the form of it felt any different, Taylor pressed his feet against the floor and stood. With a motion that by now had been a week-old practice, he stripped the short, uncomfortable couch of the bedding—a sheet, a blanket, and a pillow—and carried them to the hall closet. There, he folded the blanket, then the sheet, stacked them together and added the pillow, and tucked them onto the shelf he'd cleared for these items. He shut the door and leaned back into a stretch.

Oof. The strong ache from his neck down to his tailbone wiped whatever bit of smile he'd had right off his face, and in its place, he was quite sure, he grimaced. How long was he to sleep on that short, narrow lump of overused foam? Depending on when frost actually hit, two to three months.

Ouch.

"You really should let me have the couch." Sonora's quiet but cheerful morning voice reached him from near the bedroom.

Whipping around and ironing his posture, Taylor watched her emerge from the doorway, her face shining with morning freshness, hair braided and wrapped at the nape of her neck, ready for the hat he'd located for her to wear along with the livery uniform Gretta had materialized for them. Sonora was a breath of sweetness—like the smell of fresh-cut grass on a warm August morning.

What a sentimental bunch of nonsense. He didn't think such things.

She met his watch with a gentle grin. "Good morning, Taylor."

As had become a thing, his heart stuttered at the greeting. It wasn't intimate. But . . . wow, he sure responded as if it were. At least his secret, physical response.

"Good morning." He kept both words even. Maybe even chilled. Just to make sure he wasn't transparent. And to put his thoughts back on the iron rails where they belonged. No more thinking sappy rubbish.

Was that wise? Maybe he should be transparent? In the week and a half since she'd become his wife, Sonora continued to impress him. She was kind. Competent. Smart. Good at the job.

And beautiful.

A man could do considerably worse.

He swallowed and pushed that thought into a corner.

"I trust you slept well," he said.

"I did, thank you." She reached into the small refrigerator and pulled out the half gallon of chocolate milk she'd purchased from Island Goods two days before.

That had nearly made Taylor chuckle, when she'd placed that item in her shopping basket. *"Chocolate milk?" he'd asked.*

She turned her face up to him with a sweet charm that nearly had him leaning down to try out those lips again. To quell the urge, he frowned.

"I love chocolate milk, and I'll have you know that the calcium and protein is good for me," she'd said, defensive now. "I'm not sure why that is something you should scowl about."

He nodded, and they finished their shopping.

Now, pulling out a chair to sit at the table, he wished he'd apologized for scowling. But then that would mean he'd have to explain his reaction. That fell under sappy and rubbish, which wouldn't do.

"I won't even ask how you slept." Sonora set the full glass of milk on the table. "That low groan as you were stretching tells me everything. You should stop being so stubborn about this. I'm smaller than you and would fit better on the couch. Anyway, you should get to have your own bed."

"I'm not allowing my wife to sleep on the couch while I sprawl out on my queen mattress."

She raised a brow at his use of *wife*, and heat flared up the back of his neck. Why had he said that?

Sonora turned from the table, where she still stood. "Then at least let me get you a cup of coffee."

"That I will allow."

"That's good, because I'm pretty sure I don't want to know the uncaffeinated version of Taylor Everest."

"No, you likely would not survive."

She stopped mid-reach for the coffeemaker and swiveled her look over her shoulder and back to him. After a full heartbeat and maybe another half, her smile cracked and grew wide. "Look at you. Teasing."

His lips quirked, and the corners of his eyes tightened again.

"And a grin." Sonora turned back to the small counter and poured a mug full of black coffee. She returned to the table and set it in front of him. "I like it, Everest. How do I keep it coming?"

He cleared his throat. This teetered dangerously close to flirting, which would inevitably summon more of those soppy ideas. Unacceptable. "Just keep doing your job."

At his curt response, her grin mellowed. Those lovely eyes shifted from his face to the table, the joy in them withering like a summer flower after the first frost.

Instant regret pressed against his heart. How could he find an easy, friendly working relationship with this woman when what he repeatedly wanted was her sweet, flirty smile and those eyes to dance when they met his? It was impossible. First, because he wasn't the friendly sort. And second . . .

Skip it.

"Am I meeting your standards?" Sonora set the glass onto the table with a quiet thump.

"Exceeding." That wasn't flirting. That was honest. She did very well, and as he had been thinking before she'd emerged from the bedroom looking all adorable and making him wish this scenario held the possibility for something more than a charade, they'd settled into a routine. Working-wise, anyway. She acted the hostess as she drove, and he played the part of silent footman. Occasionally, when she'd pass him the reins, he'd take charge of the horses, and he felt less like a pathetic prop and more like himself again. He wasn't sure how she knew, but she seemed to have impeccable timing with that, rescuing him from the deepest reaches of his self-pitying abyss.

And as to having her there—she was a life saver. Or a business saver. She interacted with the tourists in the most natural and delightful way. Taylor honestly was amazed by it because he couldn't do that. Even when he tried to be hospitable and accommodating, he came off as stilted and awkward. He couldn't people—it was as simple as that.

"Glad to know I'm not a disappointment." Though she lifted a playful look, as if trying to tease a smile from him again, there was something . . . what? Something *wounded* in that.

Surely not. This woman . . . Taylor could not imagine that she could be a disappointment to anyone.

Suddenly her proclamation back on the mainland echoed in his mind. *Love is not in my story.*

Why? He'd wondered back then, on the first day. But not real hard. Hadn't mattered much to him then, as he didn't think they'd go through with this.

But now? Now he felt a compulsive need to uncover why she thought she existed outside of the romance norm.

He knew why he held the same belief about his own life. But he couldn't imagine the same situation for this pleasant ray of warm sunshine at his table. What man would reject this lovely creature, especially if she offered him her whole heart? Yet apparently that had been the case. It was simply unfathomable.

On the tail of that thought, he recalled the question that had plagued him during his last outing with Curtis before all this ensued. *Can a man ever trust again One who had so keenly disappointed him before?*

"Taylor?" The sound of Sonora's uncharacteristic insecurity jarred him back to the present.

"Not a disappointment," he blurted.

She nodded. Then she bowed her head, as she did every morning, and prayed silently. After a few moments, she took another swallow of her chocolate milk. "You're thinking something deep." Sonora leaned one elbow against the table.

"No."

"I can read you, Taylor."

"I very much doubt that." At least, he hoped not. Mostly.

"There were twin lines right here." Bracing against the table, she reached to brush three fingers against the spot between his eyebrows. "And I have been married to you long enough to know that means you are deep in thought."

Everything about what she'd just said—and done—sent his thoughts whirling about like fall leaves in an autumn storm. Taylor's mind raced, searching for something passable to tell her—something that was not *I was pondering if I could ever risk love again, which would require that I try trusting God again, which I can't, because I can't get over the disappointment. It has fermented into bitterness. But the longer I am with you, I wish . . .*

Blast it. That was not helpful, even if it was honest.

Sonora popped her chin on both hands and stared at him with patient, playful expectation.

Why was this woman so charmingly determined?

"I was thinking about the last time I went golfing." Sort of true.

"Golfing?" Sonora sat back.

"Yes. With Curtis."

"A round of golf with your friend made you look like *that*?"

"Like what?"

"Like a hungry lion stalking his prey."

"That is an exaggeration."

"False. Have you seen yourself when you look like that?"

"I don't make a practice of staring at myself in general. Particularly not when I'm thinking about . . . golfing."

"You must not like golfing."

"Not particularly."

"Why do you play?"

"Curtis enjoys it. I caddy for him more than I actually play."

"Perhaps I should caddy for you both."

"No."

"I'm not allowed to go golfing with you?"

"You are allowed to do as you wish."

"I am?"

"Of course. You're not a prisoner."

"Oh good. Then I wish to sleep on the couch."

Taylor rolled his eyes and shook his head. Then he pinned her with his most serious look. "No."

"No?"

"No."

"That would make you a liar, Everest."

He scowled hard. The hardest he'd scowled in at least forty-eight hours. "You may golf if you want. You may buy all the chocolate milk you want. You may stand on your head if you want. But you're not sleeping on the couch."

"So many rules."

"You're an exasperating woman."

Her eyes danced with laughter. "I'm going to need a definition for that."

"You know what *exasperating* means."

"Let's make sure, shall we?"

He couldn't resist, though he also couldn't withhold an irritated groan. "Exasperating: 'causing strong feelings of irritation or annoyance.'"

"Will you spell it for me too?"

"No."

She laughed. "Okay." Then she swigged the last of her chocolate milk and stood. "That was fun. We'll do it again." She rinsed the glass and deposited it in the sink. "It's a good day to have a good day, don't you think?" As she strode by on her way to the door, she paused to run her fingers through his hair.

Gooseflesh tingled down his neck and across his shoulders. Why had she done that?

Taylor remained glued to his chair while she closed the length of room to the exit, unlatched the door, and bounded down the stairs.

Exasperating?

Yes. In the most heart-throbbing, head-swimming, make-him-lose-his-breath sort of way.

Thirteen

"Have you played before?" Curtis lowered his golf bag onto the grass and selected a club.

Sonora adjusted her ball cap. "Once. It went very bad."

"Then why did you want to play?"

Taylor's dark tone made her stomach clench. They'd been doing well together over the past two weeks. Well enough that she felt comfortable with him. And had even drawn a few stiff grins from his hard poker face. Well enough that she enjoyed his company.

Well enough that her prayers had turned from *I'm sorry I was so stupid, Lord! Please don't let this man turn out to be crazy* to *Thank You for a new day in this beautiful place, and for Your provision and protection. Please help me to find Taylor's smile.*

There was no smiling to be had that morning.

Why was he so grumpy on this nearly dawn Sunday? It was their morning off, and a beautiful one at that. They had access to one of the most beautiful golf courses she'd ever seen—though that wasn't saying a lot. As stated, she'd only attempted the game once. Nonetheless, the Sanctuary Island

Golf Club was rated in the top 100 American courses by *Golf Digest*. She knew because the sign had said so.

And even if it didn't, Sonora had eyes. This place was gorgeous. The long green fairway lined by tall pines and full maples, not to mention the hydrangea bushes that seemed to be a favorite all over the island. Pockets of vibrant flower beds boasting cascading petunias, feathery ornamental grasses, and an assortment of foliage. And as the grand backdrop of it all, the deep-blue expanse that was Lake Huron.

How could a person be cranky when they got to be a part of this picture?

Sonora tipped her chin up and pinned a sassy look on her husband. "Are you going to change your mind?"

A challenging silence extended between them, as if she'd dared him to continue his grouching. And maybe she was. With every scowl he aimed at her, she'd meet with a determined grin. And she'd find a way to pull him out of his self-inflicted sourness.

Somehow, she'd defeat his grumpy demeanor. Even if just to say she won.

Taylor held a long stare on her, and the corners of his eyes twitched. "No."

Curtis stood to the side of the tee, watching this odd interaction with mild amusement. "Sonora one, Taylor zero."

"What's that?" Sonora asked.

"You win that round." Curtis grabbed his hat with two fingers and a thumb and nodded his head, as if bowing. "Impressive too. I've never witnessed Taylor defeated so easily."

"There was nothing to lose," Taylor mumbled. "Are you going to play this hole sometime before we have to go to work?"

Curtis stepped back, anchoring his club over his shoulder. He looked first at Sonora, then at Taylor, then back at Sonora. "No. I think we should let the lady go first."

Sonora snorted. "You'll regret that. It'll take me at least a dozen swings just to connect with the ball."

"Nah." Curtis jerked his head in a *follow me* gesture, then sauntered toward the women's tee box. "I'll help you. You're in good hands."

With a glance at Taylor—sheesh, another frown!—she shrugged and followed Curtis. Taking the extended club and ball, she set up the tee and then stepped back. "Okay, All State, tell me what to do."

Curtis chuckled at her insurance joke. "First, address the ball."

"Does it prefer formal or casual?"

Another laugh from Curtis. Zero from Taylor. Sonora resisted the urge to look at the unsmiling man and instead focused her smile on Curtis.

"Feet shoulder width apart, arms relaxed." With both hands on her shoulders, Curtis squared her to the ball. Then he fixed her head so that she was looking at her target. "Okay, we'll try a few practice swings so you feel the way your lead hand will draw you through." Now he was behind her, both arms around her, hands on her forearms.

It was a little cozy.

He guided her club back and then through a swing.

"Relax."

Sonora swallowed. Maybe this wasn't the best idea.

Curtis helped her reset, then moved her arms into a swing again.

"Head down. Watch the club hit the ball. Lead the swing through with your hand."

"Okay." Sonora shrugged him away but kept her voice cheerful. Maybe too cheerful. "I think I got it." She set up again, this time with the intention of hitting the ball. Before she started her swing, she glanced up and caught Taylor's expression.

Hard. Cold. Severe.

Not what she had been going for at all.

She swallowed, bent her head, and focused on the ball. Drew the club back and pulled her lead hand forward. The club made a solid crack against the little white ball, and it flew.

"A solid hit!"

Sonora laughed. It was forced, fake, and hollow. "Look at that. I was in good hands." She fixed a smile that felt like plastic and turned back to Curtis, bypassing Taylor entirely. "Thank you."

Curtis winked. “You’re welcome.”

Behind her, Taylor’s footfalls moved away. When she looked over her shoulder, she found he’d hefted his golf bag—where the club she’d used belonged—and was stalking down the fairway toward her ball. She squeezed her eyes shut. That hadn’t gone right at all.

With a small sigh, she turned to follow him.

“I’d say you play the game well, Mrs. Everest.”

She stopped and pivoted back to Curtis. “What does that mean?”

He looked at Taylor, then back at her and winked. “Hooked ’im good.”

Her lips parted, and she simply stared.

“Can’t say that I disapprove. I like you, Sonora. But I will say that he’s my best friend, and his heart has been broken before. Don’t be reckless.”

Her heart squeezed and her stomach burned. “I don’t think . . . I mean, you’ve got this wrong.”

“Do I?” The lift of one eyebrow and his tone said that he didn’t think so at all.

Sonora swallowed against the bulge in her throat. “I only wish that he would smile.”

“Ah. I see.” Curtis shook his head in direct contraction. “And flirting with me is the way to do that?”

What! She hadn’t flirted with Curtis! He’d been the one to flirt with her. Of all the presumptuous, vain, stupid men . . . Sonora pressed her lips into a tight line.

"You obviously mean something to him, and now he can't deny it." Curtis gestured toward the man of their discussion. "For that, I congratulate you. Well played. Just be wise, Sonora. That's all I'm saying. He's a good man, and he deserves a faithful woman."

Taylor rubbed the oil rag against the leather straps of the harness with more vigor than the job required. But he needed to work the energy out of his body. All day, ever since the morning on the golf course, he'd been a powder keg of irritation. Hourly, almost like clockwork, he replayed Curtis wrapping his arms around Sonora. Sonora smiling at Curtis. Curtis and Sonora bantering.

Curtis and Sonora.

He simultaneously felt like punching something—namely Curtis—and throwing up.

"They still hold evening church services." Curtis's voice entered the barn before the man materialized.

Taylor clenched the rag in his right hand as his fist tightened around the harness. "So I've heard. Going to confession?" A dumb comment. That wasn't a practice at Sanctuary Bible Church, though on occasion Taylor thought it should be. If you had to go tell an actual human the things you were most ashamed of, maybe one would think twice before doing those things.

Curtis drew deeper into the shadows of the barn. His hands were stuffed into his dress pants pockets, face tipped down, toe scuffing the dirt and straw on the floor. Everything about him said *guilty*.

At least Curtis had a conscious.

Did Sonora feel bad too?

As his thoughts drifted toward the woman upstairs, who was likely in the shower, part of Taylor hoped so. The other part demanded that he didn't care because it didn't matter.

"Sonora cleaning up from the day?" Curtis asked.

Taylor found that he'd been staring at the passage that led up to his living quarters. Jarred back to the conversation, he fixed a hard gaze on Curtis. "Yes. There a reason you're asking?"

Curtis held up both hands. "Easy, buddy. I'm here on a peace mission."

"That so?"

"Look, I know what it looked like this morning." He shoved his hands back into his pockets again. "And I'm sorry."

"Really." Taylor feigned disinterest as he put his energy back into oiling the harness.

"Yeah, really." Curtis stepped closer and lowered himself onto the lid of the grain barrel to Taylor's left.

"Great. Apology accepted." Taylor glanced up. "Feel better?"

Curtis sat stiff and unmoving.

"You can go now."

"Actually, that's a half-truth."

"What?" Taylor's grip rolled around the leather he worked, and he felt a compelling urge to plow his fist into his friend's gut.

That might be an overreaction.

Curtis smirked. "Pretty possessive for a man who isn't interested."

"What does that mean?"

"You like her."

Taylor twisted his mouth, then reinvigorated his efforts with the harness.

"That's all I wanted you to see." Curtis shifted, crossing his arms. "Because I know you won't acknowledge it to yourself. I thought I'd give you a little push."

"Let me see if I've got this." Taylor stood and set his work on the long table behind him. "You flirted with my wife for *me*?"

"You could say that."

"No. I could not."

"Why? Surely you're not going to cling to the lie that you have zero interest in her. A moment ago you wanted to sink your fist into my face."

He could read that? Taylor strived to keep his expression neutral. Clearly he was slipping up. "Not your face," he muttered.

Curtis laughed. "We're edging toward honesty." His green eyes held both amusement and challenge as he held a fearless look on him.

No one but Curtis would do this. Confront him. Dare him to be honest. Well, no one besides Gretta. But she hardly counted. The woman didn't have boundaries. Curtis though? He'd always looked out for Taylor. Even when it meant crossing into Taylor's business and getting the wrong side of his bad humor for it.

That had happened once before—about Iris. Same song—except different. Curtis hadn't liked Iris, and he wasn't the sort of polite friend who'd kept that fact to himself. And he'd been right.

Taylor should have listened.

But Curtis liked Sonora? That didn't add up. "Last time you interfered, it was because you thought I was being a blind fool."

"Right. Here we are again."

"Why do you like Sonora when you didn't like Iris?" This honestly befuddled Taylor. "They are similar. If you paid attention, you would see that."

"I am paying attention. And I don't think she's a whole lot like Iris at all."

"What do you mean? Sunshine friendly? People person? Smiles even if she has to fake it. Totally like Iris."

"No." Curtis stood. "I mean, I can see the similarities. I'll admit that they're both people people and they enjoy interacting with others. Kind of your opposite. I get that. But Sonora *doesn't* fake it the way Iris did. She's genuinely a happy person. And, Taylor? I think she genuinely likes *you*."

"Yeah, you could tell that from our charade of a marriage. I don't think so, Curtis."

"She flirts with you."

"She flirted with you too." Anger made his voice sharp. Maybe Curtis had a point—he was pretty worked up about that.

Curtis lifted his eyebrows, his expression a challenge. "If you didn't like her, that wouldn't have bothered you this much."

"Of course it would, on principle. She *is* my wife."

Curtis snorted. "I think it's way more than principle, my friend. And because I think you don't see it—because you are astronomically stubborn—she *is* genuine when she flirts with you. What happened this morning with me? *That* was fake. And she wasn't comfortable with it."

Something in Taylor wanted to grasp what Curtis was claiming and nurture robust life into it. Because yes, he did like Sonora. Had since the moment his eyes had settled on her lovely face the day they'd met. But that was just attraction.

Attraction was a very poor indicator of something worth pursuing. Something worth risking his heart for. And for the record, he wasn't interested in risking his heart again. Ever.

Curtis stepped closer and gripped Taylor's shoulder, lowering his voice. "She looked pretty genuine the other night, at the celebration, with you."

"See, that's what I'm talking about." Taylor stepped back, pushing Curtis's hand away. He smothered the temptation to take what Curtis was suggesting and run with it. "That kiss? Why did she go and do that? It wasn't necessary. That was just . . . flirting recklessly. Just like Iris."

"Um, yeah, it kind of was necessary. She was selling your marriage to everybody else."

"But she didn't have to do it quite so compellingly."

Curtis laughed, shaking his head. "Buddy, from where I sat, *you* were the one who went in for the replay."

Taylor rubbed the back of his neck while a pain throbbed through his head. Was that true? Had he been the one to take that kiss from an innocuous peck to . . . He swallowed. Yes. Yes, he'd pulled her close, leaned down for a second go, and taken it to a more convincing level.

Man, what had he been thinking? Seemed with Sonora, his brain shut off and this attraction took over.

"Look, would it be the worst thing in the world to admit that you like your wife?"

"Yes, actually, it would."

"Why? I mean, you're *married*."

"Because this isn't a real marriage, Curtis. You know that."

"I don't know that. I hear the papers are signed. Everything's legal. In the eyes of the state of Michigan, you're married. The way I see it, you have an opportunity staring you in the face." His eyebrows bounced. "Now all you have to do is woo your wife. She seems pretty willing."

Taylor fixed his fiery glare. "Stop. You know what I mean. This arrangement isn't intended to last, and Sonora and I have a clear understanding about that. In fact, we made it a pre-wedding vow. She even hyphenated her name so that when we separate, things will be easier. She's here as my employee—the marriage was just to satisfy Gretta's stupid contract. Nothing more."

"Which would explain why you were jealous this morning."

Anger fisted his chest. Man, Curtis was pushing hard, and Taylor struggled to hold his composure. "Sonora is taking Albert and Victoria to the winter grounds, and she's not coming back. She's *not* coming back."

Suddenly raw, honest emotion overtook his superficial irritation. Those last four words were the proclamation he needed to keep forefront in his mind. But also, they had become the sharp twist in this misbegotten plot.

Sonora would leave, and she wasn't coming back. Then what would he do?

"I can't do that again." He swallowed as the unwelcome flood of bitter ache surged through him. Blast Curtis for that—if he'd leave this alone, Taylor wouldn't have to remember the disappointment. The heartache of being abandoned.

He shook his head, taking up the harness again. "I just can't."

"Who says you will?"

Taylor remained silent.

After several beats of confrontational awkwardness, Curtis sighed. "About church."

With a side-eyed glance, Taylor silently warned his friend to let well enough alone.

Of course Curtis didn't. "Same time. Same place." He strode toward the door, then paused before stepping out of the shadows of the barn and into the waning evening sun. "Maybe it's time to move on. Time to start living life again. Before it's too late."

Sonora finger-combed her damp hair, wishing for the hundredth time that she'd packed a hair dryer. Surely it wouldn't be that hard to acquire one. After all, the Palace was a resort. But she always forgot until the moment she needed one, and those times seemed inconvenient to go on a hunt for one.

So she let her thick mess of hair dry as it willed, which usually meant in a chaotic, semi-wavy mess that she would eventually braid just to get it out of her way. Not that big of a deal, since she needed it tied back for work anyway.

Settled on not needing a hair dryer, she wandered from the bedroom, which one must go through to get to the bathroom, and out into the front area. As it always did, her attention landed on that small couch.

If she lay on it and refused to budge tonight, would that force Taylor to take the bed? And if so, would he sleep better and scowl less? With that thought, a rush of guilt swept through her. Today she'd given Taylor a reason to scowl—and it'd had nothing to do with their sleeping arrangements. Worse, she'd done it on purpose. Although she hadn't wanted that result, particularly.

She'd just wanted . . .

A big fat sigh deflated her chest as she dropped onto the couch. *Lord, I messed up.*

She'd wanted to see if he'd be jealous. That was so junior high of her. An apology would be appropriate.

No. An apology was required.

Why did she keep tugging on this draw she felt toward him? She'd boldly told him that love was not in her story, and she'd meant it. So soon after Donovan, Sonora really didn't think she was ready to test the waters of trust and hope with a man. Particularly one whom she had trouble reading anyway. What if Taylor showed himself to be as flimsy and untrustworthy as her last attempt at forever?

Faithful.

That was what Taylor had claimed he worked to be in life. And Sonora believed him. She'd seen nothing to indicate that she shouldn't. Then again, she'd known him all of a few weeks.

Weeks of living in the same space. Sharing the same job. Spending mornings at the same small table, her with her chocolate milk and him with his black coffee. A few weeks of pretending they meant more to each other than a contracted job so that others wouldn't question their marriage. That meant sitting together in the employee dining hall. Walking together to Island Market. And of course, sharing a love for those gorgeous animals in the stalls below.

They had more in common than they didn't. In fact, though their personalities were perhaps opposite, it seemed that what they wanted in life, and the values they lived by, were parallel.

Added all together, Sonora had to admit that this pretending felt very much like it had the potential to become real. At times, it *felt* real. Like when Taylor would carry her food tray to their shared table. Or when she'd slipped her arm through his on their walk back from the Island Farmers' Market the day before.

Her belly pulled tight as she remembered how he'd sucked in a quiet breath, stiffened, then looked down at her hand on his arm. Then his eyes connected with hers and held. She'd held her breath as his gaze softened.

Lord, am I being a fool all over again? I ran when I should have sought You first. But now I'm here, and it seems like there's something . . .

There *had* been connection. There was possibility there. And despite having been once rejected, Sonora was willing to risk her heart again. For her boss.

Sonora sat forward, her mind clear and made up. She'd go for it—and not like a junior high girl with a crush. First things first—an apology.

As she pushed up to stand, the door rattled open. In strode the man she'd been pondering, his face unsmiling, as usual. Once he shut the door, he turned to her and their gazes collided. There was a sharpness to his look, but that wasn't unusual. But then his look drifted toward the window above the small sink, and he winced.

"Taylor I—"

"There is service at the Bible Church on Sunday evenings." He spoke the same moment she'd started.

With eyebrows raised—church? He'd never mentioned that before. Nor had she—Sonora stilled her tongue.

"I'm sorry." Taylor gestured toward her. "You were saying?"

She swallowed. *I'm sorry* . . . that was what was going to happen. But she only shrugged and asked instead, "Church?"

"Yes. I thought—" He rolled his fingers into fists near his hips and cleared his throat. "You pray every day before you eat. So I thought you'd be interested. There is an evening service so that those of us who work Sunday mornings can attend."

"Do you usually go?"

His lips pressed.

Sonora took that as nerves. "Taylor, we can go. You should have said something sooner."

Slowly his gaze lifted to meet hers again. "I haven't gone in quite a while."

Ah. Something else they had in common. Sonora nodded. "It's been a while since I've gone to church too."

Work had been her excuse the past few years. But beyond her mealtime prayers and some last-minute *I need some help!* pleas, she'd grown complacent in her walk with God. Which might explain why she hadn't stopped to really pray about her situation before she'd run off to Sanctuary Island to marry a stranger.

But maybe God was still at work, even in her failures.

Though Taylor held his stare, his expression twisted into something painfully uncomfortable. Sonora stepped toward him, wondering what he would do if she tried to smooth away the furrowed lines between his eyebrows. Instead, she stopped near enough to touch him, though she didn't do so.

"Do you want to go?"

He visibly swallowed. "If you . . . will go with me."

It would probably increase their credibility as a married couple. Although there didn't seem to be any doubtful rumors about them floating around the Palace. At least not that she was aware of.

Sonora reached to lay her hand on his arm. "Let me braid my hair, and I'll be ready."

"Leave it."

She'd turned already, but his simple words stopped her. Looking over her shoulder, she saw crimson creep up his neck. He cleared his throat. "I mean, if you'd like. You don't have to wear it up all the time."

"It's kind of a mess."

He blinked. Drew in a breath. Then shook his head. That was all.

But that simple wordless action felt like a beautiful compliment.

"Jeans okay?" she asked around the lump in her throat.

"Yes."

"Will you be changing?" He was still dressed in the black suit he wore for the tourists.

"Yes."

"Then you can have the room." Sonora put lightness into her voice and moved to sit at the table.

Taylor nodded—that meant thank you, she was pretty sure—and then strode to the back room.

Her heart flitted, and her hands twitched. Church. With Taylor. It felt . . . oh, dear heaven, it felt like a life she used to long for.

Fourteen

She slipped her hand around his arm again.

Taylor instinctively stiffened as he pulled in a quick breath. His throat felt thick, and he wasn't sure if, while he paused in front of the white clapboard church with a soaring steeple and tall multipaned windows, his heart galloped because it had been more than a few years since he'd entered that little building or because the woman at his side held the power to make his insides a wreck.

A betting man would have wagered on Sonora. Taylor decided it was the church.

Her fingers tightened on his bicep. "You okay?"

"Yes." His standard one-word answer. But he didn't resume their walk toward the pair of wood doors.

"It's been a minute, huh?"

He looked down to see her concerned expression focused on him, and a squeeze of warmth eased the strain in his chest. "Yes."

"Me too."

They had already covered that ground. It wasn't normal for Taylor to indulge in inane, already-discussed topics. Then again, it wasn't normal for him to allow a beautiful creature such as Sonora Hillary-Everest to muddle his insides.

As if he could stop her.

She dipped her head close and pressed her temple into his shoulder. "We'll manage."

There went his pulse again. Off to the races.

Why had he done this? Not the marriage—he'd already berated himself about that to the point of the equine being deceased. Attending church, that was what he questioned now. All Curtis had to do was suggest he get himself there, and now there he was. Wife on his arm.

When had he become this malleable?

A moment from a few weeks past resurfaced in his memory. In the dark hours of earliest morning, he'd admitted that he'd missed God. Since that day Taylor had done nothing about it. He'd considered that the moment of self-reflection had been more because he was more terrified about getting *married* than about honesty. Or perhaps he'd told himself that. He'd been lying to himself.

He hated lies!

But he was also mad. At God.

***You* left me.**

The impression of accusation from heaven—though gently pressed—produced a sharp pain.

Iris had left Taylor. In his hurt and disappointment, Taylor had left God. Because it hadn't been the first time God had allowed something to happen that left Taylor alone and aching.

He looked up to the tip of that high steeple, then shut his eyes. Truth was, Taylor wouldn't take Iris back now. Not for anything. She'd left him heartbroken and bitter, and he hoped to never see her beautiful face again.

So why would God take him back? Is that what this wrestling was about? Not really about whether or not Taylor wanted to return to God, but a fear he'd be rejected?

Taylor rolled his fists as his throat swelled.

"Taylor?" Sonora wrapped her arm around his. "I'm with you, okay? Let's just go in and sit down. I'll be right beside you the whole time."

Did he look panicked? Is that why she was whispering these reassurances as if he were a terrified little boy about to take his first boat ride? Insult threatened just beneath the raw vulnerability that had gaped. But before it could take root, he looked down at her.

Pure sweetness stared back at him. Not pity. Not condescension. Just this lovely creature whose heart seemed as pleasant as her smile.

Where had this kind and steady woman come from? How was it that she'd breezed into his life at the exact moment he'd needed her?

One corner of his mouth eased, and she rewarded him with a squeeze of her hand. Then they were moving forward again. Through those open double doors, past the flower arrangement in the center of the narthex, into the vaulted sanctuary, and onto a sun-drenched pew. A stream of warm gold light draped across his shoulder, and for a moment of uncharacteristic levity, Taylor imagined it was the hand of God welcoming him there.

Sonora slipped onto the polished wooden seat beside him with an ease that hinted at her familiarity with church. Suddenly he wondered why she'd stopped going—as she had said that it had been a while for her too. That would indicate she'd made attending a practice at one point, wouldn't it? Did her absence from church have anything to do with her not believing that love was in her story? Had she quit going because some man had thrown her off track?

Before he could toil with that question much, the gathering of people he'd known and worked with all his life stood, and almost all pulled a hymnal from the back of the pew. As he reached for one to share with Sonora, Taylor remembered hearing from tourists that "no one uses hymnals anymore"—usually said with pleasure at the charming novelty of it.

He didn't know either way, except that he secretly delighted in sharing one with his wife at that moment.

"Let's begin our worship with 'Rejoice! The Lord Is King .'" Charles Harlowe, an elder, spoke from the large wooden pulpit up at the front—apparently another charming relic of church-past.

Meg Harlowe, Charles's wife, played a few chords to introduce the music, and then the congregation began to sing.

Taylor joined the melody, familiar with the hymn. His mind narrowed in on the words as they reached the third verse.

His kingdom cannot fail,

He rules o'er earth and heav'n;

The keys of death and hell

Are to our Jesus giv'n:

Lift up your heart,

Lift up your voice!

Rejoice, again I say, rejoice!

He stopped singing at that point, though there remained another verse to be sung, and Mrs. Harlowe was not one to skimp on a hymn. He reread those lines, and pain twisted in his chest.

His kingdom cannot fail.

But what of the disappointments in life? How could one reconcile a triumphant, sovereign king with the heartaches, the woes of this world? There was still evil. Still so much wrong. People could be hurtful. Life could be terribly disappointing.

His mind turned over that—the very reason he'd stopped coming to church and had given up on God in his personal life—while the elder and Mrs. Harlowe took them through two more hymns. At the close of the third, everyone sat down, and Charles took up his Bible. It must be his week to preach, as the regular pastor had been gone often because of an ailing father in need of care.

"Join me in Genesis, won't you?" Charles said. "I'll be reading from chapter 22, verse 1, to the end."

The hushed and hallowed swish of pages turning filled the peaceful church.

"Ah. A favorite sound. It's so good to join together to hear from the Lord, isn't it?" Charles raised his hands. "Will you stand with me in honor of reading the Word of God?"

Again, everyone stood.

"Isaac spoke up and said to his father Abraham, 'Father?' 'Yes, my son?' Abraham replied. 'The fire and wood are here,' Isaac said, 'but where is the lamb for the burnt offering?'

Abraham answered, 'God himself will provide the lamb for the burnt offering, my son.' And the two of them went on together."

Taylor winced as he listened to the story. Sacrifice his only son? What was God thinking? Doing?

God himself will provide . . .

That phrase landed in Taylor's ears and stuck. It was like a foreshadowing—Taylor knew because he was familiar enough with the account to know that Abraham didn't sacrifice Isaac. A ram had shown up just in time.

As Charles continued to read, the course of the story revealed exactly that. A ram was caught in the thicket. Isaac was spared—and Abraham was spared killing his own son. Such a bizarre series of events.

What did it mean? Why would God need to test Abraham like that?

"Friends, we come to this chapter in Genesis, and we scratch our heads. It's a strange telling, isn't it? So strange, in fact, that philosophers have pondered it, dismantled it, examined it from all angles, written books about it, and still . . . we come here and wonder. What? Why? How could a loving, good God ask such a thing of a father? Can one trust this God?"

Taylor's attention zeroed in there. Wasn't that the wrestling of his own life? How could he trust the God who had disappointed him?

"We have to honestly wrestle with this. Life is littered with hardship. Heartache is a theme of every soul. Disappointment is epidemic. What do we do with suffering, and how do we reconcile it with the God of the Bible, which proclaims in Psalm 145:9, for example, that the 'Lord is good to all, and his mercy is over all that he has made?'"

Posture like steel, Taylor sat riveted. It was like the man speaking had been inside his head. His soul. Had witnessed the defeat and resignation that had led to Taylor's paralyzed faith. Because that was exactly the question he could not resolve—how could God be good and yet life be so . . .

"But we see here something profound. Both in the discovery of Abraham's faith and in the revealing of God's provision. Abraham had been through a thing or two, hadn't he? He'd already known the deep pain and disappointment of being childless. He thought he'd die that way, until God told him otherwise. And even after that, he had a long wait and a misguided path to endure. His family suffered for his faithlessness before.

"So now here we are, Abraham with the promised son. The one his wife had named *laughter.* And there he goes, with the boy he loves, doing the bidding of the God he has discovered, over a lifetime of heartaches and mistakes and long promises kept, is *faithful* despite all that would seem to point otherwise.

"And we find out that after a lifetime of those missteps, Abraham has learned what Adam wished he'd held on to in Eden: Yahweh can be trusted. Did you get that? Read his response again: 'God himself will provide . . .'"

In the extended pause, Taylor's eyes stung. It was . . . contradictory. Abraham knew what God had told him to do—sacrifice his son. But there it was. *God himself will provide*. Why did Abraham say that?

"We have to know the full story to get this, so let us take a minute to review the case. God had called Abraham and had promised him that he and Sarah would have a son, and through that son, all the nations of the earth would be blessed. It was a unilateral promise—God was going to do it, regardless of Abraham's actions. So we fast-forward through all the convoluted messiness of Abraham and Sarah learning to believe God, and here we are. The challenging moment of truth—would Abraham believe God *here*? Because we know

Isaac is the promised son. We know that the promise extends well beyond the boy's life. So what is Abraham to think?

"Stunningly, Abraham, in this moment, takes God's promise and applies it to an unbelievable situation. In his mind there are two possibilities: God will provide an alternative sacrifice, or God will raise his sacrificial son from the dead. Those were the options. Either way Abraham shows us here that he *believes* God's promise.

"And, my friends, we should be breathless at this! Overwhelmed by the grace and goodness of God, who is the author of our faith. Because Abraham is not only holding out the example of that unshaken faith, but through his story we are pointed to the ultimate story. Because God has provided the solution!

"Both possibilities in Abraham's situation have been proven true. God provided a ram in place of Isaac. A gift of substitution. And He's given us Jesus in *our* place. Not only that—oh no! That's not enough! He raised that sacrificial Son from the dead.

"If you're of a Pentecostal bent, this is where you stand up and start singing with Charles Wesley, 'Where, O death, is now thy sting? Alleluia! Once he died our souls to save, Alleluia! Where's thy victory, boasting grave? Alleluia!'"

A stirring and a few chuckles filtered among the people. Taylor wondered if someone would do exactly that—stand and sing in the middle of the sermon. No one did, but the energy of it was felt. And his soul stretched heavenward for the first time in way too long.

"Blessed be the God who does not leave us without hope. He is to be trusted. He keeps his promises. He provides. Perhaps you come from a place today where you have been wondering, *Do You see this? Are You watching? Listening? Do You care?* Look with me now at the place from which Abraham and Isaac left together, and recall the name given to that mountain: 'So Abraham called that place The Lord Will Provide.'

"There is heartache and suffering in this world. Disappointments aplenty. Sometimes God doesn't make sense to us. But have we learned, like Abraham, that through it all, God is trustworthy. He will provide. He *has* provided.

"We can join with Wesley and say, Hail the Lord of earth and heaven, Alleluia! Praise to thee by both be given, Alleluia!

"Let us declare together our faith, no matter what we may face right now. The Lord is good to all, and his mercy is over all that he has made. Amen."

A soft echo of "amen" filled the room. Bibles slid closed. Charles finished with a prayer, and the service came to a close.

Taylor sat unmoving. Overwhelmed. While his eyes burned and swallowing became difficult, a hand, warm and gentle, slipped into his.

The Lord is good to all . . .

The concrete Taylor had poured around his heart split.

Sonora had never felt this. Was it her imagination? As she sat with Taylor, the congregation stirring around them, it was like she shared the ache she could sense from him. She had no idea why—what the source of pain was—but she was certain that's what kept him glued to that polished wooden seat they shared, staring forward. Swallowing hard.

It was an undeniable connection.

When she slipped her hand over his, she heard his sharp intake of breath, though it wasn't particularly loud. His lips rolled together, and he winced. Though he didn't move otherwise, Sonora kept her fingers sheltering his. A silent *You're not alone, whatever this is.*

Did he appreciate that, or did he resent it?

In typical Taylor Everest fashion, he kept the truth of that off his face and wholly to himself. For some reason, that didn't bother her.

"You two made it." Curtis stopped in the aisle beside the pew Taylor and Sonora shared. Though his grin was mild, without a hint of the flirting he'd brought to their round of one-hole golf, his green eyes smiled. "I'm glad to see it."

Taylor turned his hand and gripped Sonora's.

For show? To warn Curtis to keep it appropriate? Or because he wanted to?

He stood, and she followed, unable to hush the queries—nor quell the hope that it was the last of the options that motivated him. Curtis held a hand toward Taylor, and the men shook.

A truce then?

The trio filed down the aisle and out the double doors, both of which had been braced wide open. The cool evening air prickled along the skin of her bare arms. The gentle breeze smelled of crisp lake and pine and was sweetened by a citrusy rose scent, which must have drifted from the arbor smothered by soft pink blooms at the end of the short walkway from the church.

And by her side walked a handsome man. A girl might find this idyllic. If she allowed herself to slip into daydreams.

"Will you hang around town square tonight?" Curtis walked with both hands in his pockets, his demeanor at ease. "Maybe wander over to the gazebo?"

"I hadn't considered it."

Curtis leaned to look past Taylor and at Sonora. "Have you been in town at all during the weekend evenings?"

"No." Other than going to the small store or the farmers' market, her world had been the Palace or the business of the Palace. That meant driving to and from the docks, with few stops in between. Though she wouldn't have complained—she had been satisfied with that—this evening had been a pleasant breach of routine.

Curtis gave Taylor an arched-brow look. There was some sort of secret in that. He then clicked his tongue and shook his head. "If I had a wife as lovely and charming as yours, I'd be showing her off as often as possible."

Taylor's fingers slipped from hers, and she was immediately sad. Sonora braced herself for the scowl sure to come. But Taylor surprised her when his blue eyes settled on her and he asked, "Would you like to stay for a while?" There was nothing intimate in his tone. It was rather stoic, to tell the truth. But even so, Sonora's tummy squeezed.

"I would, I think."

"Great." Curtis was back to all enthusiasm and energy. He and Taylor were truly opposites. Had they really been lifelong friends? How did they put up with each other? With a fedora in his left hand—one Sonora had missed that he held until that moment—Curtis did a fun little hat flip that made her think of the show *White Collar* and settled it over his dark-red hair. "The boys and I sing at eight thirty. At least hang around for that." Then with a wink that must be involuntary for that guy—as often as he performed one—he clapped Taylor's shoulder and jogged down the cobblestone lane.

"He's always into something, isn't he?" Sonora said.

"Yes." Flat, nondescript tone.

She resisted a sigh. Was it foolish to wish for the connection back? Probably. Sonora did so just the same.

While they neared the town square, the activity seasoned the small-town vibe—kids laughing and yelling and playing a round of chase in the park and the clippity-clop of the one-horse-drawn taxis that serviced the main road through town, a community amenity outside of the Palace's more prestigious, and more limited, carriage services. And as they neared the center square where the gazebo sat, the melodic song of bows drawn across strings.

Taylor kept their stroll aimed toward the gazebo, and the musicians came into view. Four youths, the oldest no more than eighteen, Sonora would bet, sat at the center of the cedar wood feature set in the middle of the town. The kids played a quartet of stringed instruments—two violins, one viola, and one cello. Whatever they played, it was soft, enchanting, and perfectly done.

Sonora stepped off the walkway onto the mowed grass and stopped. "They're good."

"They are."

Hey—two words! That was a good sign. Sonora swiveled her attention from the quartet to the man at her side.

Taylor rolled his shoulders, as if they were stiff or sore. Then he clenched his fists.

Why was he agitated? Was it being in town that made him uneasy—more so than normal? Or was this left over from whatever had bothered him in church? Or perhaps it was left over from her stupid stunt this morning.

Ah. That. She'd decided an apology was required but hadn't followed through. No time like the present.

"Taylor." She pivoted to stand square with him, touching his elbow as she moved.

Those sharp blue eyes widened.

"I owe you an apology."

He frowned.

"This morning . . . I was . . ." Hmm . . . how to put it? She swallowed, rolled her lips in, and decided to just be brutally honest. After all, Taylor claimed that he always was—he would respect that. "I was acting like a junior high girl, flirting with Curtis. It was childish of me, and I'm sorry."

The corners of his eyes pinched as he looked down. "You like him."

"Curtis?"

That solemn gaze captured her face again. Was there pain at the far end of that distant look?

"I like Curtis fine—though he's a little over the top sometimes. But that wasn't why I flirted." Was she willing to admit the real reason she'd done it? That might be on the edge of too risky. Especially since she'd vowed this relationship wasn't destined for anything beyond their business arrangement.

Taylor's jaw shifted. Then he looked back at the quartet on stage. She braced herself for the inevitable question . . .

"Mrs. Harlowe, the woman who played the piano at church, taught them."

He . . . he was changing the subject? Overriding the small helping of relief at not having to say the truth of why she'd flirted, the sting of him ignoring her apology made her flinch. She watched Taylor's face, but he didn't return his gaze to her. Finally, she shifted with him. "Mrs. Harlowe taught those four how to play their instruments?"

"Yes. And many others in town."

"All of them violins or cellos?"

"No. She teaches piano and flute. Maybe the French horn too, though I've never seen that up there." He nodded toward the gazebo.

"She knows how to play all those?"

"I don't think she's met an instrument she couldn't master."

"Wow. That's extraordinary."

"She loves music. And loves to pass it along to the kids of Sanctuary Island. Though it feels like this place is hopping now, the reality is we have limited access to the outside world, so having Mrs. Harlowe teach music is superabundant. As you can see, she does a good job."

Despite her disappointment, Taylor's use of another uncommon, big word cracked a grin onto her lips. "Superabundant?"

He froze, and an adorable pink colored his cheeks beneath the dark stubble of his evening shadow. "Yes. Well, perhaps I extended the use of that word. I meant it as *a big deal*. As in having Mrs. Harlowe's talents here is a big deal. But it's not excessive. Just . . ."

Was the solemn and tight-lipped Taylor Everest babbling?

For a moment, amused delight touched her, but it flitted away when she considered that he might be working *super-abundantly* to brush off what she'd just said. Sonora turned back to face the gazebo again, stepping back to add more space between herself and Taylor. Her stomach twisted, and she couldn't fight the droop of her shoulders.

Was he refusing to accept her apology? Why?

Man, this shouldn't matter this much. After all, this whole situation was temporary.

But of course it mattered. She didn't want him to think badly of her, and more importantly, she'd really meant what she had said. This morning had been badly done, and she was sorry for it.

"Would you like some ice cream?"

Her chin shot up. "What?"

"Ice cream. The Pearl has homemade vanilla. It's quite good. Tourists say some of the best found anywhere."

Was he . . . was this like . . . a truce? Like that handshake she'd witnessed between Taylor and Curtis earlier?

"Maybe you're too chilly for ice cream." Taylor stuffed his hands into his pockets. "I'm sorry. I should have told you to grab a sweater. The evenings can get cool even before fall sets in." He peeked at her, hesitated, then moved to take off his sports coat. "You can—"

"Oh, I'm fine. Not too chilly for ice cream at all." Sonora's words tumbled over each other like rocks in a landslide. Taylor was worried about her being cold? He was worried about her at all?

Wait. Had he just intended to let her wear his sports coat?

And she'd rejected it?

She mentally did a facepalm.

Taylor cleared his throat. "So . . . Ice cream, then?"

"Yes. Please. That sounds yummy." Goodness, she was being an idiot. Why was she being so . . . ridiculous? It wasn't like this was a . . . date. Or something.

Not a date. He's your boss, and you have a deal.

Taylor walked toward the row of shops that lined the bricked street. His posture remained ever square, his stride ever sure. But he kept opening and closing his hand.

Sonora wondered what he would do if she slipped her fingers between his when he next flexed them wide. Her belly tightened, and she swallowed against the delightful nerves that just the mere thought of it produced. Clearly her little self-talk had meant nothing.

When they came to the Pearl, Taylor pulled the door open and held it wide for Sonora to pass through. She walked to the counter, and he followed, stopping close to her back.

"Well. Taylor Everest." The woman at the counter, wearing an apron of pink and white stripes, smiled at the man, then her widened eyes drifted to Sonora. "This must be your wife."

"It is." Taylor's voice came deep and formal. "Mrs. O'Connell, meet Sonora. Sonora, this is Mrs. O'Connell. She was my first-grade teacher."

The woman reached across the counter, which doubled as a freezer, with several buckets of ice cream tucked beneath the glass top, and offered a handshake. "I'm delighted to meet you." Her greeting and smile seemed warm and genuine. "And I was thrilled to hear that you'd married, Taylor. Though I have to say, disappointed that I was not invited to the wedding."

"We eloped," Sonora said, then wished she hadn't. At least, not in such a rushed manner. Like they had something to hide.

"I heard." Mrs. O'Connell nodded, as if there was nothing suspicious about Taylor's sudden marriage to a woman no one on the island had ever met before. "And I'm glad. Curtis tells me you've found a gem."

Sonora looked over her shoulder to find Taylor's lips lifting into a tiny smile. "Does he?"

"He certainly has. Several times. Says she balances your dower face with bright smiles, is perfect with the tourists, and makes your tough gaze softer."

Whoa. That was . . . harsh? Again, Sonora looked up at her husband, a stony feeling of defensiveness rising fast. Were all of Taylor's friends this sharp with him?

But Taylor's expression held no hint of offense. Instead, that ghostly grin became . . . whole. "That sounds exactly like something Curtis would say. You raised a rascal."

"Curtis is your son?" How was that for burying the lead? Why had Taylor left that bit of news out of the introduction?

Wait. O'Connell! Of course. Curtis had mentioned his last name that first day.

Mrs. O'Connell laughed. "He is. I only claim him when he's not getting into trouble, though." She winked. "Thankfully, he's had Taylor to help stem his penchant for mischief. Usually, I claim them both as my boys." She paused, her playful smile growing wide. "Taylor I claim *all* the time."

Ah, now Sonora could see it. Like mother, like son.

"What can I get you?" Mrs. O'Connell reached for a metal scoop from a small bucket of water.

Sonora glanced at Taylor. "The homemade vanilla is famous?"

"That's the word from the tourists."

"Then I must try it."

He nodded. "Two please."

Mrs. O'Connell dipped the ice cream, chatting as she did. Had they been to Seven Pines yet? Did they have a real honeymoon planned after the tourist season ended? Would they go to the winter grounds for Christmas this year? Had Taylor treated her to the Lantern Room yet—because he should have. Was Hope over-the-moon delighted?

Sonora had exactly zero answers for those questions—mostly she didn't even know what they pertained to. Seven Pines? The Lantern Room? Hope?

Taylor mumbled uninformative answers. Once their bowls were served, Mrs. O'Connell pinned a motherly look on Taylor. "You're not one for lies."

Sonora sucked in a breath while Taylor stiffened at her side. He swallowed. "What lie are you accusing me of?"

"Hope would be thrilled if she knew you were married. You haven't told her, have you?"

Taylor leaned back, looking toward his left hand.

"Why would you not tell your mother you got married?"

He rolled his lips together. Sonora's stomach twisted, shooting nausea through her as her mind sprinted for something to say. Something that would save Taylor from this incredibly awkward moment.

Finally, after the chilly air seemed to freeze entirely, Taylor lifted his face to look at the woman. "Mom will be crushed to find out I eloped. It's not something I want to tell her over the phone."

That sounded true. Was it true? If so, how would Mrs. Everest feel when she discovered the terms of this marriage?

Mrs. O'Connell gave them both a side-eyed look. The motherly, disapproving kind. Then her expression softened, and she nodded. "I get it, Taylor. And I know that it's been . . . strained. But you can't expect that your parents won't hear about you being married. This is a small community, and they're still part of it, even from a distance."

Taylor's lips seamed tight, and a hardness cooled those blue eyes back into steel.

Though this particular talent of his seemed to intimidate everyone else, Mrs. O'Connell didn't back down. "Call your mother, Taylor. The sooner the better."

He didn't answer. Instead, he reached into the inner pocket of his sports coat and pulled out his wallet.

Mrs. O'Connell held up a hand. "On the house." Her smile resurfaced. Gentle. Kind. "Congratulations."

Sonora wasn't sure she could enjoy the ice cream, even if it were the best in the country.

FIFTEEN

TAYLOR WILLED AWAY THE ringing in his ears. His face felt hot, like he'd just been slapped.

He hadn't been. Just reprimanded by a woman he held in high esteem. And Fiona O'Connell wasn't wrong. He should have called his parents.

The thing was, he barely spoke with them. Hadn't in years. Not since they'd up and left him. He wasn't mad at them, exactly. It was just that he'd felt blindsided.

And utterly abandoned.

It wasn't how he'd pictured his life going. But it was, as life had played out, how things went with him. People left, and he lived alone. Now there were the handful of phone calls made throughout the year—mostly to make arrangements to transfer Al and Vicky for the season. One at Christmas. The obligatory Mother's Day and Father's Day calls. And birthdays. That was all that was left between them.

"She seemed worried."

They had meandered down the sidewalk, Taylor lost in the depressing labyrinth of his thoughts, though aware of Sonora at his side. How could he not be aware of her? She stirred him—often uncomfortably so. Sometimes, as had happened multiple moments that evening, electrifyingly so. But as she usually did, Sonora had left him to think.

He liked that about her. That she could be present but not intrusive. He found her . . . soothing. In the most uncomfortable ways. How did that even make sense?

"She's probably right," Sonora continued after he'd remained wordless past the opportunity to respond. "Someone is bound to reach out to your parents and tell them that you're married."

"Yes." He'd already considered that, and every time the thought crossed his mind, his heart hammered with anxiety. It was a small miracle, in fact, that he hadn't received a hyper-emotional phone call about it already.

"But it's complicated, isn't it?" Her voice was solace, not condemnation.

"Yes." Though, did she mean their marriage? Yes, that was complicated—though it wasn't meant to be. Or was she referring to his relationship with his parents?

When he glanced down, he found her enjoying the ice cream, as if there were nothing consequential being discussed. She was neither pushy nor aloof. Simply . . . there. Offering to listen, if he'd like. Or let it alone, if that was his preference. Usually it was. But her easy silence was a compelling invitation.

The milling crowd clapped, signaling the end of a song. In the gazebo, the stringed quartet tucked their instruments into their velvet-lined cases. Noah Bryant, the oldest of the group, spoke a word of thanks into the mic, and then the four took up their cases, music stands, and stools and exited the stage. Passing them, Curtis and his three singing pals skipped up the steps to take the string quartet's place.

Sonora pointed with her cup of ice cream. "What do they play?"

"Their vocal cords."

"Oh, right. Curtis said he'd be singing."

"They're a barbershop quartet."

Sonora grinned, as if she thought that was charming, then dipped another heaping spoonful of homemade vanilla. Turning the utensil upside down, she placed it on her tongue. Her eyes shut, a delightful grin lit her face, and she let out a little groan as she pulled the spoon out of her mouth. "You're correct, as usual. This is . . . delicious? Amazing?" Her eyes dancing playfully, she looked at him. "Give me a word, Everest."

His emotions lifted from despair. "This is a fun game for you, isn't it?"

"Delightful." She made a show of enjoying another bite, then licked her lips. "A word, please, Taylor. Make it a good one."

"Delectable."

"That is too obvious. You can do better."

He chuckled, and she beamed victorious. A thrill ran clean through him at the thought that *he'd* prompted that stunning joy from her. How was that possible? Her delight was like a warm sunrise after a harsh storm, all bright and hopeful. Why would she grace him with that sort of wonder?

He had no idea, but he wanted to summon it again. And again and again.

"Sumptuous."

"Oh, that is a good one. Are you sure it can be used for ice cream?"

"Would you consider it lavish or luxurious?"

"Absolutely."

"Then it's appropriate."

She nudged his shoulder with hers. "Well then, thank you for this sumptuous homemade vanilla ice cream."

"You'll have to thank Fiona O'Connell."

"Ah yes." She held him with that open expression. The inviting one that drew him, nearly irresistibly, out from the concrete shell around his heart. The one that had broken apart earlier that evening.

Would it hurt to tell her about his family leaving him? After all, everyone around the island already knew—it wasn't like it was a big secret. Only, he never talked about it. As far as anyone local was aware, he was fine with it. Everything was fine.

Taylor swallowed against the growing lump in his throat as Curtis and the boys finished their "Ice Cream" vocal warm-up, stolen from *The Music Man*. A coincidental choice,

Taylor thought as he glanced down at his nearly finished treat.

Maybe he could just enjoy the evening and let the burgeoning emotions stirring within die back down. That would be safer.

"Ladies and gentlemen." Curtis sounded like a ringmaster. "This evening we dedicate this song as a celebration for my best pal and his new bride." With a grand sweep of his hand, Curtis gestured to Taylor.

Good grief. Come this winter, when Curtis came around bored stiff and wanting to play checkers, Taylor would drag him out to the barn and make him aid in cleaning tack instead. And when Curtis whined about it, Taylor would remind him of this night.

As clapping erupted, Taylor glanced down at Sonora. She gazed up at him, playing the part of the blushing bride. But her brows lifted, and her eyes held a silent apology. Taylor shook his head just enough to communicate that it wasn't her fault, and then as she slipped her arm around him, he draped his around her.

He leaned down to whisper, "The winters are long and harsh around here. I'll get him back when he is most desperate."

The four men on stage launched into their first song—"For the Longest Time."

Sonora lifted her chin to whisper back, "What will you do to him?"

"Maybe I'll pull the spark plugs out of his snowmachine on one of our ice-fishing excursions, then I'll just leave him there to hoof it back in the cold."

Her bottom lip popped out. "You're not cruel, Taylor Everest. You would feel terrible."

"He deserves it, and I won't feel bad."

She rolled her eyes. "You know he thinks he's being a good friend, right?"

Taylor scowled, then shook his head. Leaning close, he spoke into her ear. "He knows the truth."

She pulled back, lines furrowing her brow. "What?"

"Curtis knows."

Lines folded against her brow as she winced. Ice cream brain freeze? Couldn't have been what he'd told her—he was fairly certain from their first exchange with Curtis that she was already aware that Curtis knew they weren't a couple in love.

"Taylor." Sonora gripped the lapel of his jacket. "I really meant what I said earlier. Now more so than ever. I'm sorry that I flirted with him. I only did it to see if you'd be jealous—and because I forgot that he knew about our situation. I was thinking that he saw me as your wife, so it would be harmless."

Her words sank in slowly. Deeply. And his breath caught. She . . . she'd wanted to make him jealous?

The sweet smiles. The long looks. Her arguing with him about his sleeping on the sofa. Her hand on his at church. She'd wanted him to be jealous . . .

There had been attraction between them. Chemistry. And it wasn't just on his side. But she'd said specifically that she wasn't looking for love. Wasn't interested in a real, romantic relationship.

Was this a game?

Taylor couldn't sort through the contradiction, specifically when Curtis and the boys had moved to "Let Me Call You Sweetheart," and all Taylor wanted to do was pull Sonora close and sway with her to the music as she filled his arms.

This was madness. They'd agreed. They had a deal. He stepped back, pulling away from her and letting his arm fall to his side.

As they drifted apart, a couple who were clearly comfortable together approached them. Taylor buttoned in a sigh. Chloe he liked fine—she was a warrior for the island and he commended her for it. Derrick . . . that man he was still warry of.

"Taylor, congratulations!" Chloe reached to shake his hand, then turned to Sonora. "I'm Chloe, and this is Derrick."

"It's nice to meet you." Sonora shifted into her work mode—though Taylor was sure he was the only one who could see the difference in her demeanor. "It's good to meet some of Taylor's friends."

He wasn't sure he'd go that far. Well, yes, Chloe was a friend. Derrick still hadn't smoothed all the feathers he'd rumpled on the island, particularly of those who ran heritage businesses. Gretta, for example, was particularly frazzled about the wealthy man and his planned family adventure resort. Taylor could hardly blame her for being upset. But that had nothing to do with anything right then.

Sonora's smile wasn't quite so smooth, and her eyes held a tightness that wasn't her full cheer. Was it meeting people that had her off? No, more likely it was the conversation they'd not yet finished.

"I'd love to get together for lemonade or coffee," Chloe offered to Sonora. "I'm the chef at the Bluebell Inn, and I make a mean stuffed French toast, if you ever have an inclination to visit."

"That's kind. Thank you." Sonora seemed more herself.

"Well, congratulations." Chloe reached to hug Sonora, then Taylor.

Derrick held out a hand, and Taylor took it. They exchanged a silent nod that seemed like a truce, and then the couple wandered away.

"That was nice of them," Sonora said.

Taylor nodded. "Chloe is a kind woman." He looked down at Sonora. "You should take her up on that French toast. She uses spiced pears harvested from the island. It really is good."

"And Derrick?"

Taylor didn't comment.

"Ah. So my guess is confirmed. You don't like him."

He shrugged. "I don't know him that well."

"But?"

"He wants to build a resort on the other side of the island. Some kind of big monstrosity with a water park."

"I see. So he's a threat."

"It's not really my business, I guess. Gretta is very upset though."

"I imagine she would be." She touched his arm, causing him to stop. "Those kinds of places attract a different clientele than the Palace though. Young families with kids. It might be good for everyone, rather than a drain on the older establishments."

Taylor studied her for a long moment. "Could be. Most around here don't like the idea of becoming a Disney World type of place."

"I doubt that would happen."

He shrugged. "Like I said, it's not really my business. I try to stay out of it. And Chloe seems happy with him, so he has that going for him."

She lifted a tight smile, and then they continued their stroll.

"Hi, Mr. Taylor." A little girl with dark curls and a gap-toothed smile waved to him. "How are the horses?"

"Hello, Miss Sam." Feeling jarred as his attention was once again ripped from Sonora, Taylor nodded to the girl's mother, Jo Fletcher, who had been a year younger than him in school. "The horses are good. You haven't been out for a carriage ride in a while."

Sam's eyes went to her mother, who offered an apologetic smile. "We've been pretty busy, but we'll get out there soon. I suppose it will only be a few more weeks before the horses are gone for the winter?"

Taylor nodded. Was it obvious to everyone that he felt the time slipping away much too quickly?

Sam turned to Sonora with a shy curiosity in her expression. "Do you like horses too?"

"I do." Sonora smiled. "Very much."

"Oh good. Then you're perfect for Mr. Taylor."

Sonora winked. "I guess I am."

"And you're pretty too," Sam added.

"Well, thank you, Miss . . . Sam, is it?"

"Sorry." Taylor finally found his voice again. "This is Sam Fletcher and her mom, Jo. We grew up together."

Jo offered a hand to Sonora. "I'm really happy for the two of you. Congratulations."

"Thank you." Sonora glanced at Taylor, and over her shoulder Taylor caught a glimpse of a dark-haired man he hadn't seen in a long time.

He looked back at Jo and caught her scowl.

"Sam, let's go find some ice cream for ourselves." Jo took her daughter's hand and offered a hurried wave. "Congratulations again."

Sonora watched them hurry off and sent an inquisitive look to Taylor.

The dark-haired man approached, and Taylor groaned quietly. “Let’s go this way.” He tugged her the opposite direction so they wouldn’t run into Beckett Knox.

But it was too late. Beckett held out a hand. “Hey, Taylor. Congratulations.”

“Thanks.” Taylor returned the obligatory handshake. “This is my wife, Sonora.”

“It’s nice to meet you.”

Beckett’s gaze traveled past them, barely acknowledging Sonora’s response. “Have you guys seen Jo?”

“Oh yeah,” Sonora answered. “They were just—”

“Not sure where they went,” Taylor cut in.

“Oh.” Beckett blinked. Then he frowned and pushed past them, heading toward the Pearl.

“Why don’t you want him to find Jo?” Sonora glanced over her shoulder.

Taylor shook his head and walked forward again. Watching Beckett and Jo over the years had been painful enough when they were kids. Taylor had his own drama to focus on now. He glanced at Sonora. “Some things just need left alone.”

Sonora strolled at his side in silence. He could feel her disapproval. Because he hadn’t been overly friendly? If she knew the whole story . . .

Several moments passed, and then she tugged on his arm. "Taylor." She waited until he met her upturned look. Those copper eyes held a serious pleading. "Please forgive me."

Forgive her? For flirting. That was why she'd been off—not from meeting Chloe and Derrick or wondering why he'd been so cold to Beckett, but because he hadn't responded to her apology earlier.

He couldn't understand her. And he was terrified, because already she'd burrowed in too deep. How had he let that happen? She was going to leave, and he was going to have his heart ripped out all over again. He winced as a premonition of that pain slashed through him.

God, why again? I don't want to do that all over again!

As resentment mounted, the sermon from earlier seeped into his mind, quelling the rising anger.

The Lord will provide.

Taylor lifted his chin, meeting Sonora's eyes. He'd not been a man of faith over the past several years. He hadn't felt like he could trust God when God had let him be tossed over into disappointment more than once. By his parents. By Iris.

He lifted his eyes farther and peered at the expanse of lake and sky in the far distance.

Abraham had believed God, despite the circumstances being awful. Wasn't that what the pastor had said? The kind of faith that delivered a man from despair to hope. From death to life. Taylor was tired of despair, of hopelessness. Of living in resentment. Tired of living in a lifeless vault.

But where could he find that kind of faith? Maybe it started with small steps. Like forgiving.

Lowering his gaze from the lake, which could be seen down the cobblestone lane through the rustling maple trees that hinted a touch of bronze in the dimming evening light, Taylor found his wife wearing discouragement. Because of him.

"I forgive you," he whispered. Three small words, over a tiny thing that shouldn't have mattered in the first place.

But it mattered.

Her face tilted up, and a sheen glazed her copper eyes. And then that downward pull of her mouth relaxed. "Thank you."

He felt her sweet smile as it warmed him all the way through.

Sonora slipped her arms out from the warmth of the oversize sports coat that smelled of Taylor Everest—a hint of clean straw, a low undertone of warm spice and pungent sage, and a light note of vanilla.

Taylor wore cologne? Maybe it was simply aftershave.

Holding his sports coat—which he'd offered again as they'd walked back to the Palace, and that time she wasn't so daft—Sonora buried her face into the collar and inhaled. Her eyes slipped shut, and she smiled.

The day hadn't been ruined after all. Actually, it had turned out rather well in the end.

Sixteen

Monday started as Mondays had for the past six weeks. Early—as in breakfast at sunrise. Sonora drank her chocolate milk, Taylor enjoyed a cup of coffee, and both ate a hard-boiled egg, buttered toast, and a side of strawberries and mandarin oranges. Sonora commented on how the food was a treat—at her old job, staff usually ate stale bagels and were lucky if some soft apples were made available. At the dude ranch, all the good food went to the guests apparently.

There seemed something awful about that.

As they left the carriage house to ready the horses for the day, Taylor considered asking for his sports coat back. But he didn't need it—they had both dressed in their dark suits designated as their uniforms. Anyway, he wouldn't have asked for its return regardless.

There was something wonderful about her having it.

The day started chilly. Being the second Monday of September, that was expected. But it was a reminder that frost was drawing near. A patchy, light frost wasn't significant. But a hard, killing frost? That signaled the end. Usually, in years past, a celebrated end.

The end of tourist season. The ferry would run twice a day for one more full week and then once a day until the quickly approaching end of the season. The Palace would follow suit, and at the end of that last week, there would be a ball. The Frostmas Celebration, where the residents on the island would dress their best, feast on what was left from the delicacies brought in for the tourists, and rejoice in another profitable season and the break from it that was to come.

An end that would give way to a beginning. There was something poetic about that.

But this year? A hard frost wouldn't only signal the close of tourist season. It was another kind of end. The one Taylor had planned on. Had promised. Under the guise of taking Albert and Victoria back to the winter grounds—which was located near his parents' home in southern Michigan—Sonora would leave. And she wasn't coming back.

There was everything tragic about that.

Taylor pushed away that gloomy thought as they finished hitching the horses, checking the lines, and then looking over the carriage. All was pristine. Ready for another day. Sonora met him at the front, and he held out his hand for her as she climbed up.

She slipped her palm against his, held still for a breath, then her fingers squeezed. "It's a good day to have a good day."

Her morning mantra. It was cliché and shouldn't have the power to make his heart puddle in his chest. But it seemed with increasing severity, everything this woman did held that particular spell. The corners of his mouth lifted as he held her gaze.

"Ah. I get a grin this morning." She raised up onto her toes and planted a peck on his freshly shaved cheek. "It *is* a good day."

Goodness, by the way his insides quivered, one would think she'd just declared ardent love for him. He really needed to stop this free-fall tumble down a slippery slope.

As if he could.

She occupied nearly all his thoughts. He replayed every smile, every touch. Her laughter became his treasure, tucked safely beside the way tender concern would seep into her eyes when she thought he was upset. He was falling headlong, and he didn't even remember how that happened.

Their day was normal—except for the way he couldn't keep his gaze from wandering to her. And the way he got lost in the delightful stupor of being near her and had missed most of the conversations between Sonora and the tourists. When evening came, they rolled to the carriage house, unhitched the animals, saw to their care, and pushed the wiped-down carriage into the shelter. Just as every other day.

Except, before Sonora could take the stairs to their living quarters, Taylor touched her elbow. She turned her sweet face to him.

"Would you be interested in a ride tonight?"

She peeked around him at the carriage they'd just stored.

"Horseback."

"Do Al and Vicky work under saddle?"

"No. But Molly and Pete do, and they could use a stretch of their legs."

She bit her bottom lip. "I haven't been in a saddle in months."

The way her eyes danced told him she was not saying no. "You haven't been to Seven Pines either."

"No. What is it?"

"A nature reserve on the other side of the island."

"That would stretch their legs." She nodded toward the pair of Haflingers who sadly had spent their summers in the small paddock just behind the carriage house. He'd rather they stay at his small farm deeper inland. But from experience, he knew that if Al or Vicky should need an immediate break, the substitute pair could pull the carriage. Pete and Molly weren't as grand as the Friesians, but they could do the job. So they were assigned understudy duty, which kept them on the Palace grounds for the summer.

But tonight... near giddiness tickled Taylor. How long had it been since he'd felt that?

"Are you up for it?" He tried to keep hope from his voice but felt certain that was a fail.

"Absolutely." She lifted the black suit jacket she had draped over her arm. "I assume we should change first? Jeans okay?"

He nodded. "Of course. You can even wear that awful hat, if you'd like." He sure hoped she would.

"My cowboy hat?"

"That's the one."

"I thought you didn't like cowgirls."

"Not what I said." Certainly not what he'd thought when he'd first glimpsed her wearing it.

She held a knowing look on him, then turned to jog up the stairs.

Did she know? Could she see him recklessly racing forward, helpless to pull back the reins? Fear and vulnerability snaked through his middle. This could end at frost, and he could be devastated. Then what?

The Lord will provide.

He had the faith of a sapling. One that had been nipped off by the hard freeze of rejection and was only just now trying to bud out again. And what a poor time for that, right before frost. Self-preservation yelled for him to retreat. To flee back into that cement vault he'd lived within for way too long.

But Curtis was right. It was time to start living again. And more than that, Taylor couldn't help himself.

Sonora sat back against the cantle of the saddle, finding the fit of the seat wasn't too bad. Not as she'd expected it to be—way too large, given that Taylor was bigger than she. The saddle was his mother's, he'd said. That explained it.

With a comfortable posture, she let her hands relax. Molly had been fresh during the first quarter-mile, dancing sideways, performing a couple of unrequested spins, but Sonora sat it out, and the horse settled in. One could hardly blame the animal for her display of overexcitement—though Taylor frowned deeply and apologized profusely for it.

"She's been cooped up in barely any space at all," Sonora said, to his displeasure. "I'd do some cartwheels about getting out too." She winked at Taylor. He looked away, but by the movement of his jaw, she guessed he was smiling.

She wished he'd let her see it. This had become a game of hide-and-seek—this searching for his smile. Taylor was particularly skilled at it. But what he had in practice, Sonora had double in determination.

They rode side by side, once Molly worked out her antsy-pants. The Palace, its extensive and breathtaking gardens, and the golf course faded at their backs. At the hedge of lilacs, which would certainly be a wall of fragrant lavender come spring—and Sonora had a hankering to see it—the road on which the horses' hooves smacked became dirt, which dulled their hoofbeats into a soft tap. The manicured landscape transitioned into a wild beauty of pine and maple forest, native shrubs Sonora couldn't begin to name, and thick green undergrowth interrupted by rocky outcrops. From the canopy of trees that remained green for the most part—but hinted at some stunning fall color—sets of birds sang about the glory of creation to anyone who would be still enough to listen.

Sonora listened. And her heart stirred. It'd been a while since she'd listened to that call to worship. A while since she'd allowed it to tug on her heart.

With eyes closed, she tipped her face toward the evening sky and let the harmony of nature lift her soul toward heaven.

Prone to wander, Lord, I fear it. Prone to leave the God I love.

Words that could have been penned for her own heart. She wasn't even sure, exactly, why she'd wandered. There had been some hard disappointments in her life since high school. Her parents. More recently, Donovan. But she wasn't angry at God about either. Just . . . apathy, she guessed. Like she'd asked for a miracle once—and it had seemed like the thing God would want too. After all, Jesus said God hates divorce. But God had answered her prayers with silence.

And her parents had been divorced for six years now.

Sonora couldn't reconcile why God would allow that. In that space of unresolved questioning, apathy had grown. Up until this moment, she'd simply accepted that.

But there was a hymn of praise all around her. And that compelling sermon. And the company of this man who was mystery and somehow hope. And this budding sense of new life pushing upward.

Did she dare trust that?

Though Sonora couldn't answer the question for certain, she felt the compulsion to press into it.

She turned to the man who rode beside her. "Will you call your mother, as Mrs. O'Connell demanded?"

Dressed in jeans and a long sleeved button-down, Taylor looked nothing like the man she'd first met—all stiff and formal. Well, perhaps not *nothing*. He was, as he had been from first glimpse, easy on her eyes.

"I suppose that is a question that is asking more than the question."

One side of her mouth poked up. "You're intuitive."

He chuckled. Because he liked her use of vocabulary? She could only assume so, because a good use of words seemed to be the thing that made him happy.

His mouth eased away from that small grin, but only into a relaxed line, rather than a frown. "I don't know yet. Though I can't see how I can avoid it. Not only is Mrs. O'Connell correct about someone telling them sooner or later, but I'll need to explain why you're bringing the horses to the winter grounds."

"Whom do you normally send? Or do you go yourself?"

"No. I don't go." There was granite in that statement. Another mystery there. "We simply trust the transport crew to get them there safely." He paused. "Which I could again, if you'd rather not go to deliver them, once you get off the ferry."

"Where would I go?" A loaded question if there ever was one. Sonora held her breath.

Taylor swallowed, looked toward the forest swaying in the lake-chilled breeze. "Wherever you'd like to be."

Not what she'd hoped for. Taylor liked her. She felt certain of it. And she liked him more and more with each passing day. But did that mean they should continue with this charade past their agreed-upon exit plan?

Logic said no, that would be foolish. But there was something else, a soft nudge, contradicting that. Was that just the foolish girl in her—the same one who had believed that eventually Donovan would come around, ask her to be his forever? The needy girl inside who craved stability and passion in the vacuum left by disappointment and apathy?

She couldn't trust herself.

But God . . . The thought—prayer—ended there. An unspoken request, not for His favor on what she wanted but for His guidance into what was best.

A new approach. Where would it lead her? Where would *He* lead her?

Had God led her there—to this island, alongside this man? No. That had been her own impulsive decision. Wasn't it? Yes—but how did that advertisement land in her lap? She never read that magazine—it was Nina's thing. And why did it surface the exact moment Arabelle had told Sonora she'd be better off finding a new situation for herself?

Was that all coincidence?

"I have no idea." Sonora jarred herself back to the actual conversation between her and Taylor. "I mean, I don't know where I'll land next."

His jaw stiffened, but he nodded.

Sonora straightened in the saddle as discomfort slithered between them.

"They left when I was eighteen."

She whipped her attention from the dirt path to Taylor.

He stared straight ahead. "I had never imagined that they would want to move off the island. It was never spoken of. But after I graduated from high school, my dad gave me Al and Vicky and said I would carry on the family legacy nicely. At first I was thrilled. But then . . ."

"Then they left?"

"That fall. I was blindsided."

"Why did they move?"

"My sister is six years younger than me. She has special needs. They felt like there would be more services available to them off the island. Not to mention some medical needs that required regular attention. They're not available here."

"But . . . the southern end of the state? That seems far."

He nodded. "It's an area that they knew though. It's where we've always gotten our horses, and where Jill was born. There's an Amish community there, and they produce the best animals."

Sonora nodded, absorbing his story. Her heart ached for eighteen-year-old Taylor, suddenly cast into manhood and stripped of family in a matter of months. Suddenly she understood him—he was a quiet, tender soul. One who formed few, but deep, attachments. One who felt abandoned.

"I didn't know you have a sister," she whispered.

Taylor eased Pete to a stop. Finally, his eyes fell on Sonora, and she felt swallowed by the openness of his gaze. "I don't speak of her."

"Why?"

He pressed his lips tight and then blinked. Finally, he drew in a long breath. "She has Down's—that's why she has special needs."

Sonora flinched as angry disapproval stirred within. "You're ashamed of her?"

"No." The single word was a millstone, dropped onto Sonora's misunderstanding and shattering it. His look became icy. "I adored her. She was the joy of my youth. Funny. Enthusiastic. Outgoing. All the wonderful things that I am not."

Instant shame at her assuming the worst of him supplanted the rise of anger. Sonora looked at Molly's white mane as heat filled her face. "I'm sorry," she whispered.

For several heartbeats, a chilled silence engulfed them, broken by those singing birds and whispering pines. Summoning courage—because she did not want to see the flash of anger in his eyes again—not when it was directed specifically at her—Sonora forced herself to seek his face.

His expression had softened into sadness rather than anger. For a moment, she felt relief, but it was a short-lived thing because she felt the sorrow of his heart in her own chest.

"You miss her still. That's why you don't talk about it."

He didn't move or speak, but he didn't have to.

"Do you go visit?"

"Rarely."

"Is she well?"

He nodded, and some light reentered his eyes. "She is. Jill works for a local restaurant as the hostess. They love her, as anyone would. Her medical needs are attended to regularly, so she is healthy and happy."

"Does she remember you?"

This earned her a wisp of a smile. "Yes. She still calls me Grumpy Goose."

Sonora lowered her head and chuckled. "And what do you call her? Just plain Jill?"

"No. She has always been Jilly-Fish to me."

At that she laughed from her belly. Then she met his eyes again. "But you're still mad at your parents for taking her."

"Not mad."

She arched an eyebrow in challenge.

"It isn't anger. I knew that the move was best for Jill, once they told me of it. I just . . . didn't see it coming. And it happened so fast, and I was very young."

"It must have been lonely."

He swallowed, then looked toward something to the southwest—the direction of the lighthouse. Sonora waited for him to speak whatever was turning in his mind. But as she should have expected, Taylor kept it to himself.

Sonora swung her leg over the saddle and hopped the short distance to the ground. "Did you ever consider moving closer to them?"

His gaze wandered back to her, and then he also dismounted. "There has been an Everest driving for the Palace since it opened in the early nineteen hundreds." With the reins held loose in one hand, he walked down the path, deeper into Seven Pines. "My dad entrusted that legacy to me."

"So you're stuck here." Sonora fell into step beside him, her horse trailing her willingly.

"That sounds . . . pathetic. I don't think it's quite right."

She nudged his shoulder. "Then tell me."

"This is my home. I never had any idea of leaving it." His steps halted, and then he pointed in the opposite direction of the lighthouse and of town. "Our farm is a mile that way. I never dreamed of leaving it."

Sonora stopped beside him, so close that she could twitch her fingers and they would brush his. But she resisted the impulse.

"I just didn't imagine this solitary life." His confession was barely above a whisper, the deep tone weighted with emotion.

Time seemed to stop in the vastness of his honest gaze, and warmth enveloped her, chasing away the cool of evening. His long look was a caress on her face, stirring her heart with longing. She dared to allow her fingertips to roam, and they slipped down the side of his hand. Taylor turned toward her, his head lowering.

From ahead, and to the right, a sudden crash of leaves and cracking of sticks jolted the moment back into action. Sonora gasped while the horses snorted and danced sideways. Taylor spun to grip both sets of reins while a pair of deer hopped into view from the shrubbery off the path.

Sonora's heart leaped and pounded, and adrenaline shot through her veins. As fast as the perpetrators of their startle had appeared, they left, leaving the horses with perked ears, wild eyes, and impatient hooves. And leaving Sonora in a world of disappointment.

He had been going to kiss her. Hadn't he?

Biting her bottom lip, she peeked at him. His back to her, he flung the reins back around the horses' necks, then mumbled something about getting late and heading back. By his stiff shoulders and impassive voice, if he'd had any thoughts of kissing at all, they'd run off with the deer and were now long gone.

Sonora buttoned in a sigh. Perhaps it was for the best. This was, after all, a business relationship. She seemed to be forgetting that on a regular basis.

Seventeen

Trust me, my friend. You'll thank me later.

Taylor's brow furrowed as he read Curtis's note, which he'd found on the door to the stables.

What did it mean?

After a glance over his shoulder, which yielded only a view of the back of the Palace, void of all people, Taylor pressed the knob and let himself into the front tack room. Rather than finding the set of golf clubs Curtis routinely stored there on Saturday nights in anticipation of their Sunday morning game, there instead was a basket draped by a black-checked cloth.

"What the devil . . ." Taylor strode forward, borrowing his grandfather's common expression, and bent to lift the wicker handle. Another note fluttered to the floor.

There is an outcrop of rocks near the lighthouse. You know the place. Take your wife and enjoy the sunrise.

A stirring of something not altogether irritating—but not entirely welcome—rustled in Taylor's chest. Crumpling the note, he lifted the cloth. Beneath that buffalo-check cotton, he found two large pastries—one cherry and one blueberry—a pair of oranges, a packet of sliced cheese, a container of large purple grapes, two small crystal glasses, and a sweating glass bottle bearing the label *Maple Grove Farm and Vineyard.*

A picnic. Curtis has set his romantic mind on a sunrise picnic for Taylor and Sonora. Didn't the man understand this was a temporary situation? A fake marriage? Further, couldn't Curtis see that Taylor was desperately trying *not* to fall in love with his wife?

The last query sent a jolt of startling reality straight to Taylor's heart, causing him to suck in a sharp breath. Before he could sort through the origin and meaning of his hasty thoughts, the latch on the door behind him rattled. Basket in hand, he turned.

Her playful grin curled those tempting lips, and those rich eyes danced. Sonora passed through the doorway, in one fist a bunch of sunflowers wrapped in brown craft paper. She shut the door and leaned back against it. "Who are you and what have you done with my husband?"

Where had Curtis stashed the flowers?

Taylor's mouth went dry, and suddenly he wished this *had* been his idea. By that soft, warm expression, Sonora thought it . . . romantic.

Not a goner.

At the moment, he forgot why it was so important that remain the truth.

Ah, truth. That mattered. For all the things he was deficient in, Taylor Everest was an honest man. This fake marriage being the exception. But with Sonora, he'd never been anything but honest. His gaze, which had been feasting on the delight of Sonora's tender expression, traveled to the thick bouquet of bright sunflowers and then to the floor at his feet. His shoulders slumped.

"I see." Sonora's tone, though still bright, held the distinct quality of disappointment. "Shall I take a guess?"

Taylor swallowed, peeking at her.

An empathetic smile nearly masked the disappointment in her eyes. "Curtis did this, didn't he?"

Suddenly he was a pathetic man. A bumbling fool who was neither romantic nor smart. With a hand on the back of his neck, Taylor turned away. "I'm sorry, Sonora."

"What for?"

For Curtis making things awkward? That he wasn't more like Curtis? What was Taylor sorry for?

For himself, at the moment.

He felt sorry that he wasn't this man—the one who would think of sweet, romantic ways of wooing his wife so that she'd consider moving past this business agreement and see him as something more than a stony, awkward man who would make a poor partner in life.

"This is . . . disagreeable." *Unpleasant, offensive.* No, that wasn't the right word. Taylor shifted his hand to scrub his face. "Uncomfortable." Closer to accurate. Perhaps dead on.

Her small hand warmed his back, and he nearly knocked her over as he spun around. Could his heart stop galloping?

And this beading moisture at his hairline—was that necessary?

Business. This was all supposed to be a business arrangement. But the past week had felt like so much more. Shared silence in the mornings as they'd both bowed to pray. Days spent in perfect sync as they worked together as well as Albert and Victoria did. Pleasant evenings with a checkers board between them and a few chuckles here and there too.

It had felt thrilling and comfortable at the same time.

Sonora reached to touch him again, this time her hand covering his arm. "A sunrise picnic sounds lovely, Taylor."

The stiff anxiety in his shoulders eased, and when he allowed his eyes to meet hers, all logical protests vanished. This lovely young woman wanted to share a sunrise on the beach. With him.

Heady wonder intruded on his stoic levelheadedness.

"You will not mind that it wasn't my idea?"

She latched her arm around his and tugged. Taylor stumbled into stride beside her and then they were out the door, stepping into the crisp gray, predawn day.

They walked the garden trail, Taylor ducking beneath the arching branches of the elderberry, then pausing to allow Sonora to pass through the rose laden archway fist. She waited for him, then slipped her hand through the crook of his arm again before they followed the stone path as it curved away from the golf course and toward the lighthouse. The cry of seagulls beckoned them onward, away from the Palace and toward the gentle sound of water lapping against stone.

And the whole way, Sonora remained on his arm. As though she wanted to be exactly there.

Taylor's nerves settled as he sank into Sonora's consistent ease. She made him feel . . . wanted. Not romantically, necessarily, but as a person. Like she enjoyed his company, even if he was often silent, and when he did speak, his words came out more harshly than he intended. That didn't figure in his mind—why would such a ray of sunshine want to associate with a man who frowned more often than anything else? But even so, that thought didn't make the sensation of being sought after by her diminish. Once again he marveled at how it was possible that this lovely, kind woman had been the one to answer his desperate and ill-advised ad.

Was that the work of God?

Even while Taylor leaned into that possibility, fear had him pulling away from it. Disappointment had a long sting.

They reached the beach, and Taylor led Sonora to a cove where a flat rock would make a perfect bench, a tall shrub would protect them from the breeze, and the lighthouse in the distance would add a charming addition to the wakening sun. To the northwest, thick and steely clouds quilted the sky, and a distant rumble sounded over the crash of water against land. This sunrise picnic might get wet. Not what Curtis had banked on, Taylor was certain.

Sonora settled on the natural stone bench and smiled up at him, apparently undaunted by the gathering storm. "I've never had a picnic on the beach. You've crossed off a bucket-list item."

"It wasn't my idea, if you'll recall." He lowered next to her, setting the basket in the pebbles at their feet. "And I somehow doubt a chilly predawn picnic on a rocky beach with a storm moving in was what your bucket-list item actually looked like in your mind."

"I didn't have a picture in my mind, and this is lovely." She pressed her shoulder into his. "As to it not being your idea, if you didn't want to be here, you wouldn't be."

He couldn't help the small half grin as he looked at her. "Seems that you've gotten to know me."

"Have I? That might be my greatest accomplishment." Her smile should have been enough to chase away the storm clouds. "What do we have in the basket?" She leaned forward, pulling out food.

As they ate, Sonora leaned back, pressing her weight on one hand. In the early morning light and the breeze that swept off the lake, she seemed like a beautiful vision. A siren from his imagination—if he'd ever dreamed something so inane. But Sonora was neither dangerous nor imagined. She was truly kind. A pleasant woman with a gentle soul. And sitting right there with him.

How had she landed there, in the midst of this insane business contract otherwise named *marriage?* At his side, her sweet and lovely face tempting his fingers to explore the contours of her jawline? Other than the quick explanation that she did not want to be anywhere near her former boyfriend, she never spoke about why she'd come, nor about the people in her past. What of her family? Did they wonder where she was?

"Do your parents know?" Taylor spoke as if he'd been pondering these things out loud.

Sonora looked up with a quizzical expression, processed a moment, then shrugged while the joyful light in her eyes dimmed. "That I got married?"

It was like she actually understood him.

"Yes." She looked toward the lighthouse. "I told them my first day on the island."

"And?"

"They were upset." She flinched, popped a pair of grapes into her mouth as though that might disguise her discomfort, and then sighed. "My dad said I was making bad decisions, and why hadn't I talked to them first?"

"Why hadn't you?"

Frowning, she lowered the next set of grapes that she'd nearly popped into her mouth. "First, because I knew what they'd say—something along the lines of *are you crazy?* And second, my parents and I haven't been very close since I dropped out of college to work at the dude ranch."

"They disapproved of that decision as well?"

"Not necessarily. It was me who disapproved of them. I sort of . . . gave them the cold shoulder." She sat straighter and turned a long look on him. It was as if she was gauging how much she trusted him with whatever it was she was going to share.

Trust me with everything . . . The thought nearly came off his tongue in a whisper. Would she, if he asked it of her?

Her gaze drifted toward the lake, where white caps rolled into the shoreline with angry warning. Another rumble of thunder shook the distant sky.

"They got divorced my freshman year of college." Pain creased her forehead when she returned her look to him. "I didn't even know they were falling apart. But I guess my dad had had an affair, and they held on until I graduated, not wanting to ruin my senior year. I begged my mom to forgive him, but she said she couldn't trust him and couldn't be married to a man she couldn't trust. I understand that better now. Even so, my relationship with both of them pretty much disintegrated." A sheen glazed her eyes. "I was so terribly angry. Especially with my dad. We were really close. He taught me how to ride, then drive. I was his little girl, you know? And then . . . then he shattered our family. Honestly, I still don't know how to process that."

Blindsided. He knew that harsh blow well.

In her pause, she drew a quivering breath. Taylor longed to reach for her, to offer her comfort and shelter in his arms. But where would that leave them?

"When they reacted the way they did when I told them we got married—all worried, like I was wrecking my life—I sort of snipped off at them. I said something about how they got to make their own mistakes—and those choices involved more than just their own lives—so they could leave mine alone." She made a face that screamed regret, and then her posture caved downward. "So you're not the only one struggling with family. I'm failing hard on the honoring my father and mother front."

"At least you told them." He'd really better get on that. Especially if Sonora did decide to take the horses all the way to the winter grounds. That alone would demand an explanation, even if by some miracle they didn't hear of his marriage from someone on the island.

"You know how your pastor talked about faith in the face of hard moments?"

Taylor nodded—though Charles wasn't the pastor. That hardly mattered right then. Taylor's mind had turned over that sermon ever since that Sunday evening, and he couldn't deny the constant beckoning he sensed as he thought on it. He wanted the sort of faith Abraham had found. But it seemed too hard. Or maybe his heart was too hard.

"I wish I knew how to believe that way." Sonora admitted out loud what Taylor felt.

"Me too," he whispered. It was soul-deep honesty. A long time back, he'd walked with God, and even though he'd been introverted and often alone, he never felt . . . abandoned.

But then again, he'd had his family right there with him. He hadn't yet been abandoned. If he'd held steady to God, would he have felt the deep blow of first his family leaving, then of Iris's rejection quite so hard?

There was no way of knowing. But Taylor did know this: He *wanted* to know that God worked all things out for good. He *wanted* to trust that God was faithful even in hard places.

A gust of cold wind sent a curtain of hair across her face. She fingered it away from her eyes and lashed it all at the nape of her neck with a stretchy band from her wrist.

"It's hard to believe good things come from bad circumstances, isn't it?"

He nodded.

"Is that why you've stayed alone all this time?"

An intrusive question. But he didn't mind—after all, he'd started the personal inquisition. In fact, he'd been searching for a way to tell her about Iris. He couldn't say why he felt the need for her to know, but he did.

"I was engaged once, a few years back."

Her eyes widened, but she said nothing.

"Her name was Iris. She came here to work for a season, and I found her . . . irresistible. Beautiful and friendly and fun. We had a whirlwind romance, and I thought she was God's answer to my lonely prayers." He stopped there as bitterness once again gurgled up from the well of unforgiveness he'd tapped.

In the space of silence, he remembered thinking about finding the kind of faith Abraham had shown on that mountain—that it might begin with forgiveness. Could he forgive Iris?

"You loved her," Sonora whispered.

He nodded, swallowing hard. He had clung to Iris with a desperation that might have teetered on selfishness.

"What happened?"

"She left three weeks after the tourist season ended." He forced himself to stop staring at the lighthouse in the distance and connect with Sonora's gaze. She needed to understand this part . . . "Winters on the island are very different from the tourist season. It is very cold. And it is very quiet. The only way off the island is by a plane that flies once a week until the lake freezes solid. Even then, snowmachining back to the mainland is a long, miserable trip and one I generally don't take."

Sonora held his stare, as if she was reading what he was not saying. He wondered if she understood that he was, in fact, warning her. If she felt at all about him the way he had grown to feel about her, she needed to understand. This life wasn't like anything she could have known before. It certainly wasn't for everyone.

It hadn't been for Iris—a truth that Taylor had wished he'd discovered before he'd become so entangled. "That year, the winter was particularly cold—and came early. Our first blizzard hit the day after the last ferry ran. The reality of remote life hit hard."

"So one day, she just . . . left?"

He clenched his jaw. That had been the worst part—he hadn't seen it coming. "She said she was going to visit her family and work on wedding arrangements—we were planning an early spring wedding in her hometown, before the tourist season got too busy. Next thing I knew, she says she's not coming back."

"Did she ask you to move, to go with her?"

He shook his head. "No." And there was the blade. Because for Iris, Taylor would have considered it. He would have been willing to leave his heritage, his family legacy, and the only life he'd imagined himself in to be with her.

But Iris hadn't asked. It hadn't just been the island she didn't want. She didn't want him. To him, she was the answer to his lonely life. To her, he was merely a summer fling.

The humiliation had multiplied the ache of disappointment exponentially.

Taylor found he'd rolled his fists tight.

"I'm sorry, Taylor."

He shut his eyes and reached for steady composure. Drawing a long breath, he eased his clamped teeth and shook his head. "I shouldn't have . . . I should be able to . . . recover. It was only a breakup. A disappointment. Not a death."

A small, warm hand slipped over his clenched fist. Her gentle thumb traced along the side of his. "I don't think it's wrong to grieve over disappointments. Especially when it is something that broke your heart."

Though he felt small and shamed by his weakness, Taylor lifted his eyes to her face. So much tenderness stared back at him. Suddenly the ache of remembering Iris fell away—like ice blocks breaking away from the land during the spring melt. In its place, a warm longing bloomed.

One for her. For this happy and kind woman who was as much a wonderful surprise to his world as she'd been an intrusion at the beginning.

She turned his hand palm up and fanned her fingers over his before lacing them together. Her touch was enough to tip his desire into action.

With his opposite hand, he reached for her face. The pad of his thumb traced her cheekbone, finding her chilly skin soft. She leaned into his touch, and he cupped the side of her face, pushing his long fingers into the windblown mess of her hair. As he leaned down, she angled her face up, and their lips met with a warm timidity. When she didn't pull away, Taylor leaned in.

He kissed her with slow reverence. This was not something to be rushed. It felt . . . sacred. Like he'd been led to a treasure and had been offered the whole of it.

And she kissed him with equal wonder.

Sonora shivered in the cold wind as the sky gave them a loud warning. Taylor eased back, kissing her cheek, her forehead, her temple before he pulled away completely. His hold around her loosened, allowing the full chill of air to embrace her body instead.

Once again his palm cradled her face. "We're about to get wet," he whispered.

"I've survived worse." She reached to trace his lips with her thumb, and he kissed it.

"I don't think it would be responsible of me to allow my wife to get soaked in a thunderstorm because I like kissing her so much."

Ah! He could flirt! She rewarded his rare playfulness with a smile and leaned in to press her lips to his again.

He returned her kiss with another long, tender exploration, then groaned as he separated from her again. "It really is going to pour on us." Taking her hand, he stood and pulled her up with him. "We should go."

"Bummer." She helped him place the food into the basket, then picked up the bouquet of flowers. When he stepped away, she tugged him back. "You won't make me wait so long before you kiss me again, will you?"

His smile! Taylor was already a handsome man, but that happy look made him doubly more so. And the way he held her in his gaze, those sharp blue eyes softening . . . Sonora's belly tickled as though a million wings brushed against it.

Then his expression grew serious again. "I thought romance was not in your story."

"So did I." She lifted his hand and kissed his knuckles. "I will freely admit I may have been mistaken."

Thunder rent the air with serious ferocity, as though to say, *I warned you!* Then the clouds broke loose, sending down sheets of rain. Taylor turned, and holding her hand, he ran with her back toward the path to the Palace.

By the time they stumbled into the carriage house, they were drenched. And happy.

And he did not make her wait long at all for his kiss.

EIGHTEEN

TAYLOR'S MIND WHIRLED MONDAY morning as he hitched Al and Vicky by himself. He hadn't slept well—not that he resented that. There had been so many thoughts and sensations keeping him away from sleep.

He'd kissed her, and it had been intentional. It'd been exhilarating. And it had been profound. He'd been careful to go slow, to not give into the temptation to slip into frenzied passion. Everything with Iris had been a whirlwind. All blind emotion and no thought—which was not who Taylor ever had been. That had been part of the allure of her—she had somehow bewitched him into acting like someone he was not. But it hadn't lasted, and when she'd left, she not only broke his heart, but he'd discovered himself lost and confused.

This time, with Sonora, he wanted to be true to himself and tender with her. He wanted more than a fleeting romance. And he hoped desperately that was what she wanted too.

Please, God . . .

That prayer had circled through his heart with a steady rhythm. And with it, his thoughts would travel back to the evening before, when Sonora had held his hand as they'd shared a pew in that quaint church. In order to pay attention, he'd had to inflict some serious self-discipline at the beginning of the evening service—and who wouldn't with the beautiful ray of sunshine sitting snug at his side? But not far into Charles Harlowe's sermon, Taylor's attention had caught and held.

The man had hopped from Genesis to 2 Samuel for his text, going to David as his next example of walking by faith. Only in that particular instance, Charles was showing the failure of David's faith. It had been interesting, because Taylor had ignorantly believed that David's failure was only the episode with Bathsheba. Not the case, as Charles had pointed out—David had developed a habit of lying to gain what he wanted. The trait was subtle at first—claiming that his men needed bread. Later, that he was raiding the Israelite people when he lived in Ziklag—which was where Charles had brought them for that sermon.

He'd pointed out that David didn't seek God's wisdom. There was nothing in the context that would indicate that he gave God much thought at all. Was he successful? Yes. Did that mean God blessed his deceit? Not necessarily. Often David was too clever for his own good—and he tended to go after what he wanted on his own terms.

An interesting contradiction. David had profound moments of deep trust and faith. He refused to take Saul's life, though he'd been encouraged to do so, and after all, David was the anointed king. He trusted God to see the promise of David's throne through. But then David nearly took his own revenge on a foolish man—and was only saved from doing so by Abigail, a wise and courageous woman. If not for her quick work, David would have blood on his hands. And then at Ziklag, David tried to bring about his own salvation by lying. He fooled the king of the Philistines into believing that he was attacking his own people, and that landed him in a big problem—one that had demanded he go to battle at that king's side, against Saul. Against his own people.

David was a man who failed. He failed on a regular basis, just like Abraham. Too commonly, Taylor thought, Christians zero in on the big moments—often the successful moments—of these great examples of faith. But those men were men—and they had failures. It was God's grace that saved. It was His grace that brought Abraham to that mountain believing that the Lord would provide. It was His faithful grace that brought David to the throne and made him the most famous of all the Israelite kings. Grace, not works.

Charles's ending words resounded to Taylor's soul.

"Friend, have you failed? Have you lied your way into what you wanted? Have you taken what was not yours to have? Have you turned away from your heavenly Father because you didn't feel His favor?

"Turn back. Repent. Find His favor and grace waiting for you—as David did time and again. As Abraham did time and again. Just like the parable of the prodigal son, we find God is that faithful, forgiving Father waiting for his son's return. Come home, friend. He is waiting for you to come home."

Taylor stopped buckling straps and allowed the enormity of that message to move deeper into his soul. In the past few weeks, he'd felt *so much*. Often, it was easy to attribute this awakening in his heart to Sonora—to her ability to summon his smiles, her kind ways and gentle sunshine. But it wasn't all her. It couldn't be. And even the portion that was because of her, was that a quirk of luck?

Taylor didn't believe in luck. He believed in God—which was why he'd been so mad at God for the great disappointments in his life.

Come back . . .

But what if all the heartaches of his life were leading him to something beautiful? What if those disappointments were being worked out into something unexpectedly good?

. . . All things God works for the good of those who love him, who have been called according to his purpose.

But Taylor hadn't loved God—not well. Not faithfully.

His claim to Sonora early on in this arrangement burned in his ears—he tried to be a faithful man.

He'd failed.

Turn back. Repent. Find His favor and grace waiting for you . . .

With his hand braced against Albert's stout neck, Taylor bowed his head. "Forgive me," he whispered as a lump swelled in his throat. He slid his hand against the sleek body of the horse, and his fingers curled into the course black mane.

"Good morning, Mr. Everest." The crisp voice of Gretta Fellenbaum broke the private and emotional moment as the woman called from the open carriage-house doors.

Swallowing and blinking rapidly, Taylor rolled his shoulders straight and turned to face the Palace manager.

"Gretta." What was she doing there? She never stepped into his domain.

"I was out doing my morning rounds."

"Were you?" He wasn't sure he could believe that.

"Yes. Well, perhaps I extended my rounds on this morning."

"I see. Can I help you?"

She smiled, catching him off. The woman rarely smiled, and when she did, it was usually a tight-lipped, forced thing. This was not that—it was warm and genuine and maybe even a bit teasing. "I wanted to see how you were this morning."

"Wh . . . why?"

Her grin broadened. "Because I perceived that the flowers seemed to have done the trick."

"Flowers?"

"Sonora likes sunflowers. I fished that from Aiden, the florist. Your friendly wife has made the rounds, and several have gotten to know her."

"The flowers were . . ." His voice trailed off.

"My idea. The picnic Curtis's."

"You conspired with Curtis?"

She dipped a pleased nod. "It's good to see you happy, Taylor."

Lips parted, he stared at her. "This was . . . a plot?"

"Though I was horrified to hear how you met your wife, I am the first—or perhaps the second—to say that Sonora is good for you."

"Horrified? You cornered me into—"

Gretta held up a hand. "It doesn't matter how it happened now. All I wanted to say is that I am pleased for you, Taylor. God must have worked in the craziest way with this, and I'm delighted."

Delighted? Pleased? Who was this woman? Gretta spoke in terms of business and duties, not of personal feelings. And the sunflowers? She had sent those to Sonora on Taylor's behalf? Gretta was even less romantically inclined than Taylor was.

"Ah, Sonora." Her attention turned to the stairway that led to the living space above the carriage house. "Good morning."

"Good morning, Mrs. Fellenbaum."

"I was just telling Taylor that I was delighted to see you both at church last evening."

Was that what she had been saying?

"Oh." Sonora's footfall stopped, and Taylor assumed she'd halted her steps near the bottom of the stairs. "It was a good sermon. Things I need to think about, I think."

"Things to ponder for all of us." Gretta returned to her businesslike demeanor. "Well then, I'll let you get to work—with the rain delaying the ferry yesterday, I think we'll have an extra surge of guests arriving this morning. Oh, and by the way, I've heard nothing but compliments on the carriage service of late. Well done to you both." With a nod, the woman in her stiff gray pantsuit pivoted and clipped her way down the cobblestone path to the Palace.

Sonora appeared, stopping to scratch Albert's ear. "What was that about?"

Taylor flinched, wishing he didn't always have to be so honest. But that was who he was, and he was determined to be his true self with Sonora. "Gretta sent the flowers for you yesterday."

Sonora's brows lifted. "The sunflowers? They weren't from Curtis?"

"No." He turned and placed his hands on her shoulders. "Not from Curtis. Not from me. I'm sorry, Sonora. I regret that I didn't think of such a thing."

One corner of her mouth poked up, and she took a step nearer. "Perhaps you'll think of it on your own in the future."

He lifted his eyes from the straw-littered floor to meet hers. So much kindness stared back at him. And, could he dare hope . . . love? His heart squeezed in his chest. Did he love this woman?

Wasn't that what he'd been pleading with God for all through the restless hours of the night, tossing and turning on that lonely and uncomfortable couch? That *she* would love him. What else was there to conclude but that he loved her?

Her cool palm slid against his warm face, and she tipped up on her toes to kiss his cheek. "I poured your coffee, but it's cold now."

He covered her hand and pressed her fingers firmly against his face. "I'm sorry. I was restless, and as Gretta said, we're bound to have a surge today."

"I thought maybe you were . . . regretting yesterday."

"No." Not ever. He wanted more just like it. Her hand in his. Her smile warming his whole being. Her lips against his. Her next to him at church, in the park, in town square . . . everywhere. Always.

Could he say as much?

He couldn't, so instead he slipped an arm around her waist and pulled her against him. "Do you regret it?" he whispered.

Sonora wrapped her arms around his neck. "Not one bit."

He sighed and tightened his embrace. Her in his arms. Every day.

Please, God . . .

Taylor wasn't sure he had the right to ask God for such a blessing, especially when he'd given Him the virtual silent treatment for years. But who else could he pour out his deepest wish to?

Who else ordained his steps?

Smiling wasn't unusual for Sonora. She liked to smile. She liked to meet people's eyes, give them a friendly grin, and say *good morning* or *hello*. That was just who she was.

But her happiness that morning, which certainly must be radiating from her whole being, was much more than normal. Taylor held her hand as they walked the team of horses and the hitched carriage onto the drive and around to the front of the Palace.

He'd kissed her yesterday. Sweetly, slowly. With tenderness and carefully managed yearning that she felt all the way into her bubbling middle. And Sonora couldn't be happier about it.

So much for romance not being a part of her story. She hadn't expected her grumpy boss to be so much more than a cold, taciturn man. Certainly not one of quiet kindness and deep tenderness.

Being with him had already felt . . . comfortable. In the most energetic and life-plan-altering way. Now? Now it felt . . . complete. Right. It was like where she'd thought she'd been running from humiliation, she'd actually been running straight into her very own blessed forever.

What was it that Proverbs said? Man plans his ways, but God determines his path? That might be a rough paraphrase, but it seemed that was the gist of the verse. Had God sent her there, to this almost-off-the-map island, to this quiet, introverted, wounded man with a happily ever after planned for them both?

It sure seemed that way—and wow, was she giddy and grateful about it.

"Whoa. Stand." As he stopped walking, Taylor spoke with that hushed, gentle voice he used with his animals. Releasing Sonora's hand, he turned to adjust the harnesses, doing one last check before they began their day. Having done this dozens of times together at this point, Sonora took her usual turn around the carriage, looking for anything amiss—from a loose bolt to an unsightly patch of dust against the gleaming paint. Finding only perfection, she rounded the front of the horses, pausing to scratch each black velvety nose, and met Taylor at the side.

"All good?" he asked.

"All good."

He took her hand again, as was typical, only this time, he raised her knuckles to his lips before he handed her up. She squeezed his fingers as she climbed up the step and onto the driver's seat.

They were a matched pair, just like Albert and Victoria—the horses. Come to think of it, rather like His Royal Highness and the queen of England had been too. Different in personality and strengths, but complementary.

And in love?

As she watched Taylor pull himself up and onto the seat at her side, her heart warmed with fluttering delight. Yes, she might love him—it was a strong possibility.

He took up the reins, checked their length, and handed them to her. "Off we go."

"You don't want to drive right now?"

"No. I want to watch you." He winked.

Flirting!

Sonora thrilled at this rare piece of him—shown only to her. She gave him her warmest smile and leaned to kiss his cheek.

"No more of that." Taylor adjusted his hat and then fixed hers, his voice not anywhere close to reprimanding. "People will talk."

"I think after we wandered all through town square with our fingers laced together last night, there must be talk already. Anyway, we *are* married, so . . ." Sonora ironed her posture and put a small gap between them on the seat. "But if you insist." She elbowed him so that he would be sure to know she was teasing him.

He chuckled, then called, "Walk on, Al."

Sonora flicked the reins to parallel Taylor's verbal cue, and the horses stepped forward together.

As the rhythmic clopping of the horse's hooves against the brick ensued, Sonora gathered in the new day. The air stirred with the freshness that came after a rain, tickling a grin onto her mouth. It had rained most of the morning yesterday, and then again in the evening, after they'd walked through town square. Both times, they'd ended up wet, but she had no regrets. Who cared about a little dampness when Taylor Everest pulled her into his embrace to offer his warmth? Sonora had been rather grateful for it.

As they clipped along under a gathering of maple trees, songbirds sang about the beauty of the morning. The road leaned into the first gentle decline, and they passed those hydrangeas, now taking on fall pinks within their blooms. Loveliness surrounded her, and she could stay here forever.

She glanced at Taylor, who was, true to his claim, watching her. She could stay with *him* . . . forever. Gathering all the boldness she owned, and then borrowing more on a prayer, she plunged. "I think we should talk."

"That's always an option—and you're proficient at it." He winked, but then his brows pulled together. "But the way you put it sounds ominous."

"Not ominous. But things have changed."

"That's true." Now his expression had turned solemn. Not unusual for Taylor, but it set Sonora into uneasiness.

Maybe a kiss was just a kiss? No, that didn't measure with who she knew this man to be. He was careful, reserved, and felt deeply. He wasn't a man to treat kissing like a sport, nor a woman's emotions like they were toys to be played with and then set aside.

She guided the horses around the final bend just as the ferry docked. They would be parked at the Palace's designated pickup zone and waiting by the time their guests disembarked from the boat.

"Whoa." She gave an even, gentle pull on the reins, which might or might not have been necessary, as Al and Vicky knew their job. Either way, the carriage stopped, and Sonora leaned forward to secure the reins while Taylor set the brake.

Before he scrambled down from the seat, he turned to her. "We'll talk." And his eyes confirmed that promise, with emotion Sonora was certain he rarely showed anyone.

She couldn't resist squeezing his hand as she nodded. And that was that.

They had work to do, and they made a good team doing it.

With firm postures, hats straight, and suits unrumpled, Taylor and Sonora greeted the four guests who had disembarked from the ferry and came directly to their carriage.

"The Palace?" A silver-haired man asked, dragging a large piece of luggage behind him.

Taylor stepped forward and took the suitcase while Sonora tipped her hat and answered, "To the Palace. How many are we?"

"Four for now. The rest of our party opted for the noon ferry." A woman—presumably his wife—smiled a giddy smile. She wore a floppy straw hat—which bounced in the lake breeze—and looked like the kind of person who found life a grand adventure. "This feels like a scene from *Downton Abby*, and I am here for it!"

She beamed up at the man, who, having been relieved of his luggage, stood to the side, not smiling but not frowning either. When his wife took the place at his side, however, he looked down at her with the sweetest look.

Sonora's heart warmed and leaped. It was like looking at a hopeful future—because that dignified, solemn man could easily be Taylor many years down the road, and she could be that vivacious woman. And they could spend the next forty years sharing looks just like that.

Oh, how she wanted that to be their story!

"Mom, you're being silly." A younger woman, perhaps in her mid-thirties, laughed as she passed her luggage to Taylor, as did the man who trailed behind her.

Taylor loaded the bags in silent efficiency, but he did glance at Sonora. And winked.

Oh goodness, her middle melted right there on the spot.

She focused her delight on their new guests. "Welcome to Sanctuary Island. May I ask what brings you to us?"

"My parents' anniversary." Pride shone in the younger woman's eyes. "Isn't it wonderful that they wanted to share their trip with their children? My sisters and their husbands—the rest of our party—are the ones arriving later."

"How special." Sonora felt the sincerity of her response all the way to her soul. Along with a twinge of sad jealousy. She would never know this particular joy in life. Her parents wouldn't either.

But perhaps someday, her children would . . . She glanced at Taylor. What was he thinking?

This was going too fast in her mind. Surely he, being the more levelheaded and careful one, wasn't rushing into forever dreams the way she was. Was he?

Taylor stood, having finished securing the luggage, and found her gaze. Oh, that long look . . . it was like a silent promise, and it nearly took her breath away. Before the pause extended to the point of awkwardness, Taylor stepped back and swept his hand toward the carriage, then addressed the older of the women. "Can I offer you a hand in?"

Each of the four climbed into the velvet-lined seats, and then Taylor moved toward the driver's seat. Sonora followed him, but when she took his offered hand, something in her periphery brought her to a dead stop.

The blood in her veins froze as a familiar face appeared on the ferry. He stopped, took a long, panoramic inspection of the island, and then moved toward the gangway. Panic fired from her chest.

"Sonora?" Taylor's concerned whisper jarred her from the ringing in her ears.

She looked up at him. By his deepening furrowed look, she must have been wide eyed and pale.

"Are you okay?"

She swallowed, then shook her head. Squeezing her eyes shut for a moment, she tried to shake off the icky feeling of having been stalked.

Taylor's hand wrapped around her arm. He moved to shield her from the view of the tourists. "What is it?"

"He's here."

"Who is here?"

She flinched. This wasn't what she had in mind when she'd said they should talk. "Donovan Arlington. The man who broke my heart. He . . . they must be on their honeymoon . . ." She squeezed her eyes shut, as though this was a nightmare.

Taylor's gaze hardened and cooled. He looked over his shoulder, then back at Sonora. "The man in khaki pants, blue button-down, and a cowboy hat, coming off the *Haven* right now?"

She nodded.

He paused. Glanced back again. Then nudged her forward. "Let's go."

Though she wondered at his response—was he protecting her, or was it something else?—Sonora scrambled up onto the driver's seat, and Taylor followed. He released the brake, and she flicked the reins.

The drive to the Palace was not as leisurely as normal, and Sonora barely spoke a word. She hoped her passengers didn't notice or mind.

NINETEEN

ANGER AND ANXIETY TUSSLED within Taylor as he strode from the carriage house to the back entrance of the Palace. They didn't normally take a break after the first run to the dock, but after dropping off their passengers, he'd taken up the reins and driven to the back.

Sonora said nothing. Which added heartache to the already warring emotions.

She'd told him that she had left her old job because of an ex-boyfriend. She hadn't mentioned that she wasn't over him though.

Was she not over him?

Or was he dangerous?

Both were possibilities, by the way she'd gone white and silent the moment she'd glimpsed the man. And both possibilities made him want to be sick and punch someone at the same time.

He'd told Sonora to go up and splash some cool water on her face—she still looked ill—and then he'd set his stride for the hotel. He nearly jerked the back door off its hinges as he gained entry and stormed through the back halls until he rounded the corner near Gretta's office. From there he had a view of the long check-in counter, and it didn't take a whole lot of searching to zero in on the black cowboy hat. The man must have taken one of the taxis that worked the dock pickup. Didn't even remove his hat indoors. The buffoon.

Taylor pressed his shoulder against the corner while he watched this unwelcome stranger make his way to Curtis's counter. There, the two men talked—Curtis clearly going through the check-in routine. After several minutes, Curtis handed Black Cowboy Hat a key and pointed toward the grand staircase in the middle of the great entry.

He was a guest.

Unacceptable.

Swallowing, and with a bead of sweat lining his hairline, Taylor pushed off the wall and strode toward Curtis, ignoring the milling guests around them.

"That man you just checked in."

Curtis jerked his head up from his computer screen. "What?"

"What was his name?"

A scowl—uncommon for him—folded Curtis's brows. "You know I can't tell you that."

"Donovan?"

Now his brow lifted. But his lips pressed firm.

Confirmation enough. "Did he check in as a single or a double?"

"Taylor. You know I can't tell you these things. What is with you?"

Taylor pressed a palm against the counter and leaned in. "I need you to take the next trip to the docks."

Curtis gave him a hard stare. "I have a job to do here too, you know."

With a curt nod, Taylor acknowledged the fact. "Even so, I need you to drive."

"What will you be doing?"

"Taking Sonora out to the farm."

"Why?" Concern etched Curtis's response. "What is going on?"

Taylor held a long look on his friend as he debated what to say. Should he tell him that the man he'd just checked in posed a threat to his wife—at least to her heart? Would he tell Taylor not to overreact? Would he advise him to stay put and to have Sonora stay put?

Too much risk there.

"She needs a few days off."

"All of the sudden?"

"Will you drive for me or not?"

Curtis crossed his arms.

"I'm taking her to the farm in five minutes either way. But if the carriage is not at the docks, I'll let you explain to Gretta why."

"As opposed to me explaining to her why I'm not here doing *my* job?"

Taylor drummed his fingers on the counter and watched Black Cowboy Hat ascend the stairs, suitcase in hand. The man was alone. Or was his bride waiting somewhere outside?

That didn't make much sense. And he only had luggage for one—if he was staying a week.

Why would he stay there a week by himself?

He was there to find Sonora. Taylor was absolutely convinced of it. And by Sonora's reaction, she didn't want to be found—not by this Donovan fellow.

So then, this wasn't an overreaction. Taking her to the farm wasn't a selfish reaction either. He was protecting his wife. Any man would do the same.

Taylor turned his chin back to Curtis. "Please? Because you care about Sonora."

Still wearing a confused and concerned expression, Curtis shook his head. "Because I care about you, my friend. *And* your wife. But this clears my debt, I think."

"Debt?"

"For getting you a wife in the first place." His customary grin resurfaced. "Remember."

"Ah. That." Taylor tapped the counter one more time. "Al and Vicky are in the back by the carriage house. I'll drive the truck back from the farm."

Curtis nodded, glanced at the walkway along the second floor, and looked back at Taylor. "Is this Donovan guy dangerous?"

Taylor didn't have an answer. Well, yes, he did. Either physically or emotionally, Donovan threatened his wife—and the budding romance he'd only just found with her. But that was more than he was willing to say. So Taylor said nothing at all. He simply turned and stalked back the way he'd come.

Face cool from the water she'd splashed against her cheeks, Sonora sat on the edge of her bed and sorted through her fuming thoughts.

How on earth had Donovan discovered where she'd gone? Why on earth had he brought his new wife there? Was it all a coincidence?

It couldn't be. It just couldn't. Sonora hadn't even heard of Sanctuary Island until she'd seen the ad in the equine magazine. The island may live and breathe on tourists, but it wasn't like it was Hawaii or some other super-well-known destination. And Arabelle was a beach girl—as in white, sandy, warm beaches. Not rocky shorelines with brisk northern gusts dropping in from Canada. She wouldn't choose quaint little Sanctuary Island as her honeymoon location, of that Sonora was certain.

Donovan had found her. And followed her.

Leaning across the mattress, Sonora grabbed her phone and opened a new text to Nina.

D is here—I just saw him get off the ferry. What the heck?!

She hit Send and then stared at the delivered message. It remained . . . delivered. Not read. It was after ten in the morning, Nina would be working, and unlike the sloppy part-time hands at the dude ranch, Nina would not waste her employer's time and money by being on her phone when she was supposed to be working.

Sonora sighed. *Get it together. He's married, and so are you.* At that thought, her emotions shifted toward Taylor. Goodness, his scowl had been fierce on the way back. A lump swelled in her throat as Sonora imagined why Taylor had gone from flirting and pleasant to especially dark and unhappy.

One glimpse of her ex-boyfriend, and she'd acted like a brokenhearted ninny. It wasn't like that though. It was—

"Sonora!" Taylor's call from the stairway jarred her.

Standing and pocketing her phone, Sonora set her jaw as she determined to explain to her husband—whom she very much liked—why she'd been so shaken by the sight of Donovan in her territory.

Except then she'd have to tell him about Arabelle and how humiliating that had been. Still was. Heat burned in her face as she imagined retelling that part. She had never been fired in her life . . . and to be dismissed by a spoiled princess because of a man . . .

The pounding footfalls landed on the wood floor of their small living space. "Sonora?" This time his voice was quieter. Gentler.

Putting starch into her posture, Sonora stepped from the bedroom and met him near the small sofa. "I'm here."

His intense study held her. It was sparks and fire. "You okay?"

"Yes." She painted up a smile.

He did not. "Curtis is taking the carriage this round."

"He doesn't need to." She frowned. "I'm fine."

"I'm taking you to the farm."

"What?"

He lifted a hand, but then it fell back to his side, without touching her. "You were shaken up."

"I know that. But he wasn't on our carriage. Maybe they're staying at one of the bed and breakfasts." Sonora looked down, twisting her fingers together. "I overreacted, is all, Taylor." Looking back up, she forced herself to meet those dark-blue eyes. "And it isn't what you think. I just . . ."

Taylor visibly swallowed, then he stepped forward. "It's okay, Sonora. I know—I've been there, remember?" His palm slid along her jawline, fingers curled tenderly into her hair. "I won't let him hurt you."

While tears burned against her eyes, Sonora wondered at this surge of fierce gentleness in him. Did anyone else ever witness *this* Taylor Everest? Selfishly, she wanted to bask in it. But did he think she was in *physical* danger? That wasn't true. She was only humiliated.

She covered his hand, pressed her face into his palm, and then slowly pulled his warm touch away. "He wouldn't hurt me, Taylor. Just so you know."

Taylor's gaze lowered to the floor. Did he flinch? He cleared his throat. "He is staying here. I saw him check in and confirmed it with Curtis." He met her eyes again, and now there was a hint of a challenge in his watch. "I can take you to the farm if you'd like. It's your choice."

This felt . . . weighted. Like he was measuring her response and the balance of what had grown between them was at stake.

With the confusion that provoked, as well as the anxiety reignited because Donovan was staying there—at the Palace—Sonora felt panic rise again.

Pray. Do not panic . . . Ah. The calm whisper she didn't heed back at the dude ranch. Thankfully, God was a gracious and compassionate God, slow to anger and abounding in good. And He had brought her to good, even through her foolishness.

Lord, let me not be foolish this time . . . Especially when it felt like so much more was at stake now. All that she'd found with Taylor . . .

Sonora stepped forward and pressed her hand on his suit lapel. The heart beneath that dark jacket thumped against her palm. Did it leap at her touch? Hers did at the strength of his look fastened on her.

"What would you have me do?" she asked.

"I would have you out of his reach. I would have you never hurt by him again."

She nodded and managed a small smile. "I would like to see your farm."

Relief filtered into that stern look, and Taylor leaned down to press a kiss to her forehead. "That would make me feel better." Then he stepped back, taking her hand in his. "We can go now, then I'll make it back for the noon run."

"That fast?"

"We'll ride Molly and Pete, and I'll leave them at the farm for you. I'll drive back."

"Drive? You own a vehicle?"

He nodded. "A small pickup. There's a parking lot on the back side of the Palace, behind the lattice screened line of dumpsters, hidden behind that big bank of hydrangeas and lilacs."

While the cleverness of a hidden parking lot in such a place sank in, Sonora wrestled with this rushed plan of Taylor's. On one hand, Sonora felt sheltered and protected. Loved. On the other, she sensed there was something else at play here. That Taylor wasn't telling her everything.

But that was silly. If he was anything, Taylor was honest. Brutally so. Wasn't that what he'd warned her at the very beginning? And she'd seen the truth of it in him over the past two months. If there was something more, Taylor would say so.

She would trust him and take the shelter he offered.

While Pete and Molly maintained a steady trot toward Seven Pines State Park, Taylor was grateful they'd at least taken them out to stretch the week before. Poor animals, made to dwell in that small paddock, only to be asked to whisk them away at a moment's notice. He hoped that while at the farm, Sonora would pay them some attention.

He glanced at her, noticing her solid riding and admiring it. She used her legs, maintained a good seat, had perfect balance, and kept a gentle touch on the reins. Obviously she was as comfortable in the saddle as she was driving. Her dad had taught her both—wasn't that what she said? She'd been a daddy's girl, and horses were their closest connection.

And now her relationship with her father was strained. That was sad—as sad as his broken relationships with his family. Was every connection doomed to hardship?

At the road that would lead to the entrance to the state park, Taylor directed Pete an inland direction, rather than going toward the northern shore. Pete's ears twitched, and his head perked up. Molly gave a small, joyful whinny, as if crying "home!"

Sonora laughed—and what a wonder the woman kept proving to be. How was she always able to find a smile, even when things were more than unfavorable?

"I have a feeling I could let the reins fly, and they'd find their way all on their own," Sonora said.

"That's true. But not recommended." Taylor felt a tickle at the corner of his mouth, where a small grin poked through. How about that—she could summon a smile from him, even when he felt the thunder of jealousy and roar of anger stirring in his soul. It was like she was God's gift of grace, sent to him to calm the storms.

That was fanciful of him. Even so, he wanted it to be true.

The battle within continued to war—one part jealous of Donovan, who had so deeply stirred Sonora that she'd lost her smile and her sensible determination with once glimpse of him. One part thrilled that he could whisk her away, taking her to the farm—to his home, all the while hoping that she'd fall in love with it. And him.

Please . . .

Taylor squeezed his eyes shut, trusting that Pete would see their way safely on, and forced his mind back to the pastor's words last week: *Trust that God's goodness will carry you through. Even if His method isn't how you would prefer. Even if the way He goes seems like the exact opposite of what you would want. Trust His goodness to meet your heart. For He cares for you.*

Could Taylor trust God with his heart? With Sonora?

Disappointment had been a cruel twist in the past. But perhaps where Taylor had read a harsh *The End*, God had actually begun something new. And maybe that new thing was leading him here, now. To Sonora.

Would he change that if he could go back and have his way then?

His gaze traveled to Sonora, astride Molly, as the mare galloped across the small rise that would lead them home. She made a lovely profile in her white straw cowboy hat, honey braid bouncing with the rhythm of the horse's lope. More than that, Sonora was his match. The piece that filled the gaps where they swelled in his character.

No. He wouldn't go back and change things now. He wanted to go forward. With Sonora.

Tell her so . . .

The prompting settled in his mind as the green roofline of his small white farmhouse came into view at the end of the tall rolling grass pasture. An image of him sliding off Pete at the front gate, meeting her beside Molly as she came off the mare, and swinging her up and into his arms filled his imagination. Wouldn't that be dissonant with his usual self?

No, not dissonant—though it would definitely be jarring. But not in a harsh way. In a surprising and perhaps refreshing way.

What would Sonora do, if he dared?

"This is your farm?" Sonora's wistful voice shook him from his daydream.

Taylor eased Pete to a walk as they neared the rails that hemmed in the south pasture. At her obvious admiration, he grinned. "It is."

"It's a bit of a dream—so green, and sheltered on every side by trees. I wonder why you ever leave it."

"Something about a job."

"Ah yes. The same reason I am here."

That was a punch in the gut, though he was sure she didn't mean for it to be. "That is not why you are *here* now."

Pete and Molly walked side by side, continuing down the two-track lane toward the four-stall barn at the northwestern corner of his property. A gap of silence lapsed—unusual for Sonora not to respond.

He was pushing too hard. Hoping too much . . .

Sonora pointed across the valley. "Is that your greenhouse?"

They were changing subjects, then. "No. It belongs to my neighbors, the Klines. They farm their small acreage and a bit of mine, as well as hay my pastures while I'm at the Palace. In exchange, I have bales for winter feed and a clean house."

"That sounds like a good deal for you." Her teasing resurfaced, and that was a relief. And a disappointment.

He had things he needed to say. From his heart. And his conscience.

One of which had been bothering him since he'd found her still rattled in the carriage house. She was operating on the assumption that Donovan was on the island with his wife.

Taylor hadn't seen a woman with Donovan at any point—neither at the docks nor when the man had checked into the resort. He'd been alone and had carried a single bag.

But his wife could have been waiting outside. There was a lovely three-tiered fountain, and the charm of the front gardens that often caught the immediate attention of guests. She could have been lost in all that endearing beauty.

It was possible.

He'd rather tell Sonora the things from his heart. Specifically, how much she'd filled it in the two months they'd been married. And how much he wanted her to stay.

The horses didn't stop at the front gate, and Taylor had been so lost in the complications of his thoughts that he didn't require them to. They reached the front of the tobacco-style barn, and Pete and Molly stopped at the hitching post. Good thing they knew what they were doing.

Sonora swung a leg behind her and slid to the ground, catching her hat before it slipped off the back of her head. Hands on her hips, she turned a slow circle, taking in her surroundings. Did she see the beauty of tall, rolling grass, the serenity of a life tucked away from all but two other people? Or did she see a life of lonely isolation?

Taylor saw both. He knew both.

She pivoted to face him, tipping her chin up, which allowed him to see her expression beneath the shade of her hat.

"It's stunning, Taylor." Peace had replaced the panic he'd seen in her earlier that day.

His heart leaped as hope surged. Taylor dismounted and leaned his forearms against the swell of his saddle. "It's home."

"I bet it's quite a sight in winter, all blanketed with snow."

"It can be. It can also be a terrorist in winter. The artic winds slam us, the lake-effect snow is bone chilling, and the isolation can be . . . long."

Sonora held him with a long gaze, her silence unnerving but the warmth in her eyes stirring. What was she thinking and not saying?

He was left to wonder as she turned back to Molly and reached for the cinch. With easy familiarity, she worked through the unsaddling process, even finding the tack room at the side of the barn without inquiry. Taylor followed her lead, taking care of Pete's tack. After a good brush down—the gleaming animals had earned it—Taylor gathered the reins of both horses and walked them to the back gate. Once free of their bridles, both horses tossed their creamy manes, turned toward the empty pasture, and ran into their freedom. Pete was so thrilled, he kicked up his heels, causing Sonora to chuckle.

"Is that how you feel, coming home?"

Taylor didn't have words for all he felt right then.

If he told her she made him feel like that—running into freedom and kicking up his heels—would she think he was ridiculous? If he said that he loved her, would she forget about Donovan?

He reached to finger the brim of her hat, then traced her jawline with the back of his knuckles. He let his fingers drift down her arm until he found her hand. “Come and meet Mrs. Kline. She’ll make sure you have everything you need until I come back.”

Sonora’s fingers wove with his, and he led her home.

Twenty

Sonora chided herself for being flimsy. Wimpy.

She'd run like a girl ashamed of herself. Just like she had when Arabelle had *suggested* she'd be more comfortable with a different job at some other place.

But this wasn't entirely the same, was it? After all, Taylor had practically insisted she go to his farm and stay there until Donovan and Arabelle left the island.

Goodness, but it had been nice to be taken care of. To have someone protecting her from the emotional storm that had crashed on her. How long had it been since she'd had that sort of refuge? Not since her parents' divorce—an awful event she'd had to navigate on her own. Donovan had never been that sort of partner to her. If he'd noticed any struggle at all, he'd say she was a cowgirl and could handle it. And that had been true, so she'd taken it as a compliment. But this . . .

Sighing, Sonora lowered onto the porch swing that hung on the covered front porch. Taylor had gone back to the Palace, driving his beat-up 1990s Toyota Tacoma down the two-track dirt lane several hours before. In that time, the chipper and talkative Mrs. Kline had invited her to supper that evening and then kindly left her to settle into the farmhouse alone. In a few hours, Sonora would follow that simple lane around the back side of the barn and to the Klines' house. But for now she eased the swing into a gentle sway and watched while the wind made waves in the tall grass pasture. Pete and Molly grazed happily on the far side, the late-afternoon sun making their dark-red coats shine.

"I could stay here forever," she said to no one except her own heart. And to God. Gripping the chain, she raised her gaze toward the deep-blue sky. "Could I stay here?"

A peaceful silence answered back. She shut her eyes and turned her heart toward prayer. There was much to pray over. Her lingering anger at Donovan. The humiliation and sense of insufficiency that the mere thought of seeing Arabelle had provoked. Taylor.

Oh, Taylor Everest. Things had certainly shifted in the past two months. The man had such a claim on her heart. Sure, he was quiet and solemn. Maybe even a little glacial. But he was good and kind and honest. And faithful. Heaven knew, Sonora longed for a faithful man in her life, even if she had insisted that love was not in her story.

That had just been fear and hurt talking.

What was this?

Once again Sonora squeezed her eyes shut and set her heart free to pray. "Father, I ran when I should have prayed, but You brought me here. It feels a little bit like Ruth, finding favor in the eyes of a good man. Unexpected. But beautiful. If

I'm wrong, Lord, and Taylor and I are not in Your will, would you make that clear? Because I'm falling pretty hard for that grumpy boss of mine." With a small laugh, she opened her eyes.

He wasn't grumpy. He was introverted and serious, and he'd been shoved into a tough situation. But his steady calmness balanced her tendency for exuberance, and she balanced his tendency toward gloom.

Across the pasture, Molly walked to Pete and touched her nose to his. Just like Albert and Victoria, they were a matched pair.

A sense of home warmed Sonora's heart. A matched pair. All that was missing was Taylor there by her side.

Taylor missed Sonora. He missed how she filled in his awkward silence with the guests as they clopped along the road, her enthusiasm and kindness fitting perfectly with this job. Missed the way her hand fit in his when he helped her down from the driver's seat at the end of a run. Missed the way she worked with him, knowing exactly what needed to be done without him saying a word.

He stared at the checkerboard on the coffee table. The day was done, supper eaten, and now he was in his apartment alone. Just like he'd always been up until Sonora came crashing into his world. Strange—before her, the solitary evenings hadn't bothered him much. They'd been a balm to his tired spirit after a full day of tourists. Not so now. Now, he was lonely and bored.

Curtis was a decent checkers opponent but not nearly as appealing as Sonora.

His heart lurched, and heat rolled through his body as he thought about the last match they'd started. The game hadn't ended . . . because she'd ended up snuggled beside him on the couch. She'd asked him to tell her more about his family, and he found himself pouring out all the treasures he'd kept in his heart about them. That his mom had loved to play *let's pretend* with them when they were little, and she delighted in music. She would turn the radio up loud, and they would dance in the kitchen.

Sonora brightened at that, saying it was fun to imagine him busting a move with full abandonment. He'd blushed but smiled.

He shared about Jill—how much fun his sister had with life. She was almost always cheerful—but if she was in a mood, watch out! It could be ugly. Jill loved old Shirley Temple movies and anything that could be considered a musical. She dreamed of becoming a tap dancer and wanted, with all of her heart, to perform in the gazebo in the town square.

And then there was his dad. He worked hard and was gone during the weeks during the tourist season. But he always came home on the weekends—even though that meant he had to get up early to make the weekend runs to the dock. But he made up for it in the winters, reserving the evenings for his family to play checkers and read stories (they read all the Chronicles of Narnia every winter), and once a week they'd watch a movie. When Taylor was twelve, he started working alongside his dad on their farm. At fourteen he began spending the tourist season in town with his dad.

They'd been close. Which was why their leaving had been particularly devastating.

"They didn't give you any indication that they were thinking about moving?"

"No. But maybe I should have guessed. Jill had some heart issues that had them going to southern Michigan three or four times a year. Mom had found some other educational resources there . . . I guess I just thought doing everything by distance was working. I didn't imagine . . . but perhaps that's because I'm not good at looking beyond myself." He finished that admission on a cracked whisper.

Pure compassion filled her beautiful eyes. Her fingers grazed his face, and then she wrapped her arms around him. In that moment, he'd felt fully exposed and yet deeply loved.

Sitting forward on that lonely couch, Taylor blocked the rest of the replay of that evening, lest he drown in the memory of how soft her hair had felt, tangled in his fingers. How sweet her lips tasted as he'd kissed her again and again.

Checkers was out. He needed out of this apartment, to find someone who would get him out of his own head. The stillness of the apartment was stifling, and if he didn't find something to do, he was bound to find himself heading back to the farm.

Hmm. That wasn't an entirely bad idea.

Except that he needed to work in the morning. It was a terrible idea.

He could make it work though. He could stay in his old bedroom—giving Sonora the master that he'd taken over on his twenty-eighth birthday when he'd finally accepted that his parents weren't moving back. Then he could get up early, drive back—

No. There was a reason he stayed in the carriage house during tourist season. As it was, he rose at five thirty to ensure everything was done and pristine before his first trip to the docks. A stay at the farm would have him setting his alarm for much earlier.

It wasn't practical. Anyway, he certainly disliked the thought of leaving Al and Vicky in the stalls unattended. It wasn't responsible. His father would absolutely disapprove, and even now, with all the years and distance between them, that mattered to Taylor.

Even so, the idea niggled in the back of his mind.

Wow. Sonora had some kind of enchantment over him.

Taylor pushed off the sofa, shaking his head. Dressed in his casual dark-blue jeans and a pinstriped button-down, he'd blend as a guest. He took himself down the stairs and, after a quick check of the horses, across the back garden path and into the Palace. With any luck Curtis would be flinging darts in the employee lounge or stirring up a card game.

Before he reached the employee lounge, Taylor stopped. His attention had latched on to the man sitting alone at a table near a window in the grand foyer. Donovan Arlington had set himself up in a position that allowed him to see the back portion of the sprawling first floor of the Palace—an uncommon choice, as all the activities and lovely guest features were positioned the opposite direction, including the stunning views of the rocky shoreline and Lake Huron that stretched beyond the massive front windows and pristine gardens.

Donovan was alone—still no wife to be seen. And he was set up to watch the employees. To watch for Sonora, Taylor suspected.

Taylor's chest hardened as he stared at the man pretending to read a newspaper. Donovan's attention popped up. He scanned the back hall until his inspection landed on Taylor. The pair of men held an icy stare, and then Donovan motioned for Taylor to come over.

What? This fellow was bold!

While fire rushed through his veins, Taylor walked across the deep, intricately carved carpet toward the table where Donovan sat.

"Do you work here?" Donovan didn't even stand to speak. Simply sat there like he owned the world.

"I do." Not really. He contracted with the Palace, but whatever.

"I'm looking for someone."

"Is that so?" Taylor's fists curled tight at his side.

"She would have arrived late in the season. Cute blonde. Likes to wear a cowboy hat. Smiles a lot—the friendly type."

"No one wears a cowboy hat at the Palace. Not if they work here."

"Oh. Sure. I understand dress codes. I own a resort of sorts myself."

What a spectacular liar! How had Sonora gotten herself mixed up with this guy?

"Her name is Sonora."

Taylor kept his lips seamed.

"Have you met her?"

Taylor remained silent. He wasn't a liar. Not like this man. But he wasn't about to answer his question either.

Donovan lowered his paper and smacked the table. "I asked you a question."

"Why are you looking for this woman?"

The irritation on the man's face eased. He relaxed back into his chair. "I made a mistake. Let her go." With a conspirator's smile, he shrugged. "You know how it is—sometimes you just need to taste something different for a day or two. But now I know that was a mistake, and I'm here to beg her forgiveness."

No. Taylor did not know how that went. He had no intention of *tasting* something different.

Would Sonora take Donovan back if he asked her too? Taylor's heart froze and then cracked. Suddenly it hurt to breathe. She'd been deeply injured by this man—which would lead one to believe that she'd loved him.

Did she still love him?

"Do you know where I can find her?"

Taylor saw spots, and the room dimmed around him. He blinked. Swallowed. Then looked straight at the man who could cause his world to shatter. "She isn't here." With that he turned and strode away while his heart writhed within.

Sonora stroked the kitten curled up in her lap. Her tummy was full, and a steaming cup of citrus mint tea sat on the side table nearby. Across from her in this small farmhouse parlor, Mrs. Kline sat beside her husband on the nineties-style plaid couch.

"I haven't had ham and scalloped potatoes in forever, and never made with freshly harvested potatoes. It was delicious," Sonora said. "Thank you again for having me."

"Glad to." Mrs. Kline patted Mr. Kline's leg. "Edward is likely glad to have someone else to talk to other than me on a Monday evening. We hardly see anyone out here. He's stuck with only me until our Thursday evening farmers' market.

Then it's just us until Saturday, when we get up and do the morning market. Have you gone to the farmers' market? It's at the park in town. Oh! But maybe you're too busy. Seems Taylor works sunup to sundown driving that fancy carriage. I think he likes it that way though. He's a worker, that man. Has been ever since he was a boy. Not much for people though, which seems odd for a resort. But he sure loves those horses. And we like seeing them when they're here for the winter—but that is only Pete and Molly. Taylor is afraid there won't be enough feed to get those big Friesians through our hard winters, so they don't stay here."

Sonora couldn't quite button down her amused grin, so she wrapped her hands around that warm mug and put it to her lips.

"Oh!" Mrs. Kline barely took a breath before she plunged in again. "And of course, we like seeing Taylor too. He's a good neighbor. Gets pretty lonely out here when he's in town all summer. But then there's Sunday. Some weeks, seems we live for Sundays. Have you been to Sanctuary's Bible Church? Pastor Frank sure can preach! He leans in on the Word of God and gives it to us straight. But he's not around much these days. Off on the mainland to take care of his father, poor man."

Sonora got a nod in.

"Now, Sicilia. Let the girl answer here and there." Mr. Kline gripped his wife's hand and winked at Sonora.

Mrs. Kline blushed. "Oh, Sonora! I'm so sorry. I'm such a Chatty Cathy, especially when I'm nervous. Not that I should be nervous with you. But the thing is, we've been praying for Taylor to meet a woman who would stay. He's such a good man, even if he doesn't talk much, and after that other girl left him heartbroken, it looked like he'd be single forever. That would be too sad for words! How did you meet him?"

Sonora swallowed. What was their story again? "We . . . um. Online?" Was that a question? She was supposed to be giving an answer here. She cleared her throat. "We were both part of a horse community on social media, and I made a comment on a post that he agreed with, and we ended up connecting via private message . . . and then we met in person."

She lied. She was lying to these kind people and dragging Taylor down with her. The wonderful dinner she'd just consumed turned in her stomach. And the kitten who had been purring contentedly stood up and hopped off her lap, as if the sweet little furball knew Sonora was being dishonest and didn't want any part of it.

Mrs. Kline leaned back and grinned, as if that were the most romantic story she'd ever heard. "How about that. Those social media thingies *can* be used for good." She beamed at Mr. Kline "Did you ever imagine such a tale?"

"Never."

"Well, however you met, I'm sure glad for it. Taylor looks at you like you're the treasure he's been waiting his whole life for." She turned to Edward, placing a hand on the man's chest. "You should have been there. Remember how he stared at Albert and Victoria when Jim gave them to him? It was like that. Like all his dreams just materialized right in front of him. And when he asked me to look after his *wife* . . . I'm telling you, I've never heard such a reverent tone."

Edward laughed, eyeing Sonora as though to gauge her reaction to being compared to a pair of horses.

Sonora wouldn't be complaining if Taylor looked at her like he would have when he'd been given those Friesians. He did love those animals—and who could blame him? And she'd missed the part when Taylor had asked Mrs. Kline to look after his *wife*. She sure wished she'd heard it now.

A lull expanded—mostly because Mrs. Kline stopped talking. Sonora sipped the tea, which was good—so fresh, made from mint leaves from the garden, a freshly squeezed orange, and honey from the hives Mr. Kline kept on the back side of the property. It was their own little haven, this remote farm on the other side of the island.

A haven she wanted very much to remain in. To be a part of.

She wished Taylor were there with her. He'd blush furiously at Mrs. Kline's awkward comments. And when he did, Sonora would lace her fingers with his and squeeze to let him know it was okay. She liked his neighbors. She liked everything about his life, and she wanted to remain a part of it.

She wanted to amend their agreement—and to clear the air about why they were together in the first place. And she felt, with growing confidence, that Taylor did too. They just needed to say the words . . .

Why on earth had Donovan shown up now? Right when things had become beautifully clear in her heart about Taylor?

She should have stayed at the Palace. She should have told Taylor exactly why she didn't want to—that it was Arabelle, not Donovan, whom she dreaded seeing most—and that had to do with Sonora's silly sense of inadequacy. She should have been braver.

More than all that, though, Sonora wished she'd told Taylor what had stirred in her heart about him—about them. That those kisses they'd shared weren't simple impulse, and what had grown between them was so much more than a crush on her boss.

She could call him tonight. Would it mean less if she spoke her heart over a phone call?

"Are you okay, dear?" Mrs. Kline leaned forward, and for a moment Sonora thought the woman would reach across the space and check her brow for a fever.

Sonora fixed a smile. "I am." She finished the last of her tea. "I'm so sorry, but I think the day is catching up with me. It's time to find a bed, I think."

"Of course." Mrs. Kline nodded with firm approval, then turned to her husband. "Taylor said Sonora was feeling a little bit rundown. That's why he brought her to the farm, so she could rest." She looked back at Sonora. "So off you go, dear. Should we walk with you?"

"No." This time Sonora couldn't stifle her small chuckle. "No, that's okay. I have a flashlight app on my phone, and a quiet stroll down the lane will be good." She stood, and Mr. Kline rose also, taking her mug and offering a kind, fatherly look.

"Cell phones don't work well on this side of the island—not that that would impede your flashlight," he said. "But we have a landline, and so does Taylor. I'm sure our number is somewhere beside the phone in the kitchen."

"Yes!" Mrs. Kline was on her feet now as well. "I made sure it was right there, freshly penned—it was so faded before—and clearly marked. Please don't hesitate to call us if you need something."

"Thank you." Sonora nodded, tucking away the disappointment about the cell phones not working. She could use the landline to call him . . . but then again, there was something romantic and alluring in the idea that he would call her. Especially if Mrs. Kline was right about the way Taylor looked at her. Didn't every girl want to be pursued?

It was decided. She wouldn't be calling Taylor that evening.

Which left her with a long night of prayer ahead of her—and the delicious hope that her husband would ring her on that landline. Not bad alternatives.

No, not bad at all—particularly with the first. It was high time she laid her whole heart before God and listened to what He had to say about things.

Twenty-One

The following day, Taylor kept a close eye on Donovan. The man made his rounds, taking the carriage to town on Taylor's midmorning run to the docks.

"You're sure she isn't here?" Donovan asked from the backseat.

"She's not here," Taylor responded, his back to his passenger and lead in his voice.

Donovan sat back and rode in silence. At the drop point at the edge of town, Taylor didn't bother hopping down to play the role of footman. Donovan was his only passenger, and the man could get himself off the carriage without help.

Ah. How easy it was to slip into his old, cold ways without Sonora at his side, gently pushing him to be more. No wonder their tips had more than doubled in the past couple of months. Conviction pinched, and Taylor cleared his throat, turning to speak to Donovan, who was now on the ground.

"I come back this way in thirty minutes, if you need a ride back."

"Won't be necessary. I plan to do some poking around for a while, and the taxis run all day, right?"

Pressing his lips together, Taylor nodded. No need to guess what Donovan was *poking around* for. Anger burned fresh, alongside another bout of panic. And guilt. He should call his wife and set the record straight—about Donovan and about the reason Taylor had rushed her off to hide. He swallowed hard—that sort of conversation should be done face to face. Which meant that he should go back to the farm and tell Sonora that Donovan was there to speak with her. To apologize to her and to beg for another chance. Which would indicate that the man was *not* there with a wife—that he wasn't married after all.

Sonora could see her ex-boyfriend with all the facts, then proceed without misunderstanding.

And Taylor's heart would be in her hands. Two days ago he hadn't thought that a precarious situation.

Donovan wandered down the main street, his gait screaming arrogance. Or perhaps that was Taylor's bitter prejudice.

"Walk on." Taylor flicked the reins and set his face toward the docks. He had a job to do. One that wouldn't allow him to stalk the unwanted fellow searching for his wife, nor could he make another trip to the farm and tell Sonora what he'd discovered.

The first was the truth. The second . . .

Taylor hardened himself against the discomfort of a lie.

Sonora spent the next three days wandering the farm and the grounds beyond. Keeping in mind Taylor's quiet request that she exercise the horses, she alternated riding Pete and Molly. Each time saddling only one, she felt bad about leaving the other behind. They were so buddy bound, and she knew it was good for them to work on their own, but hearing the one being left cry out their *come back!* whinnies pricked her heart.

One such moment, while she was atop Molly, she patted the Haflinger's red neck and ruffled the thick white mane. "I get it, sweet girl. But I won't keep you apart forever. Don't they say absence makes the heart grow fonder?"

A cliché proving true. She sure missed Taylor and grew more certain about where her heart had gone concerning him with each moment they were apart.

For the first minutes of that ride, as she trotted in the general direction of Seven Pines, she pondered the nightly phone calls from Taylor. On the landline, of course. She would grow giddy, waiting for those calls. Exactly at eight forty-five, the kitchen phone would ring and that low, quiet voice would send a thrill through her system.

Except, he sounded off. Like something bothered him.

He would ask how her day was. If she'd gone exploring—which she had. The first day to Seven Pines, the second to a rise south of the farm, where she had discovered a beautiful but hauntingly abandoned château-like mansion. Taylor had told her that had been a nunnery in the early nineteen hundreds but had stood untouched for decades now.

"No one wants to restore that beautiful thing?" she'd asked.

"I don't know—I generally stay out of affairs that aren't mine."

She'd laughed. "Yes. That about sums you up. Taylor Everest keeps to himself. Do you have a fancy word for that?"

She'd thought he'd chuckle—maybe even blush a little, though she couldn't see it—and give her a short vocabulary lesson. He'd done none of those things. The line between them went still with his silence.

"Taylor, I'm teasing you."

"I know. I hear it in your voice."

"Are you okay?"

Long pause. Cleared throat. "Everything is fine here."

That was . . . not reassuring. "Taylor?"

"There's an old dairy on the other side of that rise. You might enjoy exploring that."

He changed the subject? Something was not right. "Taylor?"

"I'm here."

"I miss you."

Silence.

Her heart dropped clear to the pine plank floor.

"Sonora . . ." His voice trailed off, strained with emotion.

"I'm listening."

"I'll come back for you tomorrow. We need to talk."

She felt dizzy, and hot tears pricked her eyes. "That sounds ominous." Would he appreciate her choice of vocabulary? Why would he care in this moment—and why would she think he would? This had the makings of a *it's not you—it's me* conversation. Not really a time for a playful game of lexicology.

Sonora swallowed, banishing emotion from wobbling her voice. "Okay. Something you can't tell me over the phone?"

"No." Definitive. And maybe a little harsh.

"I see." Disappointment slipped into her sigh as she slumped onto a chair. "I guess we'll talk about it tomorrow, then. Good night, Taylor."

"Sonora." Was that desperation replacing this chill in his tone?

She fingered the grain on a well-worn plank of the farm table. "I'm still here."

"I miss you too."

With that, the call ended. And a tear slipped onto Sonora's cheek. Once again she spent the sleepless hours of the night in prayer.

Taylor remained true to his word and made his way back to the farm, even though it was not yet the weekend. Once again Curtis drove for him, only this time, his friend didn't tease.

"You look upset," Curtis had said. "I thought you'd be antsy to go get that girl back."

Taylor had rubbed the back of his neck. "That man I asked you about?"

"Yeah?"

"His name is Donovan Arlington. Sonora dated him for two years. He's back here looking for her—to try to get her back."

Curtis shrugged. "Tell him she's married."

Taylor held a long, frustrated look on him. "Our marriage isn't like that."

"Sure looks like it's running in that direction."

Looking toward the docks, where Donovan would be heading to catch the evening ferry in just a few hours, Taylor shook his head. "I haven't told her."

"Told her what? That you love her?"

Taylor winced. "That Donovan still wants her."

"Why would you do that?"

"Because she came here after he broke up with her. Don't you understand? If she still loves him and he wants her back, then I'm in the way."

Curtis examined that for several quiet moments, then slowly shook his head. "Doesn't seem right." His expression grew more convinced, and his voice carried more conviction. "I watch you two together, Taylor. She loves you. And you're good together. In fact, I'd go so far as to say you need her."

That didn't help much. Taylor stepped back and held up a hand. "I have to tell her." Once again he looked in the direction of the harbor. "And I need to do it before he leaves. I should have done it days ago . . ."

But he'd been selfish. He'd lied.

He hadn't been the man he'd promised her he was—brutally honest about all things. That was not how love worked, not how it was supposed to work.

Feeling defeated and dreading what was to come, Taylor drove his old truck back to the farm. Sonora's exuberant greeting only pummeled his already sore heart, though he couldn't help wrapping her tight in his arms when she slipped hers around his shoulders.

She pressed her face into his chest and inhaled. "You smell good."

"I'm sure I smell like sweat and horses."

"No. Like Taylor and horses. Both good things." She lifted her face and propped her chin on his chest. Her gaze up at him was sweet and warm and happy.

She was killing him.

Swallowing, Taylor dropped his hold and stepped back.

Her brow knit. "I have some coffee still warm. Do you want some?"

The knife in his heart twisted further, but he nodded. She slipped her hand in his, and they walked to the house, up the steps onto the covered front porch, and into the kitchen.

With all his selfishness, he wished he could simply enjoy this beautiful moment—Sonora, his *wife*, happy to see him as they entered this home together. A home he'd loved forever. A home they could share forever . . .

But he needed to be honest. She deserved to know the truth.

She poured two mugs and handed him one. Taylor strained to know what to do—where to begin.

"It's nice out." He fumbled. "Want to sit on the front porch?"

Her smile would have pooled his heart into delighted goo if it weren't thrashing with the truth of what he needed to tell her.

She led the way back out the front door and sat on the wooden swing hanging at the far end of the porch. Taylor leaned against the railing.

For several heartbeats the only sounds between them was the call of birds in the distant trees and the click-clack of the chains holding the swing as it gently swayed beneath her.

Finally Sonora sighed. "Taylor, what's going on?"

He gulped. A quick memory flashed from that sermon a few weeks back: *The Lord will provide.* It was time . . .

Lord, help me to trust You . . . and to do the right thing.

Sonora's pulse raced as she watched the man she was in love with wrestle in silence. Something was very wrong, and her gut told her that he was about to end what they'd only just found.

What had happened?

"I need to tell you something." Taylor took her coffee mug and placed it on the railing. He then braced himself on the front porch, his right hand rubbing the back of his neck and his eyes not meeting hers.

Sonora braced herself for whatever it was that Taylor needed to say. As she sat on the swing after a long, weighty pause, Taylor forced himself to connect with her eyes. Remorse filled his expression. "Donovan wasn't here with his wife."

Sonora stopped the swing with her foot against the wood slats of the deck and stared at her husband.

Taylor leaned against the railing that surrounded the covered front porch, a deep sigh escaping while his shoulders slumped. He braced his hands on his knees. "You told me you thought he was here on his honeymoon. But he wasn't. He was alone."

"How do you know that?"

"I kept an eye on him. He was never with a woman. And he asked about you several times, of several different people." He looked down at his hands and then peeked up at her. "He asked *me* about you, Sonora. And when I asked why he was looking for you, he told me he was here to tell you he'd made a mistake letting you go. That he wanted you back."

Misery etched Taylor's brow. But then he blinked, straightened, and schooled his expression into that emotionless, distant mask.

Sonora absorbed this news in silence. Donovan . . . wanted her back? How did he even find her? And why wasn't he married? None of it made sense.

After another length of silence between them, one that felt strained and hard, Taylor cleared his throat. "I'm sorry, Sonora. I suspected he was alone from the beginning—he checked in by himself. I should have told you before I brought you here."

Taylor had wanted to protect her. He had wanted to keep her heart safe. Sonora couldn't fault him for it. But if she had known that Donovan was there by himself, looking for her, she would have confronted him. She didn't want Donovan to think she was *afraid* of him. In fact, she would have relished the opportunity to tell him she was fine. That she didn't need him.

Maybe that was spiteful.

Either way, frustration gripped her. And when she looked up at Taylor, it was with a grimace. "Yeah, you should have told me. You said you were always honest."

He flinched. Nodded. "I know. I am sorry."

Even while she pondered the oddness of Taylor's lie, questions about Donovan overcame her mind. Not married? That hit all kinds of wrong chords. It didn't add up at all. She pulled out her phone, clicked on Nina's phone number, and sent off a quick text. *Are you getting my texts? Donovan came to the island—looking for me! He says he's not married . . . What is going on?*

Knowing that her plea for information was likely going nowhere, because the cell service at the farm was bad, she lowered her phone and then pinned her attention back on her husband.

Once again, he wore cool indifference.

Back to that. That part actually hurt. Hadn't they come farther than that? Than this cool detachment? Or had she misunderstood those tender kisses and the long, intense looks they'd shared just a few days back?

Perhaps this was purely self-defense, because this bothered him as much as it upset her.

Sonora didn't have the capacity to try to find her way past Taylor's walls at that moment, nor to understand his intentions. All of her emotional energy wrapped around Donovan and how mad she was at him. How dare he . . . stalk her! Show up and try to flip her world wrong side out again.

She came to her feet with a sigh. "You know what? It doesn't matter."

"It doesn't matter?" Taylor lifted his chin.

"No. It doesn't matter." Sonora reached for the mug Taylor had taken from her at the beginning of this conversation. If Taylor was going to play at apathy, she was going to try it too.

It would be better than giving Donovan any more emotional real estate. The manipulative snake had already taken way too much of it.

She shrugged. "He's gone now. And that's that."

"Well . . . not quite." Something edgy pushed away the indifference in Taylor's voice. "He's not gone yet, Sonora."

She eyed him. "I thought he was leaving today. That's why you came here to get me."

"He is, but not until this evening."

"You know this because you were spying on him?"

"Yes, I was." He swallowed visibly. "I asked him if he needed a ride to the ferry this morning. He said he was going to delay his departure until the evening. Probably hoping for one last chance to find you."

Her phone vibrated in her palm, and she turned the screen up to find Nina had replied. Huh. She hadn't tried the phone on the front porch. Was this a moment of divine intervention?

Oh girl! That man is a piece of work. He's married, all right. Told Arabelle he had to go to a conference this week. She's here pining for him like some lovesick teenager.

Nina's answer sent white heat through Sonora's chest.

So. Donovan was still on the island? The attempt at not caring fell straight into a deep pit. If he wanted to see her, then so be it. Apparently, they *did* have something to discuss.

"Well then." Sonora stood up from the swing, swallowing the last of her coffee. "Let's give him that chance."

Taylor stood as well, though his shoulders remained slumped. Resigned. His face turned away from her, and he stared across the windblown pasture in the direction of town. “Yeah.” He shoved his hands into his pockets and clamored down the front porch steps. “I think you should.”

Sonora followed him to his pickup. Her thoughts fuming, entirely focused on confronting Donovan.

The drive back toward town was spent in silence.

TWENTY-TWO

TAYLOR HAD BARELY STOPPED the carriage before Sonora was out the door and pounding her way toward the docks. The *Haven*'s last trip back to the Havensport left in less than fifteen minutes, and passengers would already be boarding. She wasn't about to miss this opportunity to confront the snake she'd somehow believed was a decent man.

How had Donovan been so thoroughly deceptive?

Her jog to the dock left her winded but not any less determined. After a quick scan of the people milling around the docks, she spotted him, just stepping onto the gangway.

"Donovan." Her sharp call cut through the lake breeze.

He turned. Spotted her. And grinned.

Sonora scowled as she crossed the space between them. He walked toward her as well, and they met at the edge of Harbor Way.

"Sonora." He stepped closer, as if he had the right to be in her space.

Sonora crossed her arms and glared at the man she had hoped never to see again. "What are you doing here?"

Donovan looked at her with a hint of a smile, like he thought her little outburst was cute. "I missed you."

"What?" Her disbelief came out as a breathy chuckle. This man was absolutely . . . despicable.

He dared to reach for her, gripping both of her shoulders. His gaze became intimate and intense. "You left. I couldn't believe you just . . . were gone. My whole world became empty, and I knew I had to find you. To get you back. It's taken me all these weeks to find out where you'd run."

What a load of garbage. Sonora stepped out of his hold. "Yeah, I left. Why would I stay, Donovan? You dumped me and five minutes later got *engaged*." Not to mention Arabelle's little power-play stunt. But she wasn't going to throw that into this. This was about this awful man and Sonora telling him to get out of her life forever.

Donovan looked toward the dock and then crammed his fingers into his windblown hair. When his focus came back to her, it was with a guilty and regretful expression. "Yeah, the thing is that maybe I just needed some clarity. I think maybe I was just scared, Sonora."

Scared? She couldn't believe what she was hearing. Afraid of what? Commitment? Clearly. Of having to work for the rest of his life? Also likely—and neither issue was her problem. What had she ever seen in him?

"What we had—what we *have*—it was so overpowering. I've never felt that much . . . that deep for anyone. I was afraid—"

Sonora rolled her eyes. "You broke up with me because you were *afraid* of how much you loved me?" She shook her head. "I don't think so. You made it perfectly clear exactly why you and I broke up when you got engaged two weeks later to a pretty girl with loads of money."

"Come on, that's not fair. You know me better than that, hon." He dared to reach out to touch her again.

"Don't." She pulled away before his fingers could grip her elbow. "I know exactly what you were doing."

"Look, Sonora, I didn't go through with it. I told you I missed you. And I'm not afraid anymore. I came here to tell you that. I don't want to be with her. I want to be with you. I'd rather be with the poor girl I love than the rich girl I barely care about."

This guy! He was an epic liar. Had he always been a liar? Had she been a fool for two solid years and never even suspected it?

Could be why he'd never met her dad—always made an excuse to get out of it. And when her mom had met him . . . she wasn't impressed. Mom had said he seemed slippery and self-centered.

Sonora had blown that off, telling herself that Mom didn't trust men after what Dad had done, so she'd probably say that about any boyfriend.

Man, Sonora had been so stupid. So blind.

Sonora's head spun, and annoyingly, tears burned her eyes. Donovan didn't deserve her tears. She lifted her gaze to meet his so that he would feel the ferocity burning inside her. Know that the moisture in her eyes was pure anger and nothing else. "When you broke up with me, you said it was because you didn't have what you thought I deserved. And you know what? You were right. I want a man who can make a promise and keep it. A man who is faithful. You are *not* that man."

"Sonora, you and I had two years together. They were good years. Can't we just hang on to that? Forget the mistake that I made?" He closed in on her space, and this time both his hands cupped her arms. He leaned down, narrowing that intimate gaze on her. "Please, hon. We're so good together. You make me feel so . . . rich. So alive."

How could he do this to her? How could he try to manipulate her and break her heart all over again? Did he have no shame?

Obviously not.

Sonora glared and let the silent gap in the conversation widen. She'd moved on. She'd found a *faithful* man, and though she hadn't deserved it, God had gifted her with a marriage that was working.

This man needed a swift kick back into her past, and he needed to stay there.

She shook her head, and with one firm hand to his chest, she pushed him back. "It's too late, Donovan. Besides, I'm married." Dang it, but her voice cracked. Why did she have to cry when she was angry? But she wasn't done putting an end to this farce. She dug out her phone from her back pocket. Tapped the screen a few times and brought up the text. "And I happen to know that you are too."

She turned the screen so he could see it. His eyes scanned the words and then widened as his face paled. His lips pressed hard together as his jaw clenched. When he did look back at her, it was with an expression of being caught.

Iron entered her spine, and ice ran through her veins. "You and I are done. Forever. Get on the boat, Donovan, and don't ever come back."

She spun away and walked the slight hill back to her husband, grateful that she'd ended up with the right man after all.

Taylor told himself to turn away. Seeing his wife standing so close to a man she had cared for—possibly loved—staring up at him while he gazed back at her, was one of the most painful experiences he could recall.

The lump in his throat seemed baseball sized. His eyes slid shut, and through the chaos that turned in his frenzied mind, churning pain in his heart, Taylor reached upward.

You are the Lord who provides. Please give me faith like Abraham. To hold up to You what I love most and let her go, if that is Your will.

This was the thing—the prayer he should have summoned so long ago, when his family had moved south. The move had been for the best, specifically for Jill. From the limited interaction he kept with his parents and sister, little Jilly-Fish was thriving. How could he not be happy about that?

God had provided for Jill . . . and Taylor had dug into selfishness and found resentment.

Please forgive me . . .

"Let's go." Sonora's fingers slipped over his exposed forearm.

Blinking against the heated glaze in his eyes, Taylor searched her expression. She wore a cold, unreadable mask—so unlike her. That was *his* default—*hers* was warm sunshine and brilliant smiles. It sent him topsy-turvy to see coldness on her.

"Sonora?" He reached for her arm and gently tugged her back, as she'd already started up the hill toward the parking area.

"I'm fine."

With a bent finger, Taylor lifted her chin so that she would meet his eyes. "No you're not."

After a visible swallow, she sniffed.

Taylor pressed his lips together hard, then glanced over his shoulder. The *Haven* was still docked, the gangway not pulled up. With a quick plea for strength, he brought his gaze back to her. "There's still time. You can get on the ferry."

Her brows folded inward. “What?”

“You can go. If you want.”

Tears glazed those beautiful eyes that should be dancing with love and joy. After a long, silent stare, she shook her head. “I’m not going with Donovan.” She swallowed hard again, then cleared her throat. “I’m married to you.”

Relief and agony dropped with equal weight in his heart. She’d not go back on their agreement, because she was a faithful woman who kept her word. And he . . . he might be keeping her from reconciling with the love of her life.

His breath quavered as he exhaled. “Sonora—”

She held up a hand, cutting him off with a firm shake of her head. “I just want to get out of here, okay?” Then turning back toward the truck, she marched away.

In a muddle of such big, mixed emotions, Taylor could do nothing but follow her. And pray for the endurance and resolve to trust God with an open hand.

Twenty-Three

The last week in September turned cool with telling speed. Fall was upon them, and soon enough, the first killing frost.

Sonora loved watching the island slip into its fall glory. The maples and oaks turned their brilliant oranges and bright reds. Saturated yellows and the rich green of the evergreens dotted the color palette, creating a background that could only be described as splendid.

Yet the days became long and uncomfortable. Stilted.

Taylor had pulled away, and Sonora couldn't understand why. Several weeks ago their evenings had been full of games of checkers or quiet, amicable silent reading. More recently—and wonderfully—evenings had been spent snuggling on that small couch, and a few times, kissing. This past week, though, Taylor had taken himself down to tend the horses after dinner, and then he'd disappeared. When she'd asked him one evening where he'd gone, his simple answer had been, "For a walk." And then he'd given her his back, said he was changing for bed. That was it.

He'd closed himself off to her again.

What had she done? The confusion made her angry. Why was he upset with her? She'd sent Donovan packing, leaving no room for anything to sprout between them ever again. Shouldn't that make Taylor happy?

Or was he scared now? Had they become too much too soon, and now Taylor wasn't sure?

It would help if they could just have a conversation about it. But that would require Taylor to be around her when they weren't working. He managed to avoid that. Somehow they always had passengers—even on their first morning run. Sonora couldn't help but suspect that he'd recruited them—which was certainly not his normal practice. Perhaps it should have been—the extra tips were nice. But it wasn't.

For a full week he'd evaded her, and she grew more upset.

On the second day of October, they woke up to a light frost. The zinnias and dahlias that had been a riot of color in the garden between the carriage house and the main building of the Palace wore a dusting of diamonds in the early morning sun. While the effect was brilliant, Sonora's heart sank. She turned from the window that overlooked the garden, catching Taylor as he strode from the back room to the door from which he'd make his silent escape. Again.

"It frosted," she said.

Taylor became a statue, his hand partially raised, reaching for the door. His profile became rigid, though she thought he winced. Then he lowered his hand and crossed the space between them to look out the window.

His exhale seemed part relief, part sorrow. "It's not a killing frost."

"The flowers will recover?"

"Not the ones that got nipped, but if you look beyond that patch"—he pointed to the garden that bordered the path toward the golf course—"you'll see that those have not been touched."

"So it's not the frost that determines Al and Vicky's departure?"

Taylor shook his head.

Sonora studied him, her heart lifting at his nearness. He hadn't stood this close to her since the moment he'd asked her if she was all right down at the harbor. Did he miss her touch as much as she missed his?

Goodness, but she longed for those affectionate blue gazes. The thrill of his fingertips skimming her arms, her fingers, her face. The tender smile he seemed to reserve for only her. The sweet, reverent way he kissed her.

"Taylor." Her whisper cracked between them.

His face turned to her, and those blue eyes melted from cold and distant to warm and gentle.

She dared to close the space between them, slipping her fingers into his hand. "Why have you shut me out?"

He visibly swallowed. "Our time together is coming to an end."

"But—"

He shook his head. Squeezed her hand. "The horses need to go back south the day after the Frostmas Celebration, and you're taking them. That was the deal. That was what we . . . promised."

"No. Something happened last week, and you're not telling me what it was. Ever since Donovan showed up, you've been rebuilding walls between us."

Taylor's face tipped toward the floor, and he reopened the gap between them. After a long pause, he nodded. "I don't want to be the reason you don't get to have a second chance with him, if that's what you want."

"You're not." Sonora crossed her arms. "He's married."

Taylor's eyes flashed up. "That's not what he—"

"And even if he wasn't, he's a liar. Not to mention unfaithful. I don't want anything to do with him."

He winced twice, as if she'd fired those first two accusations at him, then he rubbed the back of his neck. "I wasn't honest with you either."

"When?"

He straightened, forced his eyes to connect with hers again while he laid his hand on the windowsill. "When I didn't tell you he was here alone—and that he was looking for you and wanted to win you back."

"That's not the same." Sonora stepped forward and gripped his arm. "Taylor, I know you were trying to protect me, and I wasn't mad about it. I wasn't one bit upset with you."

His jaw shifted.

"Is that what this is? You thought I was mad?"

"No . . . I don't know." He sighed. "I wasn't happy with myself about it. I wasn't honest—and I promised you that I would be. You're right—I wanted to protect you. But it wasn't just that. I wanted to . . . keep you from him. For myself. I was protecting myself as much as I was looking out for you—likely more."

This was agony for him—that he was human. It was almost . . . adorable. Sonora slipped her hand up his arm. "So you're saying you might be selfish at times?"

"It's not funny."

"It's a little bit funny."

He smirked—which was close enough to a smile for her to count as a win. But as quickly as it came, the traces of amusement faded from his expression. "Sonora, I want you to stay with me. I want, more than I can say, to keep running headlong into this glorious whirlwind we're caught up in."

"Why do I sense a *but* coming?"

"Because there is one. I don't want to be your rebound mistake. And I don't want you to wake up some day and wish we had slowed down."

"Why do you think I will?"

"I just think we both need to take some time to really search our hearts. And to pray."

And to pray? Her brows lifted. "That . . . sounds like you're willing to trust God again."

Emotion twisted his expression—a painful yielding that broke her heart and lifted hope all at once. "I read something the other day about God asking us to trust Him with our emptiness as much as we would with our abundance. I want that. I want to be a man of faith who isn't tossed around in life by circumstances. To hold up what I love most and say, *Your will be done.* I want to be able to forgive my mom and dad—and beyond that, to see that there was *good* in their move. For them and for my sister. And even for me. Because there was. It was selfish of me to hold it against them all this time."

Wow. How had this turned from a conversation that felt like it was careening toward a breakup to this? So much hard honesty . . . Surely he wouldn't open his heart like that if he didn't trust her. If he didn't love her.

"I love that, Taylor. I want the same—to work on trusting God more with the things that have been disappointing."

He nodded. "You seem to be pretty good at it. You live with this unquenchable joy, and I love that about you."

Love . . . about her. Did he love her though? "Where does that leave us?"

He touched her braid, resting on her shoulder, then settled an honest look on her. "I want more. More from myself. More for you. More faith and depth and joy. I think that requires time and prayer."

She bit her bottom lip, struggling to process all that. What she really wanted was all the feels that had flared between them before.

But she also wanted what they'd found to last. And . . . she wanted the *more* Taylor was talking about too—the faith and depth and joy. From herself. For both of them. And between them and God.

So perhaps that meant he was right, even if she didn't love it. On a slow exhale, she nodded.

Taylor brushed the side of her face with the back of his knuckles and then walked away.

Taylor hitched Al and Vicky alone, as he'd done for the past week, while Sonora changed into her uniform. After he secured the last buckle, he paused, bracing his forearms against Al's shoulder. Bowing his head, he reached for the practice he'd been working on making a habit—prayer.

Lord, give me the faith to trust. You do good. You provide. Let Your will be done.

He felt his reemerging faith waver, like a sapling bending against a fierce gale. This was hard—not gripping Sonora with everything he had. What he'd said to her upstairs had been the truth—he desperately wanted her to stay. To scratch the deal that she'd take the horses south and that would be the end of their marriage of convenience. He didn't want their marriage to end at all.

But like the killing frosts that they celebrated on the island, perhaps one thing must end for another to begin.

That idea had seeped into his heart as he'd taken his long, solo walks the past week on the path that wound through the golf course and led to the rocky shoreline near the lighthouse. He'd landed at the very place he and Sonora had gone for their sunrise picnic—the spot where he'd kissed her.

There he had sat, the lake winds combing through his hair and his heart intentionally laid bare before God. Through prayer and reading a book he'd found in his mother's collection—a library of old prayers called *Through the Valley*—he had found solace and a fresh way of thinking.

Where he'd thought to try to convince Sonora to stay—which apparently wouldn't be necessary—he'd found the conviction to let her go. To encourage it, even.

Only—he hoped—not forever.

They both had things they needed to reconcile. Old wounds that needed the attention of the Great Physician. And relationships that needed mending. Perhaps then they would have a real shot at a deep, loving, lasting forever together.

If that was what Sonora still wanted.

That last part was the hardest. If he let her go, would she come back? And if she didn't, would he go back to giving God the cold, silent shoulder?

To the last question, he prayed fervently that the answer would be a wholehearted *no.* Actually, to both, he prayed for a favorable answer. But it was paramount that he find, grow, and live in a much more stable faith. One that would allow him to be the faithful, good man he wanted to be no matter what happened or didn't happen.

It was in these times of quiet, independent soul offerings the whisper of hope had come. The killing frost signaled the end of the busy tourist season—which was the lifeblood of the island. But everyone there celebrated it—because one season must end for another to begin. So, perhaps, it would be with his marriage.

The marriage of convenience must end, and then, he prayed, a new, real one could begin.

October 9.

That was the date of the first hard frost on Sanctuary Island—thus, it was Frostmas. All around the Palace, echoes of *Happy Frostmas* peeled from every employee—seasonal or full-time resident alike. Smiles, equal in enthusiasm to Christmas Day, shone from every worker's face. Some tourists would cast a puzzled glance here and there, eventually asking, *What's going on?* And a cheerful longtimer would say, *It's Frostmas!* and go on grinning.

Sonora tried to fit in with the rest of the Palace employees, returning the *Happy Frostmas* calls with equal gusto. She was certain her efforts fell flat. Summoning that sort of excitement felt about as impossible as swimming back to the shores of Havensport. She didn't even really have the desire to try.

The Frostmas Ball—attended by all the Palace employees, as well as many of the residents on Sanctuary Island—would be held on Saturday. Gourmet food would be served, as the next week was sure to be a down week in terms of tourists—until the special-event weekend for the Pumpkin Carving Extravaganza the weekend before Halloween. The special foods remaining in the Palace kitchen would not be used.

It was not to be wasted though. And thus the annual Frostmas Ball had been born—this according to Candi, the woman who'd trimmed Sonora's hair last week. Candi knew *everything*—some of it true, much of it exaggerated. That had been Taylor's warning when Sonora had told him she was getting her hair done. At least with the Frostmas Ball, the woman's facts seemed confirmed. Sonora's marriage circumstances, however, had certainly been, uh . . . embellished. She'd had to set the record straight.

No, she was not a mail-order bride from Russia, escaping political persecution.

No, she was not part of WITSEC, and yes, Sonora was her real name. (Though Candi didn't seem to entirely believe her on that.)

No, Taylor did not have cancer and only had a year left to live, thus he'd sent for a wife to carry his child so his name would not die. (Could anyone imagine Taylor Everest doing such a thing?)

Sonora didn't give the honest version of how her marriage to Taylor came about though. As with every other time, she repeated the meeting-online version. In other words, she'd lied.

The guilt of that charade joined the agony of knowing her time on the island, and with Taylor, had come to an end. What was Happy Frostmas to everyone else was Sadly Leaving to her.

But it wouldn't be forever. Sonora had tasted her forever, and it was there on the shores of Sanctuary Island, with Taylor Everest. She would come back.

With that thought as her refuge, she summoned her best smile and repeated the greeting to others. *Happy Frostmas* to Rachel in the dining room—Candi's sister, and hence from whom the news of Taylor's marriage had traveled from the Palace to the chatty hairstylist. *Happy Frostmas* to Ethan Chamberlin, the head groundskeeper at the Shore View Palace and the one who had carefully cut several of the best blooms over the past week so that Aiden, the Palace's florist, could make some stunning arrangements for the ball.

Happy Frostmas to Gretta, who returned the greeting with a reserve that hinted she knew Sonora's false cheer. And *Happy Frostmas* to Curtis. Curtis did not return the greeting. He simply lifted his brow, held a steady look on her, and then tilted his head as if to ask silently, *Is it?*

No. But she would get through it.

Sonora's acting continued through the day, and by the end of it, her face hurt from the effort of maintaining a smile.

Taylor noticed. "You look tired," He kept the comment between them at the table in the employee's dining room.

Sonora held a long look on him, letting her heart bleed into the silence. "It doesn't feel like a happy Frostmas."

He reached across the small space between his hand and hers and covered her fingers. "I know." He squeezed her hand, then his thumb caressed her palm. "Would it help if I officially ask you to go to the Frostmas Ball with me on Saturday night?"

Though she still wanted to cry, she chuckled. When he flirted, Taylor Everest was adorable. "It might. A little. It would justify the dress I borrowed from Chloe."

Lifting her hand, he kissed her knuckles. "Sonora Hillary, will you do me the honor of attending the Frostmas Ball as my date?"

"Can I go as your wife?" She raised her eyebrows, anticipating the deepening of those dark-blue eyes.

He did not disappoint her. "That was the deal." His voice cut on the end of that, and he visibly swallowed.

Sonora had to overcome her own swell of emotion. "Then ask me as Sonora Everest."

Taylor pressed her hand to his heart. "Sonora Hillary-Everest, will you be my date to the ball?"

With a disapproving tilt of her head at the use of her hyphenated name, she made him wait several heartbeats for her answer.

He leaned close, his lips hovering near her ear. "Please."

Sonora's heart stumbled and her tummy did a flip, as his lips were the barest touch on her skin. "Yes."

Taylor leaned back, then lifted her knuckles to his lips again.

Sonora's head swam in a muddle of delight and dread. How was she supposed to say goodbye to this man when he held her whole heart?

Taylor walked through the week like he was barely alive. He barely heard what others said—and only responded with a nod or a shake of his head. Sleep was a thing not to be had. Eating . . . ghosts didn't need nourishment, apparently. The only moments the dead numbness faded were in the predawn mornings, when he took himself out for a walk near the lighthouse, spending the time in prayer and meditation, and the evenings spent with Sonora.

She would snuggle against him on that blessed small couch, snaking her arms around him. He fingered those soft tresses of honey. Sometimes they would talk—she shared more about how much distance she'd put between her and her parents, and that she regretted it. He told her he wanted to spend Christmas with his family this year—a first in over a decade. But the topic of their marriage . . . neither broached it. He didn't want her to feel pressure from him, if he brought it up. As for her silence on it . . . Taylor couldn't say why for sure.

And so the rest of the week went.

Now . . . she was leaving. Tomorrow. But they had the ball—one final evening together. As he dressed in the one suit he owned that was not his uniform, nerves ran like cars on a super-freeway, zipping and weaving and causing his hands to tremble as he fixed his tie.

He'd not had a date to this ball in years—and hadn't particularly cared about that. Most times he made an appearance, because Curtis would pester him if he didn't, and that was about it. The next day, his practice was to load Albert and Victoria onto the *Haven*, ride the ferry with them to Havensport, and then transfer the pair to the transportation company he'd arranged to take them south for the winter.

And that was the case this year too. Except this year, Sonora would ride the ferry in his place and see the horses all the way down to southern Michigan.

Without him.

A tap came from inside the bathroom. "Taylor? Are you decent?"

"I am." He cast one last glance at himself in the mirror before he exited the bedroom that Sonora had occupied for the past two months. With a quick inhale, he locked in the memory of her scent—something warm and lemony that made him think of summer sunshine. With a hard exhale, he put away the swell of emotions. "I'll meet you in the front room."

He'd barely reached the fireplace on the far side of the small living room when the swish of skirts had him turning around. His heart stalled, and all he could do was stare. Sonora stopped a few steps away.

Certainly she was the most beautiful woman he'd ever seen.

Likely he'd forget that the dress she wore was a full-length wine-colored confection, leaving her creamy shoulders exposed to tease his fingers. He wasn't keen to remember that she'd let her hair drape around her neck in soft drifts of loose curls. He might even forget that she wore earrings—small drops of pearls that drew attention to the skin just beneath them in the most agonizing way.

But he'd never forget that his wife was stunning.

"Will I do?" Hesitancy laced her soft voice.

Likely because he'd been mute—dumbfounded and lost in a heady haze—for an uncomfortable space of time.

"You are beautiful." Taylor shook himself into action and stepped forward. He took both of her hands in his and bent to kiss her cheek. "I have thought so from the beginning, you know."

"No, you didn't." She leaned back and laughed. "You said you had no use for a cowgirl."

"That was only because I saw you from the gangway and my heart did some kind of ridiculous fluttering thing and my head felt light. I knew then that bringing you home was trouble."

She tugged her hand free from his and cupped his jawline. "Am I troubling you, Taylor Everest?"

He shut his eyes while his fingers traced the length of her bare arm. "I can't think straight at the moment."

And then his lips were on hers. Their kisses grew in fervor, and Taylor allowed more than he ever had in the past. He kissed her with fire and unbridled passion, as he'd wished he could all week. Where before he'd kept a firm grip on self-control, now that discipline faded quickly, and he found himself caught in the strong tide of desire.

He couldn't say where he found the strength to pull back. But he did—which was pure torment. Even if it was the right thing to do.

Sonora didn't care that her dress—borrowed from Chloe at the Bluebell—was being crushed. Or that her hair would be a mess. Or that her carefully applied makeup would likely be smudged. She only wanted Taylor, and the depth of his passion for her was breathtaking.

But then—

With a low growl, his kisses ended, leaving her lips tingling, her heart pounding, and her body chilled as his warmth no longer pressed against her.

A small cry cracked from her throat as Taylor put space between them. She curled her fingers into the lapel of his suit coat. "We're married," she whispered.

Those intense blue eyes, full of passion and yet restraint, locked on hers. His right hand moved from the gentle hold he'd had on her arm to cup her face, and he traced her cheek with the pad of his thumb.

Sonora covered his hand with her own, turning to press a kiss into his palm. "This can be real, Taylor. *We* can be real."

He nodded, though his brow folded, as if he felt pain. "I can't tell you how much I want that." His voice came low and hoarse, and then his wince deepened as he shook his head. "But I don't want to be one of your regrets."

His words pierced her heart, and tears burned in her eyes. "That would never happen."

Taylor didn't move. His hold remained gentle, though he firmly kept a gap between them. His stare was both tender and fierce. After several throbbing heartbeats, he finally leaned forward and kissed her forehead. Then he moved back, letting his hand fall away from her face. Though he remained close enough to twine her fingers with his, the space between them felt like the distance between Sanctuary Island and Havensport.

"Taylor—"

He shook his head and squeezed her hands, cutting off her argument before she could begin. "We need to think."

"But—"

"We had a plan. We made a promise."

Her heart crumbled, and a tear leaked from the corner of one eye. "Scrap the plan. There is a lot between us that wasn't part of the plan."

"Yes, there is so much between us." He caught her tear with the back of his knuckle and wiped it away. "And no, it wasn't part of the plan. This was a beautiful surprise."

She lifted her head, hope surging upward.

"But emotions can be fickle, especially in heated moments."

She couldn't argue the heated-moment part . . . Those kisses had been fire. But what was he saying? "This thing between us doesn't only exist in the heated moments. You're the first thing I think of when I wake up, and I wonder how many times I can make you smile, because it thrills me. And I hope that I make your life better."

His furrowed brow smoothed. "You do make my life better. Infinitely better. But we need to think clearly about this"—he motioned between them—"because once I give a promise, I aim to keep it."

The love she felt for him only expanded. "Till death do we part."

He nodded, his steady gaze searching her.

Maybe she needed to lay it all on the line.

"I feel like there's a *but* coming." This was feeling like a conversation they'd already had.

"No. No *but* attached to that." He lowered his head, cradling her face between his hands. "There's so much about you that I . . ." He drew in a deep breath. "I'm pretty sure I'm in love with you, Sonora."

Closing her eyes, she smiled. "I'm pretty sure I'm in love with you too, Taylor." She opened her eyes and found him studying her. And what he was saying became clear. This was Taylor, after all. Scheduled. Precise. Responsible. Faithful. She couldn't not fault any of that. "You want to be certain."

"I want us both to be certain."

Which was why he'd suggested they stick with the plan. She would take Albert and Victoria to the mainland and see them to the winter grounds. They would take the time apart to think.

It didn't thrill her—not the way those kisses had several minutes back. But it wasn't a bad plan. No, in fact, it was a responsible plan. And in doing so, they both could hold up their heart's desires to God, open handed, and trust Him to provide direction. Even if it was excruciating to do so.

She blinked against the moisture in her eyes and nodded. "Okay."

"Okay?"

"I'll take Al and Vicky. We'll leave on the ferry tomorrow."

He didn't smile—not the way one would when they'd won. In fact, a touch of fear sneaked into his dark-blue eyes.

Sonora lifted to her toes and kissed him. "I'm not going to change my mind."

Taylor pulled her in close and held her tight. Like he really didn't want to let her go. After several minutes, he stepped back. "There is a ball tonight, and my wife is too lovely not to show off."

Sonora accepted his offered hand, and together they walked into the chilly fall evening. Off to the Frostmas Ball. Her first . . . of many if she got her way.

Twenty-Four

The lake was choppy, as an autumn storm stirred the waters. Morning had dawned gray and sullen—appropriate, Taylor decided.

Molly and Pete had been retrieved from the farm—he and Sonora had gone on Friday night in preparation for Albert and Victoria's departure. Now the smaller pair waited patiently on the side of Harbor Way while Taylor and Sonora walked Al and Vicky to the docks. A cold gust blasted in the unhindered harbor, robbing Sonora of the hood of her jacket.

She let it fall and stay. Taylor reached to tug it back up over her braid.

Once at the docks, they walked to the gangway and went single file onto the waiting ferry. They followed the top deck to the ramp that led down to the lower level, where Al and Vicky would ride in a stock stall that was rarely used. Setting both animals in was done with quiet words of reassurance to the horses—but nothing between Taylor and Sonora.

Not until goodbye was necessary. Which came far too soon.

Taylor turned and faltered. But Sonora didn't hesitate. She took his hand, stepped into his space, and lifted to her toes so that her mouth would reach his. For a moment Taylor leaned in and indulged in the lingering flame that had been a raging fire the evening before. But then he lifted his head, breaking the last kiss.

"I guess . . ."

Sonora shook her head and smiled. "Not goodbye. I'll be back."

His lips pressed tight. He wanted to believe her. Mostly, he did believe her. But this scene felt too much like déjà vu. It shouldn't have—not to the extent that it did. After all, Iris had left by plane, and she never would have walked one of Taylor's giant Friesians onto the ferry, let alone ride with two of them on her own to Havensport.

Even so, the woman he'd hoped to spend forever with was going, and there was a possibility that she might stay gone.

Lord, help me to trust You, no matter what . . .

He forced a tight grin and nodded. "Not until you're truly ready, and if you find that it isn't right—"

With a scowl she gave him a vehement headshake.

The ache in Taylor's heart eased by degrees. *If* Sonora hurt him, it would not be done carelessly. He took her hand and pulled it up to his chest. "Sonora, I know you feel certain now, as do I, but *if* . . . if, through prayer and time and careful thought, you find that it isn't right, all I ask is that you tell me. Don't ghost me. Just be honest."

Those lovely copper eyes turned to warm summer evenings and sweet, gentle songs as she held him in her gaze. "Okay, Taylor. I promise to be honest with you. No matter what."

He could trust her for that. And it felt good.

Taylor leaned in for a last kiss goodbye and turned to leave the ferry as the departure horn blew.

The day he'd been dreading had come. He'd survived. Tomorrow would be a new day.

As he walked the gangway and then strode toward the smaller carriage and waiting Haflingers, he thought on the psalm he'd read just last night—a verse found in chapter 31: *But I trust in you, O Lord; I say "You are my God." My times are in your hand.*

He climbed up to the driver's seat and stole one final glance at the *Haven* as it puttered out of the harbor to open water.

"My times are in Your hands." He pushed back the impulse to panic—to thrash and demand that God make sure that his wife come back to him—and instead firmly placed his heart in the palms that held heaven and earth.

Jill Everest was exactly as Sonora had imagined, based on Taylor's description. The day she arrived at the Everest home, Sonora came face to face with the bubbly young woman wearing a pair of boxer-braids, trendy bib overalls, and the most winning dimpled grin that Sonora had ever seen.

"Hi!" Jill had opened the front door wide at Sonora's knock and looked like she was ready to meet another new friend. "Can I help you?"

"Are you Jill?"

She giggled, her feet moving in a little dance. "That's me! How did you know that?"

"Your brother says that you are the happiest person on earth and would never meet anyone with less than a luminous smile." Sonora winked, loving that she got to use one of Taylor's less-than-common adjectives.

Jill laughed and clapped her hands. "Oh yes—Taylor would say that. He uses *outlandish* words. He taught me that one when I was little! Isn't it a great word?" Her enthusiasm paused as she suddenly realized she didn't know the woman she was sharing joyful memories about her brother with. She leaned in dramatically. "How do you know my brother?"

Sonora leaned in, mirroring the dramatic pose. "Between you and me, I married him."

"What!" Gleeful energy reemerged as Jill's blue eyes grew moon sized. "Shut the front door! Get out of town! No way! You married my brother? That's . . . that's wild!" She spun on her heel and left the door hanging wide open and empty. "Mom! Mom, guess what!"

Oh boy. Maybe Sonora should have thought that through more carefully. But she'd thought that Taylor had told his family by now. Hadn't they talked about it when they'd had ice cream in town square?

Within a minute a lovely woman in her late fifties appeared at the door, Jill bouncing behind her. The woman had dark hair, like Taylor's, streaked with silver that glittered in the sunlight as she stepped onto the front stoop. Concern lined her brow. "I'm Hope Everest." She smiled, though there was a tightness to it. "I think my daughter has misunderstood something."

"I'm sorry." Sonora fiddled with her hands behind her back. "That is my fault. Not that Jill misunderstood." Heat rushed into her face. "It's just that I shouldn't have sprung that sort of news on her—on you—like that. It wasn't well thought out. I'm sure Taylor would not be impressed—"

"You're saying it's true?" Mrs. Everest's eyes grew to the same size Jill's had moments before. "You're . . . married? To my . . . to Taylor?"

Mentally, Sonora face-palmed her forehead as all her gusto deflated. She'd spoiled everything. What was she thinking, springing this on this poor woman? What mother would be thrilled to have a stranger show up at her front door saying she'd married her only son? But *Taylor!* Why hadn't he told them?

Sonora drew a breath and nodded. "Yes, ma'am. I am your son's wife."

"Taylor . . . is married?" The woman blinked. Stared. Blinked again. Swallowed. "When . . . how long . . ."

Sonora bowed her head and shut her eyes. At least she'd already sorted this part through—that she would be honest with Taylor's parents about the circumstances of their marriage. Mostly because she had assumed that Taylor would have already spilled the whole story. She was still reeling with shock that he hadn't. But this was the field she was playing in.

Sonora raised her eyes and met her mother-in-law's. "We were married in August. Taylor put out an ad in an equine magazine for . . . a wife. A woman who could drive the Friesians and who would be willing to enter a temporary marriage so that the clause in his contract with the Shore View Palace would be satisfied. He and Gretta had a little . . . conflict, and the marriage clause came up."

"That clause is still . . ." Hope Everest shook her head. "How could that . . ." Clearly the woman was too baffled to complete a sentence. "Taylor advertised for . . ."

"Curtis talked him into it, and Taylor didn't believe anyone sane enough to marry would answer it, so he thought nothing would actually come of it." She shrugged. "I guess he deemed me *not crazy* enough, and here we are."

"Ohmigosh!" Jill squealed. "That's the most romantic story I ever heard of in real life! And it's *my brother's* story!" After feigning a swoon, she pushed past her mother and latched on to Sonora's arm. "I guess that makes us sisters, right?"

Sonora gave Jill a grateful smile, though she eyed Mrs. Everest's reaction. "It does."

"The marriage—is it to be temporary? I mean, is that what you agreed to?"

"Obviously not, Mom!" Jill bounced. "Or why would she come here to tell us?"

Mrs. Everest's brows lifted.

"Jill is right—things changed between Taylor and me. I . . . love him."

The lines in the older woman's brow eased, and a genuine, albeit small, smile replaced the frown. "I think you'd better come in . . . uh, I'm sorry—what is your name?"

"Sonora." She sighed with relief. "Sonora Hillary-Everest. Though I intend to drop the Hillary part."

"I have a sister!" Jill leaped away from Sonora and went into a little impromptu dance. "I have a sister. Her name is Sonora. I get to keep her. Foreva and foreva!" She covered her mouth and giggled. "That doesn't actually rhyme. Don't tell Taylor."

Mrs. Everest laughed. "Your brother would not correct you, Jilly. Never you."

Ah. So Mom had kept the ties alive between Jill and Taylor, even though Taylor had let them slip. Gratitude welled in Sonora's heart on Taylor's behalf. As he'd said, there were fences to mend, but it might not take as much with Jill as Taylor had feared.

However, they were going to have a chat about this not-telling-his-family-about-their-marriage issue.

As she followed the two women into the charming craftsman-style house, Sonora focused her thoughts on the moment. Mrs. Everest seemed kind. After all, she didn't freak out. Better than Sonora would have likely done. She could have done worse when it came to in-laws. Once again, it appeared that God had shown favor on her life, even in the reckless, foolish choice that she'd made.

And she was grateful.

Taylor rarely used FaceTime. Then again, he rarely called anyone. But when Sonora's name, along with a picture of the two of them together at the ball, flashed on his screen, he didn't hesitate to answer. Though he did discipline his expression not to appear too desperate to talk to her again. That wouldn't align with his parting speech about taking time to seriously think and pray, and all the rest.

"Hello." He spoke with quiet seriousness.

"Wow. I don't even get a smile?"

One corner of his mouth rebelliously poked up. "The game is always on for you, isn't it?"

"Unearthing your smile is one of my favorite pastimes."

"That is a strange fascination."

She shrugged. Then winked. "Guess what?"

While a sensation of thrilling pleasure zipped through him at her unbridled flirting (*with him—how was he that lucky?)*, Taylor maintained his unaffected mask. "You made it safely."

"No." She rolled her eyes. "I mean, yes, I made it safely—and we need to talk about something related to that in a minute."

Oh boy. That sounded serious.

"But that's not the thing you're guessing."

"No? Fine. I give up."

"What?"

"I surrender."

"That is a mediocre word. Try again."

"I acquiesce that I am the loser of this game. Please tell me what it is I cannot guess."

Her snort-laugh was one of the most charming things he'd ever heard. "That is an acceptable answer. Don't you think, Jill?"

Suddenly his sister was on the screen, grinning with all the delight of life unspoiled. His heart squeezed with pain and joy. His baby sister . . . and Sonora? They were together? That meant . . .

Oh. Oh man. He was in trouble. Why hadn't he considered that Sonora would go see his family after she took Al and Vicky to the winter grounds? Granted, it would not be something that he would do if the tables were turned, but Sonora? Of course she would.

He knew why though.

Jill brought the phone up close to her face so all he could see were her dancing blue eyes.

"Jilly-Fish, that's too close." He tried to disguise his discomfort with the situation with a gentle tone. "I can't see your face."

"I was just checking to see if that's really you. I haven't seen you in *forever!*"

The dagger sank deeper. "You can't see me any better by holding the phone to your nose. And I called you on your birthday."

"Yep. And I got your present. Know what would be better than a gift card?" She paused only long enough to breathe. "You coming to see me instead. We had ice cream cake, Taylor! Ice. Cream. Cake. And you missed it. Again."

This video call was turning into a full guilt session. "That sounds delicious. I'm sorry I missed it."

"Delicious? No, Taylor. It was *scrumptious.* You are losing your touch."

"Oh."

"I have a question." Jill didn't leave much space for him to respond to that either. "Why are you not here with your wife? That is weird."

And . . . his heart stalled. Sonora had told them. Of course she'd told them—she'd gone to meet them. But. Man. This just kept getting worse. *This is why you don't lie!*

He hadn't lied. Sort of. He'd just not . . . told the truth. He hadn't said anything at all.

"Sonora said you didn't have a wedding." Jill popped the gum in her mouth and shook her head, then she moved the phone so that Sonora was also in view behind her. "I think we *definitely* have to fix that."

Taylor focused on Sonora's face beyond Jill's. She was pink with a blush and mouthed *sorry*. He kept his eyes fixed on her, silently asking what to do next.

Sonora stepped closer to Jill, and by the shift of the picture, he guessed she'd taken the phone back. "A marriage doesn't require a wedding."

Jill turned and gave Sonora her classic one-raised-brow-I-don't-believe-you look. "That is false."

Sonora laughed, bopped Jill's nose with her finger, and then hugged her. "Can you give me a few minutes to talk with your brother? I'll make sure he calls to talk to you more after supper."

Jill looked at the phone—at Taylor. "Promise?"

"Pinky-promise, Jilly-Fish."

She pressed her pinky finger to the camera on the phone. "Are you pinky-ing?"

Taylor couldn't help but chuckle as he did as his sister demanded. "I'm pinky-ing. But that is not a real word."

Her finger vanished from the screen, and her grinning face was back in view. "It is now!" Jill blew a big kiss—one at

Taylor and another at Sonora. "See ya later, tater!" And then she was gone.

Several silent moments beat by like a low drum while Sonora closed the door to the room his parents kept for him, for his rare visits. She settled on the bed, leaning against the headboard, and held a long look on him.

He was definitely in trouble. As he should be.

"You went to meet my family."

"Yes. I did."

"And told them."

"I thought that you had already told them."

Pressing his lips tight, he looked down, shaking his head.

"Taylor, you knew I was coming this way. You *sent* me. Why wouldn't you tell them?"

He met her stare on the screen. Surprisingly, she wasn't livid. She was . . . confused? Concerned?

"I didn't want to explain what happened if you didn't come back."

Sadness dampened her expression. "You really think I won't, don't you?"

"I really want you to do what you believe is best for you. I want you to have the freedom to choose, to not feel trapped. That was the original agreement—that you would be free after—"

"You keep going back to that. Is it because you feel trapped?"

"No." The thought that she even had an inkling that he didn't want to stay with her broke his heart. "No, Sonora."

"Tell me what you want, Taylor."

He thought hard on that—not because he didn't know what he wanted. "I can't think of anything I want more than a life with you. Perhaps to be a better man, but after that, I want for you to be my wife. For real, forever."

"Why is it so hard for you to believe that I want the same thing?"

Because he didn't deserve her. Because he was the sort of person people left behind. Or didn't understand. Or didn't want to be around. Because if he believed that she would come back to him, and it wasn't the truth, he didn't want to fall back into the sort of disappointment that led him to be a bitter, unpleasant person.

But that was his choice either way. He could believe that God had his heart, his times, his hopes, his dreams, and his disappointments, and no matter what, he could trust God to see him through. Then he wouldn't have to be cast into the darkness of bitterness and loneliness.

"Taylor."

He refocused on the beautiful woman on the screen. His wife.

"I love you." She said it with such clear conviction.

Taylor blinked against the overwhelming emotion of loving and being loved in return. Even in the midst of a situation that he shouldn't have allowed, she was kind and loving to him. Though he found it hard to breathe with so much swelling in his heart, he forced the words free. "I love you too."

Her smile was soft and made him wish he was there with her. Then she drew a sharp breath. "I'm glad we got that cleared up. You need to call your parents. Taylor, they miss you. And they love you. And . . . maybe you don't realize this, but they've allowed the distance between you and them because they thought you would not forgive them. They didn't realize that your silence was pain, not hard anger. And also, they made sure Jill knew nothing about the strain between you and them. They only ever say good things about you to her and have worked to keep you fresh and wonderful in her heart."

Taylor's heart burst, and tears swelled in his eyes. Twelve years of bitterness and loneliness broke free. Why had he allowed it all to fester? He hadn't realized . . . hadn't seen.

But for this woman. No, she was the instrument. But it was bigger than her. Bigger than them.

But for the grace of God.

He nodded, finding that tears stood in Sonora's eyes, mirroring his.

"New beginnings start now."

Again he nodded.

"Me too." She cleared her throat. "I'm going to be gone a couple weeks. I need to go mend my own fences with my parents."

"I think you should."

"But I'm coming back, Taylor."

Lightness entered his heart, like the breaking of the sun after a storm. Warmth and peace took the place of tumult.

Taylor smiled. "Take your time. I'll be here, waiting."

Twenty-Five

There it was. Little Sanctuary, its shores edged with a dusting of light snow. From the air, the island looked like a small green blob against a dark-blue-and-white canvas. Eager palpitations thumped in Sonora's veins as Angelica, the pilot, told her to prepare for landing.

Oh. She was *so* ready!

Two weeks felt simultaneously like forever and a blink. It had been time well spent, reestablishing a firm relationship with both her parents—first her mom and then her dad. The time spent with Dad had been harder and more emotional. But it'd been worth the struggle, and they were on much better terms. Dad had apologized for his unfaithfulness, for the pain it had caused both her mother and herself, and for breaking apart their family.

Things weren't perfect—but when were they, really? They were so much better though. And by her daily conversations with Taylor, his relationships were well on the way to restoration as well.

And as for the rest of those phone conversations . . . The interval of distance had somehow pulled their hearts together tighter. Sonora nearly swooned every time she reflected on how their calls ended—with Taylor asking if she'd mind if he prayed.

Could there be a more attractive thing in a man than a heart bent before God? She thought not.

With a fluttering of wings tickling her chest, Sonora stepped off the *Sky Angel* and met Angelica on the solid surface of the ground.

"That was one of the smoothest flights ever," Sonora said.

Angelica grinned. "I aim to please."

"Thanks for doing this. It was impulsive, I know."

She could have taken the ferry—the *Haven* was still running on a *weather pending* basis. But the *Haven* wasn't doing multiple crossings this time of year—too much fuel and not enough passengers. That meant she'd have to wait, and she just couldn't. Impatience had overcome practicality. She'd called Angelica, whom she'd met a few times on the island, and asked if she could charter a flight as soon as possible. With a knowing laugh, Angelica said she'd be there in thirty minutes.

The pilot laughed. "Some things can't wait." She patted Sonora's arm and stepped out of the way.

Curtis waited with his vehicle on the other side of the landing strip—another phone call that Sonora had made after she'd secured a flight.

Sonora grabbed her luggage—which was only one bag of several that she'd packed, but the others would cross on the ferry later. After it nearly dropped to the ground, she hefted it toward the vehicle.

Curtis left the car and jogged to meet her halfway. "Let me get this."

She smiled with gratitude. "You didn't tell him, right?"

"He's expecting you on the boat in about four hours."

Giddiness filled her. "Perfect. Is he still at the Palace?"

"Nope. Went back to the farm to help the Klines with the pumpkin harvest."

"Also perfect."

Curtis loaded her suitcase into the trunk of his SUV. "I take it this means you'll be staying with us."

"Correct."

He crossed his arms and chuckled. "I knew it would all work out."

Sonora smacked his shoulder. "You knew nothing of the sort—and don't pull that sort of thing with anyone else. It's irresponsible."

"I am an expert matchmaker."

"You didn't even know me."

"But as soon as I met you, I knew it was perfect."

Sonora sighed, but then she laughed. "You know what happens to people who try to play cupid for everyone else?"

"People love them and keep them close with undying loyalty?"

"No. They end up in their own convoluted romance, and it's always amusing."

Curtis held his hands up. "Nope. This redheaded Irishman is only good at flirting. Anything more would be terrifying."

She eyed him, wondering what sort of story he had that would lead him to that brazen claim. But right then, she had a man to see about forever, and Curtis was not the guy.

Taylor shut the tailgate on his pickup so that he could load the final pumpkins without risk of squishing them.

"I can't thank you enough for helping us," Sicilia Kline gushed. The woman always gushed.

"You're welcome, as always."

"You always help us. Such a kind young man. I'm so glad you found a nice girl to marry. Where is your wife these days? Is she still visiting her family? It's been a couple of weeks. That seems like a long visit. Especially after you've only recently been married. Maybe you should go too, Taylor. After all, a couple should be a part of each other's lives in all areas. It's important. How are your in-laws? Do you like them?" Sicilia paused.

Great. She expected an answer to that question.

Taylor stretched his back. "I haven't met them yet."

She frowned. "Didn't you ask her father for permission to marry her?"

"I did not." Heat tinged his cheeks, more than that of the work he'd been doing. He felt his patience slipping. Sicilia was always excessively chatty, but usually he didn't allow irritation a foot forward. She was his neighbor, after all, and she and her husband took good care of him. But holding on to patience had become quite a task the last few days.

He missed his wife. FaceTime and texts were not enough. For all his noble claims of waiting, he was sick to death of it, and it was making him grumpy. He wanted Sonora here, at his side, or better still, in his arms. Now.

Not in four hours. Right. Now.

But none of that was Sicilia Kline's fault, so Taylor strained for forbearance. And, to her question, honesty.

"I wish I had done things differently with Sonora, but we only have to go forward now."

"Ah." She patted his shoulder. "That's the truth of it. Forward is all we have. We can't change the past, but we can make amends."

He wasn't sure if she was hinting at something, but the sound of a vehicle bouncing along the dirt lane distracted him from examining the possibility. With a turn of his neck, he saw Curtis pulling up to the front of his house on the other side of the field. Taylor only had a sliced view of the car, but the man exited the driver's seat, disappeared from view, came back, shut the trunk, and pulled away.

"What was that about?" Sicilia asked. "He didn't even look for you. Wouldn't he know you were in the pumpkin patch? Surely he would. Everyone knows you help us with the harvest—how else are we going to get everything done in time for the extravaganza?"

Taylor didn't answer. He strode across the field, his heart strumming as suspicion captured his mind. The idea was so compelling, he broke into a jog. Rounding to the front of his house, he searched the front porch.

And there she was.

His wife was a beautiful woman.

"Sonora," he breathed.

Her laugh made his heart take flight, and before he was on the top step, she was in his arms. Nothing had ever felt so amazing as holding her. She smelled of lemony sunshine, and her lips were the closest thing to heaven he would ever know this side of death.

"You came back."

"I told you I would."

"I mean early." He pulled back to look at his lovely bride. God had not made a more beautiful creature in all of creation, he felt certain. "I planned on picking you up at the docks this evening."

She gave him a cheeky grin. "Surprise."

"That is a stupendous surprise."

She twisted her mouth and wrinkled her nose. "Hmm. I think you can do better."

"Scintillating?"

"I'm not sure what that means, but it doesn't sound right."

"Satisfying."

"Weak."

"Exquisite."

She laughed and leaned in to kiss him again. "Enough. I have other things to discuss."

"Oh?" That sounded . . . much too serious for this elated moment.

Sonora stepped out of his arms. "Yes."

"Am I in trouble?"

"No." She grabbed his hand and held it. "But I have a few questions."

"All right . . ."

"First, have you thought and prayed seriously about us?"

"I have." He stepped up the final riser.

She stepped back. "And?"

"And I have not changed my mind. Have you?"

She tried oh so hard to hold a stern expression. But her eyes gleamed with mirth.

"What are you up to?"

Suddenly she dropped to one knee. "Taylor Everest, will you marry me for real? Please?"

He stared at her, not sure if he was pleased or mortified that she was down on one knee proposing to him. "We . . . we are still married, aren't we?"

"Answer my question first."

"Sonora—"

She cut him off with a tilt of her head and a serious brow lift. "You're making me uneasy here, Taylor. Do you want to marry me or not?"

"Yes. I want to be married to you. But I thought we already were."

"*Yes* will do." She kissed his hand.

He pulled her back to her feet. "So we're not married?"

"Taylor. Stay with me."

"I'm trying."

"One question at a time." She tipped up and kissed his cheek. "Will you marry me . . . tonight? At the Palace?"

Oh . . . She wanted a *wedding*. Of course! He smiled down at her, cupping her face. "Ah. Yes, my love. I would marry you tonight or tomorrow or any other day you choose, wherever you would like."

Her smile warmed from playful to loving. "Good." She landed one more kiss on his mouth. "Meet me at the ballroom at nine, if you please. Wear your not-a-uniform suit. And don't forget to pick up our families first."

"Pick up—" Taylor stopped, mouth gaping as she bounced down the steps and began down the road.

"Wait," he called. "Where are you going?"

"Curtis is waiting to give me a ride to the Palace." She blew him a kiss. "Don't be late!"

Taylor stood there dumbfounded. And then he realized he was staring at an empty lane, with a sure-to-be-ridiculous grin on his face.

Married! He was getting married to the woman he loved *tonight!* And his family would be there! Mom and Dad and Jilly-Fish—they were all coming on the *Haven* that evening.

"Grace upon grace!" he called to the heavens.

"What's that?" Sicilia called back, standing on the road between his house and hers.

"God gives good gifts—grace upon grace!" he answered.

"Well, isn't that the truth!" She clapped her hands, then leaned forward. "But are you okay, Taylor?"

"I'm . . . rapturous!"

"What?"

"I'm getting married. Tonight! Nine o'clock at the Palace. I hope you'll come."

His chatty neighbor laughed and nodded, and for the first time in Taylor's memory, the woman was delighted speechless.

And that made two of them.

There had never been such a glorious night.

As he stood in a circle of white pumpkins, dried-flower chains, and flickering candles in the middle of the ballroom, Taylor drew in a long, steadying breath. To his left stood Curtis and Jilly-Fish, along with his mom and dad and several friends from the island—including Gretta. To his right, Sonora's parents both smiled with pleasure. He'd enjoyed meeting them—and having the opportunity to ask her dad for his blessing—which the man gave with a stern warning: "Don't break my baby girl's heart."

Taylor promised that he wouldn't, and he intended to live that out.

Now, there was only lacking his bride . . .

Sonora made her way into the dim room with the sound of the string quartet playing Bach as her usher, and his heart nearly burst.

Taylor's wife was the most stunning woman he'd ever seen.

Likely he'd forget that she wore a champagne gown that exposed her soft shoulders and floated down her frame. He might even forget that she wore her hair in a loose braid that drifted down one side of her neck in a mass of tempting softness. Or perhaps he'd not remember that she carried a bouquet of fall-tinged hydrangea blooms the color of frothy wine.

But he would never forget staring into those wonderful copper eyes, filled to the brim with love and joy. He'd always remember promising her forever and being amazed, yet again, that she returned her own promise to him. And he would forever call to mind that his family and hers gathered around them as witnesses, making their joy full.

Grace up on grace. Even after falling into a dark pit of disappointment. Even after allowing that tumble to turn into bitterness. He had been given grace upon grace.

God had provided. He'd given generously. And He did indeed give good gifts.

And that, Taylor determined, he would never forget again.

The End

I hope you've enjoyed this fourth book in our Love on Sanctuary Shores series! Would you please leave an honest review to let other readers know what you thought of Running into Forever? Thank you!

Did you know that there are five other books in the Love on Sanctuary Shores series? You'll find them in order listed below:

Tumbling into Tomorrow by Juliette Duncan

Fighting for Her Heart by Tara Grace Ericson

Surrendering to Love by Kristen M Fraser

Running into Forever by Jennifer Rodewald

Trusting His Promise by Valerie M Bodden

Wishing for Mistletoe by Robin Lee Hatcher

Find them all on Amazon!

And be sure to join the Small Town Christian Romance Reader Facebook Group to chat with the authors and other readers, and hear about new releases in this genre!

And finally, I would LOVE to have you join my newsletter! I share life updates, lessons from my studies in God's word, pictures of the flowers I grow on my little flower farm, and news about books! It would be an honor to have you join me on the journey—and I'd love to offer you a free copy of my Christmas novella, Ordinary Snowflakes. You can find out more on my website at authorjenrodewald.com.

Printed in Great Britain
by Amazon

55930171R00199